Pr[illegible] [illegible]gainst his chest, and unsheathed his bowie knife. Carefully but quickly, he cut her po[illegible] her neck and should[illegible] skin—and the ragged [illegible]ing down her chest.

Prophet made a fa[illegible] wound, which meant [illegible] where. And she was bleeding like a stuck pig.

"Oh, god." She sighed, flopping against him. She turned to see the wound, and her face turned white as bleached flour. "Oh, god . . . I'm bleeding."

"Don't look at it," Prophet warned, unknotting his neckerchief. He'd known her long enough to know that, while she didn't mind the sight of others' blood, one glimpse of her own knocked her cold.

"Oh, god, Lou," she cried, "I'm . . . I'm . . ."

"Don't pass out, Louisa!"

Then she was out, sagging against him . . .

PRAISE FOR

PETER BRANDVOLD:

"Takes off like a shot, never giving the reader a chance to set the book down."

—Douglas Hirt

Berkley titles by Peter Brandvold

THE DEVIL GETS HIS DUE
ONCE LATE WITH A .38
RIDING WITH THE DEVIL'S MISTRESS
ONCE UPON A DEAD MAN
DEALT THE DEVIL'S HAND
ONCE A RENEGADE
THE DEVIL AND LOU PROPHET
ONCE HELL FREEZES OVER
ONCE A LAWMAN
ONCE MORE WITH A .44
BLOOD MOUNTAIN
ONCE A MARSHAL

Other titles

DAKOTA KILL
THE ROMANTICS

THE DEVIL GETS HIS DUE

PETER BRANDVOLD

BERKLEY BOOKS, NEW YORK

This is a work of fiction. Names, characters, places, and incidents either are the product of the author's imagination or are used fictitiously, and any resemblance to actual persons, living or dead, business establishments, events, or locales is entirely coincidental.

THE DEVIL GETS HIS DUE

A Berkley Book / published by arrangement with the author

PRINTING HISTORY
Berkley edition / February 2004

Cover art by Bruce Emmitt.
Cover design by Jill Boltin.

For information address: The Berkley Publishing Group, a division of Penguin Group (USA) Inc., 375 Hudson Street, New York, New York 10014.

ISBN: 0-425-19454-X

BERKLEY®
Berkley Books are published by The Berkley Publishing Group, a division of Penguin Group (USA) Inc., 375 Hudson Street, New York, New York 10014.
BERKLEY and the "B" design are trademarks belonging to Penguin Group (USA) Inc.

PRINTED IN THE UNITED STATES OF AMERICA

10 9 8 7 6 5 4 3 2 1

For Stella, Buck, Thor, and Wild Bill
In memory of Old Shep (198?–2000)

For we are strangers before thee,
and sojourners, as were all our fathers:
our days on this earth are as a shadow,
and there is none abiding.

—1 CHRONICLES 29:15

Draw me after thee.
We will run.

—SONG OF SOLOMON 1:4

1

GRIPPING HIS SAWED-OFF ten-gauge in both hands, Lou Prophet ran through the brush and hunkered down behind a rock. He was about to step out from behind the rock and make his way to the farm cabin yonder in the night-cloaked ravine, when he felt the cold steel of a knife blade press against his throat.

A voice in his ear said, "One move, amigo, and I'll carve out your voice box and feed it to the crows."

Prophet froze, heart thudding. Then he realized the voice, smooth as silk and as cold as a Dakota winter, belonged to a girl.

He sighed with relief, his muscles slacking. "Hello, Louisa. I figured we'd meet out here, sooner or later."

He turned to the seventeen-year-old blonde he'd dubbed The Vengeance Queen. She stared at him, but it was too dark for him to see clearly her china-doll's face with its long lashes, pouty lips, and delicate nose and jaw. Her hazel eyes were shadowed ovals beneath her brows on which the silvery starlight played. She wore a round-brimmed felt hat, the thong swinging loose beneath her chin.

Louisa Bonaventure pursed her lips with mild chagrin. "Sorry, Lou," she whispered, careful her voice wouldn't travel. "I was hoping you were him."

She removed the blade from Prophet's throat and slid it into her belt sheath. Prophet looked around and said with incredulity, "How in the hell did you sneak up on me like that, anyway? No one sneaks up on Lou Prophet. I pride myself on that."

Louisa shrugged. "A girl on her own on a frontier teeming with lusty men learns how to walk softly if she doesn't want to become the victim of rabid passion."

"Yeah, but no one sneaks up on Lou Prophet. I'm a bounty hunter, dammit. I can't have girls or anyone else sneaking up behind me."

"Pride is a sin," she said. "Besides, I was on the other side of this rock." She smiled, self-satisfied.

"Pride is a sin," he mocked. "You track him here?"

"Yep. Lost him for a day, but he's here, all right. His horse is in the corral just over there." Louisa Bonaventure drew her Colt through the slit in her skirts—she concealed a cartridge belt, holster, a knife, and God knew what else in her undergarments—and with one delicate finger gave the cylinder a spin. "But he's all mine, now."

"He's all ours," Prophet corrected her. "There's reward money on him. We'll split it."

"You know I don't care about the reward money." Louisa cemented the phrase with a dark look and turned toward the cabin.

Prophet grabbed her arm. "Wait a minute. We need a plan. You check out the barn, and I'll check the cabin. Don't make a move without me."

"Same to you."

Without reply, Prophet ran crouching toward the privy silhouetted by starlight.

Handsome Dave Duvall and his Red River Gang had slaughtered Louisa's family in a Nebraska raid, and she'd spent the last year tracking them down, killing gang members one by one, sometimes two by two. Fate had thrown her and Prophet together over in Minnesota, after the gang had raided the town where Prophet had been holed up waiting for the reward money for another pair of dead cutthroats he'd turned over to the law.

Handsome Dave Duvall was now the last of his once twenty-strong gang, and Prophet knew Louisa would kill him on sight. For that reason, Prophet wanted to take Duvall down alone. He'd always believed in giving a man—no matter how evil—a chance to be taken alive. It was part of the code necessary in an occupation where, if you weren't vigilant, you could easily become as depraved as the men you hunted.

Besides that, the bounty hunter had grown protective of the overzealous queen of vengeance, and he didn't want to see her hurt. Not that she hadn't proven, over and over, she could take care of herself and then some, but everyone's luck ran out, especially when you pushed it as hard as Louisa often did.

Prophet sidled up to the privy, the ten-gauge held at the ready, its leather lanyard around his neck. He looked toward the cabin sitting about fifty yards away, nestled in knee-high weeds. It was a tall, narrow, two-story affair, sitting catty-corner from the barn, which was only slightly larger than the cabin. This was the back side of the place, and there were a few implements and cream cans and the like, that Prophet would have to skirt around as he made his way to the cabin, so as not to trip and make his presence known.

Carefully, he headed that way. When he made the cabin, he crouched beneath a window, then shuttled a cautious glance within. It was too dark for him to see much, but this looked like the sitting room. The bedrooms were probably upstairs, which was going to make it impossible for Prophet to tell which room Duvall occupied, if any, without going in and kicking down each door.

That would be too risky. If he wasn't in the barn, Prophet and Louisa would have to wait till morning, until Duvall came out on his own.

That decided, Prophet glanced toward the barn. Someone poked him from behind, and he gave a start, jerking around. It was Louisa.

"Goddamn it!" he rasped.

He grabbed her arm roughly and led her away from the cabin. When they were far enough away that their conversation wouldn't be overheard, he said, "Will you stop sneakin' up on me? What are you tryin' to do, give me a heart stroke?" Without waiting for her to respond, he continued, "I've never known a girl as cocksure and downright disrespectful in my life. Do you know that?"

"He's in the barn."

Prophet stared at her, still burning. "What?"

"Come on."

She turned and walked toward the barn. Scowling, Prophet followed. When they came to one end of the log structure, the bounty hunter said, "How do you know?"

Louisa shushed him and walked softly through the grass toward the barn's closed front doors. As they walked, Prophet heard something inside the barn. At first he thought it was roosting chickens or pigeons. He stopped and cocked an ear to the chinking between the logs.

The sounds were clearer now, more distinct, and it was obvious they were not made by chickens.

"Oh, oh god . . . oh god," a girl said breathily.

A man sighed and grunted and sighed, then grunted again.

"Oh god, oh god, oh god . . . !"

Prophet turned to Louisa, grinning. She did not return

the grin but drew her silver-plated Colt, wheeled, and moved deliberately to the doors.

"Now don't get crazy," Prophet told her. "Don't shoot unless he shoots first."

Prophet grabbed the handle of the left door. Louisa grabbed the right. Prophet nodded, and they yanked the doors wide.

Prophet shouted, "Freeze or you're jerky, Dave!"

Two lamps were lit within the shadowy barn, revealing a man and a woman in a hay pile against the wall to Prophet's right. The woman lay on her back, fully clothed but with her skirt pulled up to her waist and her blouse open, revealing her breasts. A slender man lay between her spread legs, her knees pulled high against his ribs. The man's denim breeches were down around his ankles, and the flat slabs of his bony white ass were aimed at the rafters.

Her frightened eyes jerking toward the intruders, the girl screamed.

The boy—and that's what he was, a long-faced boy with freckles, about seventeen or eighteen years old—rolled off the girl. Awkwardly jerking his denims up from his ankles, he cast a horrified glance at Prophet and Louisa.

"Please . . . please . . ." he muttered, voice quaking, while the girl covered herself with the horse blanket they'd been lying upon.

Prophet and Louisa stepped cautiously into the barn. Prophet was puzzled. "Who in the hell are you?" he asked the boy.

"Who in the hell are you?" the girl, a round-faced brunette, piped up, her voice filled with contempt. "And what in the hell are you doin' in my poppa's barn?"

Prophet looked at Louisa. She looked at Prophet, her full lips pursed with disgust.

Turning back to the girl, who sat her ground, grasping the blanket firmly, Prophet said, "Where's Dave Duvall?"

"Who?" the girl said.

Prophet indicated the lad, who was still trying to get his denims up over his ass, with his shotgun. "This ain't Handsome Dave Duvall," he told Louisa.

Ignoring him, Louisa said to the boy and the girl, "A scallywag by the name of Handsome Dave Duvall has left his horse in your corral. Are you giving him shelter in the house?"

The boy was too terrified and too busy with his fly buttons to answer. The girl's eyes widened even further as they shone now with befuddlement as well as contempt. "What . . . *who* . . . ?"

"Who left that horse in your corral out—?"

Prophet's question was cut short by a voice lifting in the distance. "Who's out there? Who's in my barn?"

"Oh, god!" the girl squealed, turning to the boy. Her fear had returned in earnest. "It's Poppa!"

The boy scrambled to his feet, grabbed his shirt and boots, and hightailed it to the door, pushing between Prophet and Louisa. Before he made it, however, a lanky man with a gray beard, who was wielding a shotgun, appeared between the open doors, scowling. The boy stopped, lifting his hands in a gesture of fear and pleading.

"Ronnie Kilgore," the old man growled deep in his throat.

His angry eyes brushed past Prophet and Louisa as if they weren't there, landing on the girl still lying in the hay and covering herself with the blanket. One naked knee was exposed.

The old man's face turned crimson as he turned back to the boy.

"No, Mr. Doggenfeldt!" the boy cried, dropping his boots and shirt, bolting past the man and into the night.

"Boy, I told you what was gonna happen next time I found you with my daughter!" the farmer raged, turning toward the retreating boy and bringing the shotgun to his shoulder.

"Poppa, no!" the girl screamed.

Watching the old man with surprised fascination, Prophet put his fingers in his ears as the old man tripped one trigger on the double-barrel and then the other, the hollow booms filling the barn and rending the quiet night.

The old man slowly lowered the gun as he squinted off in the direction in which he'd shot. "Damn," he growled. "Missed him. . . ."

Gradually, his gaze found Prophet and Louisa. As if seeing them for the first time, his eyes acquired a curious, suspicious cast. "Who in the name of Jehovah are you?"

Prophet cleared his throat, "Sir, my name's—"

"Wait a minute," the old man snapped, spying his daughter trying to slink around him. "Tillie, you go back to the house and tell your ma what ye done! And then the two of you open the Good Book and read! If I ever catch you out here with that Kilgore trash again, dancin' the devil's dance, I'll peel the hide off'n you slow!"

The girl had already bolted through the door and was running off through the darkness, sobbing.

The man stared after her, lips pursed, shaking his head darkly. "What am I gonna do with that girl? In spite of her good, God-fearin' upbringing, she's lost her way. . . ."

To remind the man of his and Louisa's presence, Prophet cleared his throat. The man turned to him, anger still etched on his bearded features, skepticism slitting his eyes. As if he were seeing the strangers for the first time, he said, "Who are you?"

Deciding to skip to the chase, Prophet said, "Have you given shelter to Handsome Dave Duvall, sir?"

"Handsome Dave *who?*"

"Famous badman. Mean son of a bitch. His horse is in your corral yonder."

"Horse?" the farmer spat, swinging toward the corral. "What horse? I don't know what in the name of God's mercy you're talkin' about."

Prophet brushed past the man, heading for the corral. Warily, the farmer followed him, and Louisa stepped in behind him. They headed toward the corral in which four horses stood with their backs blue with starlight; Prophet ducked inside. He approached the tall, white-socked chestnut, ran his hand down its trim neck.

"This one here," Prophet said. "He's still got sweat on him."

The bearded farmer approached the corral and stood there, the broken-open shotgun in the crook of his right arm. He stared into the corral, swinging his gaze right to left. Louisa stood beside him, her hands on the top corral slat.

"That ain't my horse," he grumbled. Swinging his gaze around the corral again, he said, "And one of mine's gone. Ole Jeeter, my paint. Hey, what's goin' on here? Where's my horse?"

"Shit," Prophet said to Louisa.

"He switched horses," she said.

"Damn! He's got a fresh one."

"Let's trade ours," Louisa suggested.

Prophet looked at the three other, aged, swaybacked ponies spread out and facing him in the darkness, pricking their feeble ears. "For these nags? I ain't givin' up Mean and Ugly for one of these nags. And your Morgan could outrun any of 'em with hobbles on.

"Shit," he cursed again, ducking out of the corral. He clumped off in the darkness, and Louisa turned to follow him.

"Hey, whose horse is this?" the farmer called after them.

"Yours," Prophet said without turning around.

The farmer turned to the big chestnut and rubbed his jaw with pleased speculation. "You don't say. . . ."

2

PROPHET AND LOUISA separated to retrieve their horses, then joined up again west of the farmstead. They searched for horse tracks, but it was too dark for tracking. Because clouds were moving in, obscuring the stars and threatening rain, Prophet selected a campsite on a low hill in a wide, shallow valley stippled with rocks, spindly ironwood trees, and brush.

When he and Louisa had tethered their horses to long lines in deep grass, Louisa took a canvas bucket down to the creek, and Prophet gathered kindling and dead ironwood and built a fire. He was slicing salt pork into a skillet when Louisa returned from watering the horses and filled a percolator for coffee.

While the pork fried, she and Prophet sat back against their saddles and drank coffee from battered tin cups, the light from the fire playing on their faces. They were tired from the seemingly endless hunt for Dave Duvall. When two motley coyotes came sniffing around the shadows of the camp's perimeter, eyes red in the fire glow, Prophet chucked rocks at them. A few minutes later, indignant howls rose eerily from a nearby bluff.

When the howls faded, Louisa said dreamily as she stared into the fire across from Prophet, "My brother had a dog that was part coyote."

When she offered nothing more, Prophet said, "Oh?"

"Mike liked coyotes," was all she added in her dreamy way, remembering the coyote dog, Prophet knew, and a whole lot more of the life on her family's Nebraska farm before the Red River Gang had snuffed it out.

She stared into the fire, and Prophet gazed at her, the smooth, golden skin of her face, blonde hair wisping about her cheeks. Her nostrils were sensuously flared, her upper lip slightly curled. Her eyes were the hazel of a winter's day. As always, Prophet was amazed by her beauty. Anyone seeing her for the first time would have bet she was a preacher's daughter or the daughter of a prominent businessman, given to frilly dresses, hair ribbons, books, and piano recitals in the parlor.

Not a puredee, sewn-in-the-saddle, sharpshooting, blade-wielding polecat who'd laid waste to half the Red River Gang single-handedly.

Prophet poked the pork around in the skillet. When it had cooked a little longer, he set several strips on two plates, and he and Louisa ate while the grease sputtered in the still-hot skillet, the percolator gurgled, and the horses stomped around in the brush beyond the fire.

Louisa said nothing as she ate; neither did Prophet. She'd acquired the haunted, faraway look that often crept into her face at night, and he knew from experience it was best to leave her to her silence.

When they finished, Louisa rose without a word and took the dirty utensils down to the creek. Having seen lightning in the southeast, Prophet erected a crude shelter from his tarpaulin and several long branches. He was drinking coffee and smoking a cigarette under the tarpaulin when Louisa reappeared with the cooking gear. She stowed the utensils in her and Prophet's saddlebags, then poured herself some coffee and lay down beside Prophet under the tarpaulin.

She drank the coffee in silence, then tossed out the dregs and snuggled down in her blankets. Prophet wanted to put his hand on her shoulder to comfort her, but he was never sure how she'd take a man's physical ministrations after what she'd seen men do to her mother and sisters back in Nebraska.

He settled for "Night, Louisa."

She returned with "Good night, Lou," and rolled onto her side, away from him, raising her knees and flipping her long hair out from her collar.

Prophet smoked another cigarette and drank another cup of coffee, watching the lightning grow and smelling the sage on the freshening breeze. The sound of Louisa's breathing deepened. He'd flicked the quirley stub into the fire and was settling into his own blankets when he heard what sounded like a sob.

He raised his head. "Louisa . . .?"

A high-pitched sigh escaped her, and then she turned to him so quickly, fairly bounding against him, that he found himself stiffening as though setting himself for violence. Only a dimwit would not take heed when Louisa Bonaventure sprang on him like that. But then he realized she was not attacking with a knife or a pistol but with her fists clutching at his shirt as though to rip it from his chest . . . as though to extract from him a comfort, a balm to her endless pain that no man—or woman, for that matter—could ever oblige.

Clutching at the shirt and digging her fingernails painfully into his chest, she wept and sobbed and cried aloud, ramming her head between her fists, against his tear-soaked shirt, venting her pain and outrage and unplumbable sadness. Prophet knew that all he could do was hold her tightly, rock her in his arms, and coo gently in her ear while she relived it all again: the screams and pleas of her siblings and parents, the thunder of the horses, the hoots and yells of the attackers, the pops of the pistols, the smell of the smoke, the wind of the burning cabin against her face, stinging her eyes.

She'd been returning to the farm from selling eggs when she'd seen the smoke. She'd hidden in the weeds and, frozen with horror, she'd watched her father and brother butchered, one after the other. She'd watched her mother and two sisters dragged into the tall grass by the stream, and the Red River Gang, led by the handsome, diabolical Dave Duvall, had whooped and hollered their pleasure.

She'd been able to do nothing but watch, horrified beyond the brain's ability to comprehend. Prophet knew that horror. He'd lived it himself while fighting for the Confederacy during the War Between the States. He knew what slaughter looked like. He'd heard the screams, smelled the smoke and putrid odor of burning bodies and blood. Watched as his friends and family fell to minié balls and bayonets.

And he'd been awakened by such dreams as that which had awakened Louisa now.

"Hold on, girl," he said, as her sobs slowly faded and her fists released their taut grip on his shirt. "Just hold on . . . it's all ye can do. . . ."

Finally, her muscles relaxed, and she slumped against him. Her face on his chest, she slept. Cradling the fine-boned girl in his arms—she couldn't have weighed much over a hundred pounds—he, too, slept, waking only occasionally to the thunder and lightning of the short-lived storm, hearing the tarpaulin snapping above his head.

He woke the next morning to Louisa standing over him, fists on her hips. The sun was rising, and the sky was clear. The air was fresh and cool.

"Are you going to sleep all morning, Mr. Prophet?" she said, prodding his ribs with a boot toe. "I don't know what time you Georgians crawl out of the tick, but we Nebraskans rise with the sun."

Blinking sleep from his eyes, Prophet gazed up at her hovering over him like a schoolmarm, her brows ridged, her hat hanging down her back by a horsehair thong. Her storm had passed without a trace. Her pluck was back, and, in spite of the rude awakening, Prophet was happy to see it.

Unsteadily, he reached for his boots and began pulling them on. "Louisa," he drawled, funning her, "we got a term for women like you down South: brass-plated ball buster."

She'd turned and was tending the corn cakes she was frying on her breakfast fire. "Your language only serves to illustrate the fact that you are and always will be an unreconstructed vulgarian."

Prophet chuckled. "If I'm so damn unreconstructed and vulgar, why in the hell did you take up with me?"

"Well, 'cause," she said, her voice softening, "I guess we're sort of alike." She looked up from the smoking skillet, her eyes no longer haughty but pensive. "I mean, we're both alone, with no other friends or family. And we're both manhunters—you, by profession, and me, by circumstance." She flushed and turned her gaze back to the skillet, scraping the corn cakes off the pan with the fork and flipping them. "Besides," she grumbled, frowning again, "you threw in with me."

Prophet watched her, wondering how it was that God or whoever was tending things down here could have allowed life to turn so sour for a girl so basically good and sweet. But then, he'd asked similar questions about the war, and had received nothing even close to a satisfying answer.

Finally, he stomped into his boots and said, "I'll rig up the horses," as he donned his hat and walked away through the brush.

After a hurried breakfast washed down with Louisa's pungent coffee, they rode back toward the farmstead, where they hoped to pick up Duvall's tracks. Louisa rode the black Morgan she'd confiscated from one of the gang members she'd turned toe down. Prophet was in the hurricane deck of his trusty hammerheaded lineback dun, Mean and Ugly. Thus mounted, they tried for a half hour to break Duvall's sign; then Prophet halted the recalcitrant dun and scowled with frustration.

"Nope—that shower last night was just enough to wipe out his tracks."

"Surely there's sign somewhere."

Prophet shook his head. "Lady, I can track a snake across a flat rock. If I say there's no sign, there's no sign."

"I hope you don't intend to give up," Louisa said huffily, knitting her blonde brows together. Her eyes were shaded by the round brim of her hat.

"Who said I was givin' up?"

"If you're not giving up, what do you intend to do?"

"Peck, peck, peck. Is that all you women ever do?"

"I've found that most men are laggards, in need of constant cajoling."

"Is that so? Who saved your crazy hide back at the Red River Gang's hideout, for chrissakes?"

"Isn't it just like a man to gloat instead of taking action?"

Prophet only stared at her, partly dumbfounded, partly amused. A more changeable nature, he'd rarely encountered.

"You know this country," Louisa said. "Where do you think he's headed?"

Prophet was thinking it over. "Bismarck."

"Why?"

" 'Cause it's the largest town within a reasonable distance."

"Which way and how far?"

The bounty hunter pointed. "Southwest about a hundred miles."

"Well, don't just sit there," Louisa cajoled, heeling the Morgan into an instant, ground-eating gallop, spraying Prophet's horse with dust. "We're burning daylight!"

Prophet stared after her, bemusedly shaking his head. "Mean and Ugly," he said, patting the horse's beefy neck, "that girl's a handful."

Two days later they were riding due west when Prophet halted his horse suddenly and stared, lowering his hat brim to shield the afternoon sun from his eyes.

Louisa pulled up beside him and followed his gaze to a low, rocky ridge about two hundred yards ahead.

"Smoke," she said, watching the thick, white puffs rise from the ridge and unravel skyward. "Cook fire?"

"Could be." Prophet was thoughtful.

"Handsome Dave?"

Prophet looked around and chewed his lip. "I don't know."

"Well, let's find out." Dismounting, Louisa led her horse to a spindly cottonwood and tethered him, then shucked her carbine from the saddle boot.

"Just hold on, girl," Prophet cautioned. "That so-called 'cook fire' could be a trap. Hate to admit it, but I've walked into one or two."

"Or it could be Handsome Dave settled in for a cup of coffee," Louisa pointed out, jacking a shell in her rifle's breech and off-cocking the hammer.

As she started walking toward the ridge, Prophet said, "Maybe so, but we do this my way, or we part company here and now." He meant it. She may have single-handedly laid waste to half the Red River Gang, and her success may have been partly due to skill, but a good deal of luck had been involved, as well. She'd been damn lucky that her overzealous nature and tendency to throw caution to the wind hadn't gotten her beefed.

She turned to him angrily, opening her mouth to object. Then, realizing he was only trying to keep her from getting killed, and happy to have someone caring about her again, the lines in her suntanned forehead planed out, and she said demurely, "No need to get huffy about it."

Prophet dismounted and tied his horse with the Morgan, admonishing the horses not to fight. Then he shucked his Winchester '73, leaving the ten-gauge hanging from his saddle horn, and started walking slowly toward the ridge. Louisa followed a few steps behind. When they came to a depression about a hundred yards from the ridge, Prophet stopped.

"You go around that way," he said, pointing to the northwest. "I'll go this way. We'll work our way around the ridge and come in from the sides. Keep your head low, and don't get too close to the ridge. If it's a trap, he'll probably try to bushwack us from the top."

When Louisa had turned and begun walking away with her carbine in her gloved hands, Prophet hefted his Winchester '73 and tramped east, keeping a wary eye on the ridge around the smoke, watching for reflections off gun barrels or spyglasses—anything that might tell him he and Louisa were walking into a death trap.

When he'd made a wide half-circle around the ridge, he came in from behind it, walking slowly, his rifle in his hands, swinging his gaze from left to right, wary of a concealed gunman. When he'd stepped around a sage bush, something rustled a clump of bromegrass to his right. Heart thudding, he whipped his rifle that way, seeing only a gopher scamper into a hollow log.

He turned back toward the camp smoke, which had thinned considerably since he'd first glimpsed it. When he was less than a hundred feet away, he stopped, crouched behind a shrub, and gave the campsite a thorough scanning with his naked eyes. He couldn't see much for the rocks and shrubs, but there didn't appear to be anyone around the fire. Hair prickling under his collar, he stood and began walking again.

He'd taken only two steps when a rifle cracked ahead and to his left.

Prophet dropped to his knees and looked in the direction from which the rifle had sounded. Smoke puffed, and another crack cut the prairie silence.

Prophet bolted to his feet and ran toward the gunsmoke, head low, leaping shrubs and low rocks. More gunfire sounded directly ahead, in a hollow, but he didn't stop. When he saw a horseback rider, he dropped to a knee. The rider was galloping away on a paint horse, kicking up dust and stones in his wake.

More gunfire sounded from just ahead, and Prophet again ran toward it, dropping into the hollow. He saw Louisa lying on her side amid several sage clumps, her rifle lying nearby. Her hat had fallen down her back, and her hair hung loose. She held her revolver in her slack right hand.

"Louisa!" Prophet yelled as he approached.

"That son of a bitch!" she screamed, raising her silver-plated Colt and firing three times toward the disappearing rider. "He dry-gulched me, the son of a *bitch!*"

She fired once more and then the hammer clicked on the firing pin. She gave a frustrated yell and threw the revolver at the rider, who had disappeared behind a hogback. The gun flew about fifteen feet and landed in the turf with a plunk.

"Where you hit?" Prophet dropped beside her and saw

the blood just below her left shoulder, even before she indicated it with her hand.

"He dry-gulched me," Louisa cried, gnashing her teeth, her face pinched with pain. "I did just what you warned me not to; I walked right into it!"

"Easy, easy," Prophet said.

He took her in his arms, letting her rest against his chest, and unsheathed his bowie knife. Carefully but quickly, he cut her poncho, dress, and chemise away from her neck and shoulder, revealing her smooth, porcelain skin and the ragged hole from which blood leaked, gushing down her chest.

Prophet made a face. It was bad. There was no exit wound, which meant the bullet was still in there somewhere. And she was bleeding like a stuck pig.

"Oh, god," she sighed, flopping against him. She turned to see the wound, and her face turned white as bleached flour. "Oh, god . . . I'm bleeding."

"Don't look at it," Prophet warned, unknotting his neckerchief. He'd known her long enough to know that, while she didn't mind the sight of others' blood, one glimpse of her own knocked her cold.

"Oh, god, Lou," she cried, "I'm . . . I'm . . ."

"Don't pass out, Louisa!"

Then she was out, sagging against him like a hundred pounds of cracked corn.

3

PROPHET KNEW THE girl needed a doctor, but where in hell was he going to find a doctor out here?

The nearest sawbones was no doubt in Bismarck, still a two-day ride away. Even with Prophet's bandanna shoved in the bullet wound to stem the bleeding, he doubted she'd make it.

The bullet had to be removed quickly. Prophet would attempt removing it himself only as a last resort. First, he'd look around for a farm or ranch in the area. Living as isolated as they did, some ranch women were often better medics than the medics themselves.

He'd decided on the plan while carrying Louisa back to their horses. Now he tied Louisa's Morgan to the tail of Mean and Ugly, then scooped her up in his arms and gently mounted, setting the comatose blonde before him on the saddle. He heeled the horse into a walk, balancing Louisa between his shoulders, her head lolling against his chest.

He'd had to leave their rifles where Handsome Dave

had bushwhacked her. He retrieved them now, dismounting and holding the girl in the saddle with one hand. When he'd slid both rifles into their saddle boots, he remounted and heeled the dun into a lope, heading west, leading the Morgan and scouring the countryside for a settlement.

He'd ridden for twenty minutes when he found himself on a hogback looking into a ravine opening on the north. A creek threaded the ravine, sheathed in box elders and cottonwoods. In the trees, spindly wagons and carts were parked, and seven or eight ponies grazed from a picket line.

Travelers. If there wasn't a half-decent medic among them, they'd have hot water and blankets, at least.

"Come on, Mean and Ugly." Prophet reined the dun down the hill. But the horse walked only sluggishly, jerking his head and rattling his bit in his mouth. He turned a white-ringed eye to his master and snorted.

"Come on, Mean," Prophet carped. "This is no time to get ornery. What the hell's the matter with you, anyway? Drift, dammit!"

Prophet was about fifty yards from the trees when the recalcitrant mount stopped so suddenly that Prophet and Louisa nearly flew over his head. "Goddamn you, M—!"

Seeing two people step out from the trees, Prophet froze. They were Indians—an old man and a boy. The old man wore a black bandanna with white polka dots, and his coarse gray hair cascaded over his shoulders. He wore a muslin shirt open halfway down his dark brown chest. Buckskin breeches were held over his modest paunch by snakeskin suspenders. In his arms he carried an old Spencer single-shot.

The boy was about ten, with neck-length, jet-black hair. He was clad in only cut-off breeches, and his roan skin was mottled with insect bites. The inside of his right wrist was scraped, as though he'd been squirreling around in briars. His lips were drawn back from square, white teeth, and his big, black eyes were fixed on Prophet warily.

"Whoa," the bounty hunter said under his breath, reprimanding himself for not heeding his horse's warning. Mean rarely reacted like that to anything but diamondbacks, Indians, and preachers. "Shoulda known . . ."

It was too late to turn back now, so Prophet manufactured a smile and raised a hand in greeting. "How."

"How-do," the old man said with a curt nod, his hair breezing around his face.

"You speak English?"

The old man nodded once.

"I have an injured girl here." Prophet glanced down grimly at the unconscious Louisa Bonaventure lolling against his chest. Her face was pale and her lips moved, but she said nothing. He wasn't happy about riding into an Indian camp, but Louisa didn't have much time left. This old man might be her only chance.

Prophet lifted his gaze to him, beseechingly. "If there's anyone in your camp can help her, I'd be mighty obliged. She's lost a lot of blood."

The old man and the boy stood side by side, regarding Prophet with mute skepticism. The boy expectantly shuttled his puzzled gaze between Prophet and the old man.

"What happened?" the old man asked.

"She was shot by an outlaw named Handsome Dave Duvall. He and his gang killed her family. We been trackin' him."

The old man stared at Prophet hard, a brown light flickering in the depths of his flinty eyes. Then he turned to the boy and muttered something in guttural Indian. The boy turned and ran back through the trees.

To Prophet, the old man said, "Come," and then he, too, turned and started into the trees.

In the ten years Prophet had been on the Western frontier, he had steered clear of Indians. He'd tracked a couple breeds in the Staked Plains a few years back, but he'd never tangled with a war party. That was soldiers' work. Nothing there for a bounty hunter. Besides, he felt Indians in general were getting a raw deal, with the whites moving onto their ancestral lands, killing their buffalo, and crowding the natives themselves onto reservations of the worst land imaginable.

It was the way of the world, he knew. Survival of the fittest. Dog eat dog. Still, he wanted nothing to do with it. And he'd never wanted anything to do with the Indians themselves, whom he understood about as much he understood little blue men on the moon.

As he gigged his reluctant horse ahead, he felt his stomach turn sour and his neck grow stiff with fear. Indians killed white men on sight. Everyone knew that. But he couldn't very well turn tail and run when there was half a chance that someone here could save Louisa.

Who was it told him that Indians were good healers?

He kept thinking about that as he rode, Mean and Ugly's reluctant feet snapping twigs beneath him, the sounds loud as gunshots in the quiet woods. Sweat trickled under Prophet's arms, down his back.

Soon the encampment opened before him: five tepees in a clearing traversed by the creek, and three cook fires over which meat roasted or kettles hung. Children stopped their play to stare warily at the visitor. Dogs barked. Old, prune-faced women sat here and there about the ground, sewing or cooking or hammering raw meat with mallets. They looked up as Prophet approached, halting their chatter to frown and stare dully. No braves appeared anywhere in the vicinity. Maybe they were hunting, Prophet thought with relief. But they'd have to return sooner or later, and then what would happen when they saw the white man and the pretty blonde?

Prophet had to saw back hard on his horse's reins to get Mean and Ugly stopped. The horse fiddle-footed angrily, not liking the current situation one bit, and Prophet fought him with one tight hand on the reins.

"Settle down, Mean . . . goddamn you, horse!"

The old man sidled up to the horse and extended his arms. "Here, I take to Ka-cha-e-nee."

Prophet looked at the old man warily for a moment. He wanted to carry Louisa into one of the tepees himself; he was reluctant to turn her over to these dark-skinned strangers until he was certain she'd be safe. But with Mean and Ugly acting up, he didn't think he'd be able to climb out of the saddle with her without falling.

He eased her down to the old man, who must have been stronger than he appeared, for he held Louisa's weight easily, one arm under her neck, the other under her knees, and moved off toward one of the tepees, where an old woman stood in a dark blue dress adorned with colored beads, waiting. The woman's nearly black face was scored deep with wrinkles. Her eyes were tiny marbles in the weathered foxholes of their sockets, but her hair bore not a speck of gray as it fell in two thick braids down her shoulders.

As the old man approached her, the crone turned and ducked through the flap in the tepee. The old man followed her in.

Prophet tore his eyes from the tepee and slipped out of the saddle, still holding fast to the skittish Mean's reins. He turned to the boy, but before he could say anything, the boy yelled, "Wasichu! Wasichu!" and ran off across the meadow. The half-dozen other children, appearing to range from age three to thirteen, followed, repeating the clarion call, "Wasichu! Wasichu!" half in jest, half in fear.

Prophet turned to the three old women working nearby. A young girl had joined them, a smoky beauty in a soft hide dress adorned with porcupine quills and bear claws and beads arranged in the shape of the moon and stars. Her face was high-boned and softly chiseled, and her eyes and hair were of the same obsidian. Her form was as fine as her face, and nearly all of one supple, brown thigh was revealed by the slit in her skirt as she sat.

She returned Prophet's stare with an only mildly interested one of her own, then haughtily covered her thigh with her dress, whispering something to the old woman beside her. The old woman nodded, glanced at Prophet, and turned away, snickering.

Feeling as though he should introduce himself, Prophet clumsily removed his hat and said, "Name's Lou Prophet. I come in peace. My friend there—Louisa Bonaventure's her name—she was wounded by a scoundrel named Handsome Dave Duvall. You probably never heard of him, and lucky for you ye haven't, but he's one of the worst badmen currently on the dodge in these parts."

Prophet stopped. Only one of the old women so much as glanced at him. The others were sewing and tanning and cooking as though he weren't even there. The girl was watching him, however, looking him up and down with a hard-to-read expression in those pretty black eyes. She mumbled something to the old woman beside her and smiled. She glanced at Prophet again, appraisingly, and returned to the herbs she was grinding in a wood bowl.

"Well . . . okay, then," Prophet muttered, feeling stupid and self-conscious. "I'll just put up my horses. . . ."

He untied the Morgan from Mean's tail and led both mounts away from the encampment, where the smell of the Indians wouldn't be as sharp in the wily dun's keen nose. He tied both horses on long ropes to trees where the bluestem was lush and high, and walked backed to the encampment. He stood around the tepee for a while, trying to listen to what was happening inside, but heard only hushed guttural voices and occasional whimpers from Louisa. As the old women and the girl were not far away, he held his hat in his hands—did Indians recognize such niceties?—as he paced nervously before the tepee, eager to find out whether or not the old woman could help his wounded companion.

Finally, the flap lifted, and the old man appeared. "Ka-cha-e-nee is with her now. If she can be helped, Ka-cha-e-nee will help."

The old man started away, but Prophet grabbed his elbow. "Who's Ka-cha . . . Ka-cha—?"

"She is medicine woman. The powers of mother earth and father sky work through her for the People. If the girl can be saved, Ka-cha-e-nee will help. If not"—the old man raised his hands and lowered them in a gesture of supplication—"she will pass on."

He turned and walked away between the tepees.

"Where you going?" Prophet called. The old man was the only one here he appeared able to communicate with, and he wanted him near.

"I hunt. Our cache is growing thin." The old man turned and said something to the women, then walked away, his Spencer carbine in his arms.

Prophet turned to the women, feeling alone and out of place and worried about Louisa. The girl got up, went away, and returned with a bowl. She filled the bowl at the cook fire over which hung a large iron pot, and brought the bowl to Prophet. Without raising her eyes to his, she offered the bowl and a wooden spoon.

Prophet took them, said, "Obliged, miss," and watched the pretty Indian princess walk away and gracefully retake her seat with the old woman by the cook fire.

Prophet found a log near the tepee in which Louisa lay and sat down. After examining the food in the bowl—chunks of deer meat and pale, spongy guts in a thin yellow broth specked with green herbs and other things he could not identify—he brought the spoon to his lips and began eating.

Not bad. Bland, but not bad.

Time passed slowly. When he finished the food, the girl brought him a weak tea, again without looking at him. When he finished the tea, feeling heady from whatever herb it had been brewed with, he rolled a cigarette and smoked.

The old woman came out of the tepee, and Prophet stood eagerly, but the old woman did not so much as look at him. She called to the girl, who got up, grabbed a bucket, and walked off toward the creek. Then the old woman disappeared back inside the tepee.

The girl reappeared a few minutes later, with the bucket now filled with water, and went into the lodge. She came out without the bucket, went to another tepee, and returned with a hide sack and a handful of roots of several different shapes, sizes, and colors.

Prophet watched, worried and perplexed and wondering what kind of mumbo jumbo was going on in that tepee . . . wondering if he shouldn't just dig the bullet out himself. For all he knew, Louisa would have as much of a chance with him as with these women and their plants.

The aroma of the smoke wafting through the hole at the top of the lodge smelled musky and fetid and not at all like any medicine Prophet had ever heard of.

When he couldn't stand the suspense any longer, he marched over to the tepee and swiped the flap aside, peering into the dark depths in which a fire flickered and a pot gurgled. Louisa lay near the fire on a buffalo robe. Her nude, white body shone in the darkness. Her head moved slowly from side to side, and she was mumbling something unintelligible, but her eyes were closed. The old woman crouched over her, the Indian princess at her side, silently observing.

Prophet was about to step inside when the old crone straightened, lifting her bloody hands. In her left hand, she held a long, thin knife covered with blood. She looked at Prophet and cackled, showing her near-toothless gums.

She held up something between the thumb and index finger of her right hand.

The bullet.

Relief slackened Prophet's muscles. "Is she going to be all right?"

The crone didn't say anything. She just dropped the bullet in a bowl and gestured to the girl for a spool of gut thread, cackling deep in her throat. Not knowing how else to take it, Prophet took the crone's laughter as a promising sign, and went back out.

To pass the time, he took water to the horses, then wandered around the encampment, relieved but puzzled to find no sign of any other men but the old man and the two or three young boys.

Where were the braves? Where was the rest of the band? Surely this small gathering of the very old and the very young wasn't all there was.

4

PROPHET SPENT THE rest of the afternoon near the lodge in which the old healer crooned over Louisa, mumbling and sighing and muttering words Prophet couldn't understand. They sounded half like songs, half like prayers.

Whatever they were, they made the hair on the back of the bounty hunter's neck stand straight up in the air. He felt a bona fide fever chill when she came out of the tepee and circled the lodge while shaking a rattle and dancing to a song that sounded as though the devil himself had written it and was singing it through the crone.

He checked on Louisa later, though, and she was alive. Feverish, but alive.

He realized early that evening, when the old women began grumbling over their meager food stores, that the old man had not yet returned from hunting. Since there was nothing he could do here for Louisa, Prophet decided to go looking for the man, and do a little hunting of his own.

He rigged up Mean and Ugly, who snorted happily at

the prospect of getting out of there. Leading the Morgan, he rode eastward across the creek, through the trees, and up a low ridge swathed in midsummer wildflowers including Indian paintbrush and balsam root. He shot a nice buck on the other side of the ridge, gutted it, and draped it over the Morgan, securing it with rope.

He'd just finished tying the last knot over the buckle when the lineback, having swung around and sidled up behind him, gave Prophet's back a painful nip.

"Ouch!" Prophet cried, swinging around. "Goddamn you, Mean. Why in the hell did you do that?"

The lineback jerked his head back and twitched his ears, a pleased gleam in his copper eyes.

"Happy to be out of the Indian camp, that it? Well, you got a funny way of showin' it! You continue that behavior, and I'm gonna offer you up for their stewpot. What do you think of that?"

As if in reply, a distant rifle cracked.

Prophet swung around, facing west, where the sun was tumbling, pushing shadows this way.

The rifle cracked twice more.

Staring westward, Prophet frowned. Who could that be? The old man? Had he finally shot something?

Another report echoed on the freshening breeze. This one belonged to a pistol. Two more just like it followed.

Curious, and hearing a warning bell toll far back in his head, Prophet mounted up and rode westward, trailing the Morgan, the gutted buck flopping against its sides. Twenty minutes later, the bounty hunter climbed out of the saddle and tied Mean to a scrub oak in a purpling canyon.

Shucking the Winchester, he climbed the gravelly canyon wall to the ridge stippled with sparse brush, pines, and cedars. Staying low and removing his hat, he peered down the ridge into the narrow gorge on the other side, where three men dressed in ratty trail garb surrounded another man—the old Indian—tied to the trunk of a dead tree that had been topped by lightning about twenty feet up from its base.

Two of the gunmen held pistols. The third held a rifle. Their laughter rose from the canyon floor, which the sun brushed with salmon and gold.

They'd found an old Indian with only a single-shot Spencer, and they were having a good time out here, where good times were few and far between.

Hearing the sporadic gunfire and the hoots and howls of the old man's antagonists, Prophet donned his hat and made his way along the ridge, trying to get behind the gunmen while keeping out of sight from below. When he'd walked a ways, he took another peek over the ridge. Satisfied with his position, he traced a circuitous route through shrubs to the canyon and hunkered behind a rock and a chokecherry shrub.

One of the gunmen chuckled. "Now lookee here, JC. Watch this shot. I bet I can hit that knot there just left of his big, black, ole, Injun eye!"

"No way you can, Dick. You'll take his eye out!"

"Wanna lay some money on it?"

"Two dollar."

"Jacky, how 'bout you?" the sharpshooter said.

Jacky said, "I got five says you shoot the ole redskin's eye out the back of his head. You ain't no marksman, Dick."

"Well, to hell with you, Jacky," Dick said. "Watch this."

Prophet stood, took one swift step to the left of the rock, and extended his Peacemaker .45. "Watch this, you three brainless wonders." Their backs to Prophet, the three gunmen stiffened and froze. "I bet I can shoot one eye out of each of ye from the back. Wanna lay money on it?"

The men jerked and twitched as they turned, their rawboned, pugnacious faces blanched with fear and surprise. "Hey, now . . . who're you?" one of them said.

They held their weapons stiffly, having the good sense not to jerk them in Prophet's direction.

Prophet's anger swelled a confluence of veins in his forehead, just beneath his hat brim. "I'm the one wonderin' just what in the hell you three vermin think you're doin' to this old man."

"What the hell do you care? He's just an ole Injun. We caught him huntin' where we hunt fer the railroad."

"Railroad hunters, eh?" Prophet grunted. "Human vermin is what I call you. I s'pose you were plannin' on killin' this man when you were done funnin' him." The bounty hunter smiled knowingly and without mirth.

The man in the middle—a short, sandy-haired man missing his two front teeth—said, "What in the hell's it matter to you? He's just a thievin' ole Injun!"

"Yeah," the man on the far left said. "Didn't you hear what they done to General Custer?"

Prophet lifted his head to speak to the Indian tied with his arms behind his back to the dead tree. "Old man, did you have anything to do with that idiot Custer's demise?"

"Nope," the Indian said without inflection.

"See there," Prophet said. "He had nothing to do with it. Not only that, but he helped me out earlier today. And for that reason, my trigger finger has gotten awful itchy." He half-closed one eye as he aimed down the Peacemaker's barrel. "I might be able to control it, though, if'n you three dumbasses lay those guns down nice and gentle and get the hell out of here."

The three men glanced at each other tensely. Prophet could see the rocks rolling around in their heads.

"Well, I reckon since ye got us dead to rights, that's what we'll have to do, all right," Toothless said, his bottom lip twitching.

"Yeah, I guess that's what we have to do, all right," the man on the left said.

"Damn . . . I guess there's no other way," opined the man on the right.

Prophet smiled and lowered the Peacemaker to his waist.

The three men before him shared one more glance, sighed and carped again and shrugged, and slowly began lowering their weapons. "Well, here goes," Toothless said.

His gun was down around his knees when he stopped suddenly, lifted his head, and jerked the revolver at Prophet. He was dead before he could fire it. And so were his two companions—blown back off their feet with bullets through their foreheads and chests and rolling in dead heaps at the Indian's mocassined feet.

Prophet had dropped to a crouch, extending and fanning the Peacemaker till all six chambers were empty. Now he straightened and peered at the dead men through the powder smoke wafting around his head, stinging his eyes.

"I had a feeling they'd pull something stupid," he groused. He dropped the gun in his holster and moved to the old man. "It's been my experience that the born dumb die dumb." He moved around behind the tree and cut the Indian's tethers with his bowie. "What do you think?"

The old Indian stepped away from the tree. Massaging his wrists, he stared down at the three bleeding, glassy-eyed gunmen, then turned to Prophet without expression. "I think you're handy with a pistol. That's what I think."

The gunmen had shot the Indian's cayuse out from under him, so the Indian mounted behind Prophet, on Mean and Ugly, who snorted and pranced as he craned his neck around to get a look at the savage on his back.

"Don't mind my horse," Prophet told the old man. "I don't know why he doesn't like Indians. I don't think he's ever had any run-ins, unless it happened before I got him."

"That's all right," the old man said, holding his Spencer in his right hand. "I'm used to it."

"Sorry."

"That's all right."

"Come on, Mean. Settle down and drift, you ornery son of a bitch!"

"That's a nice buck you shot," the old man said when Mean had finally settled into a fast walk toward the Indian camp. "I been out here all day hunting, but my eyes—they're not so good anymore. My aim is even worse. I should have brought one of my children along. Mad Wolf is a good shot, but it's not good to depend on your children for game. The women lose respect."

Prophet smiled. "How many of those kids are yours?"

"They are all mine."

Prophet turned his head to look at the sober old man. "All?"

The old man nodded proudly. "And all the women are my wives. All but Ka-cha-e-nee. She is the mother of my wife, Cha-lo-why-ka-nee."

Prophet sawed back on the reins, halting the horse. "Wait a minute," he said, incredulous, looking back at the old man again. "You mean to tell me that whole group is your family?"

"Yes."

"Well, I'll be damned." Staring at the ground, Prophet thought it over. At least one of the old women must have been younger than she looked, to have had the youngest of those younguns. "I guess that explains why there aren't any warriors."

Prophet gigged Mean and Ugly into a walk, and the old man, whose name was Three Buffaloes, told Prophet in a desultory way about his life growing up with a band of Sioux along the Missouri River. When he was seventeen, he went to work at a large ranch as a hostler and a drover, and the cook taught him to read and write and to cipher. He became so good at horse gentling that he spent twenty years on the ranch, living among white people, making good wages.

"But I never felt right, living among the whites," he said. "I always felt homesick. So when I was forty, I went back to my own people and took wives and had children—the children you saw in the camp."

"That pretty girl, the older one—she your daughter, too?" For all Prophet knew, she might have been a wife.

Prophet sensed a proud smile on Three Buffaloes' face, heard him inhale deeply. "Yes. She is my firstborn. Her name is Me-the-um-ba. In English it means Sunshine. She was born during the bright summer days of the sun dance."

"A beauty, that one," Prophet said, rushing to add, "no disrespect intended, Three Buffaloes."

The old man put his hand on Prophet's right shoulder. "None taken, Mr. Prophet."

"Lou."

"You may call me Three for short."

Three went on to tell Prophet that he'd left his band a year ago, when they went on the warpath against the whites. "I do not like what your people are doing to my people, Lou," he said, "but killing will do nothing but cause more killing."

"I guess your people and my people have proven that already," Prophet grimly allowed as they crossed a creek in a shallow canyon, the dark water splashing silver against the rocks.

The sun had set, and the western sky had turned a painter's colorful palette, layered with high clouds.

"Yes. We have to learn to live together or not live at all."

"That's how I see it," Prophet agreed.

There was a pause as they climbed out of the canyon and cantered across the prairie toward a low ridge at the base of which was a black line of trees. In the trees lay Three's encampment.

"So you and your family are on your own, following the buffalo?" Prophet asked.

Three Buffaloes sighed. "On our own, yes. But the buffalo are all but gone. Around here the herds have been thinned to nothing by railroad hunters, like those who were using me for target practice. No, we follow the deer now, and the creeks and the rivers, and stay out of the way of the white people, though that gets harder every day."

They rode into the encampment twenty minutes later, when it was nearly full dark. The children flocked around their father, and the women cooed around the big buck draped over the Morgan. They wasted no time in cutting the ropes, yanking the carcass off the horse, dragging it over to the big, sparking fire they had going, and starting to work with their butcher knives.

When Prophet had unsaddled his horses in the trees, and fed and watered them, he went to see Louisa. He stepped into the tepee in which a low fire glowed, smelling the steam, tanned hides, and woodsmoke. Seeing that the crone wasn't there, he knelt beside the robe-cloaked figure near the fire and was relieved to hear her breathing.

She was unconscious, and her skin was pasty, but he listened to her heartbeat, and it sounded strong. There was a thick burlap compress on her shoulder that smelled as though it had been soaked in horse piss. It oozed brown liquid.

He touched her tangled blonde hair, caressed her smooth cheek with the backs of his knuckles, then stood and went outside, where the old women chattered happily as they worked. They already had two large shoulders roasting on spits and gleaming juicily in the firelight.

Three Buffaloes was there, too, lying propped against robes beside the fire, two little boys snuggled against his chest, sound asleep. When he saw Prophet, Three lifted a crock jug.

"Lou, join me."

"What do you have there, Three?"

"Rhubarb wine. Got the recipe from the cook who taught me how to read. It is a staple with me, like meat and fry bread. I seldom have a meal without it."

The old man grinned broadly, showing brown, crooked teeth. His eyes flashed in the fire's glow.

"Well, I never was one to turn down a drink," Prophet allowed, sitting beside the old man and crossing his legs Indian style.

He took the jug, sipped, and smacked his lips appraisingly. The wine was tart but refreshingly bubbly, and its warmth and alcohol bite fought off his fatigue. "That ain't bad, Three," he said. "Not bad at all." He tipped it back.

"I hope you don't mind one thing," the Indian said as Prophet handed him the jug.

"What's that?"

"I told my women I shot the deer."

Prophet waved it off. "No problem."

The old man hesitated, looking chagrined. "And one other thing."

"What's that, Three?"

"I told them it was I who saved you from the railroad hunters."

Chuckling, Prophet reached for the jug. "I wouldn't have it any other way."

"Tonight, Lou, and until you leave here, you must sleep in that tepee there. I will bed down with my children."

"I can't turn you out of your tepee, Three."

"You must. It is the Indian way. Besides, I have an old man's pride to thank you for."

"That's not neces—" Prophet stopped and raised his eyes as the lovely Indian princess, Sunshine, walked before the fire, the slit in her dress revealing a succulent, golden thigh. She glanced at him with cool disinterest and disappeared in the shadows between the tepees.

Seeing the look on Prophet's face, Three Buffaloes laughed with delight.

After partaking of a goodly portion of the buck, cooked until the skin had split and the dark meat was lightly charred and rife with flavor, eaten with his hands and washed down with wine, and after several more hours of Three's delightful conversation under the cold, bright stars, Prophet moved his gear into Three's tepee, undressed, and rolled up in a bearskin.

He didn't know how much time had passed before he heard a tap on the closed tepee flap.

"Who's there?" he said, keeping his voice low, believing it might be Three returning for something he'd forgotten to move into his children's lodge.

"Shh." It was a female voice. One of Three's wives?

Prophet was baffled as he watched the figure-shaped shadow move into the lodge and heard the sibilant sounds of cloth rustling. He smelled bear grease and the subtle, flowery musk of a woman. A young woman.

A girl?

"Who is it?" Prophet said again, louder this time, his hand near the gun and cartridge belt coiled up beside him.

Finally, the figure squatted beside him, lifted the bearskin, and slid down next to Prophet, who felt the unmistakable caress of a young woman's hair and naked flesh against his own. Slender arms encircled his neck. There was a warm, moist whisper in his ear:

"I came to repay you for saving Papa's life."

"Sunshine?"

The girl laughed huskily, running her hand down his chest and hard belly, finding him, and squeezing, and laughing again, but it was more of a delighted squeal this time.

Prophet didn't know what to do. Shocked and baffled, he slid a few inches away from her, but there was nowhere to go. "Jesus, I didn't know you spoke English. Jesus, what're you . . . what's happening here? What if your father . . . ?"

But then she'd crawled under the bearskin, the long, strawlike strands of her hair brushing his belly. She took him in both hands—her soft, exploring hands—and then her mouth was over the end and sliding down, down . . . down. . . .

And Prophet shut up and fell back with a deep-throated groan of surrender.

5

BEFORE DAWN, SUNSHINE got up and began building a fire. Hearing the soft snaps of the kindling, Prophet awoke and opened his eyes.

Silently, he watched the naked girl build the fire in the lodge's tawny shadows. When she'd coaxed a flame into being, she waited until it had grown, cracking and snapping, then set two small pieces of cottonwood atop it. Crawling on her hands and knees, her black hair swinging from side to side, she slid back under the bearskin.

Seeing that Prophet was awake, she nibbled his ear and giggled. Prophet smiled but shook his head. "You best leave before your father finds you here."

She fondled him. Despite his anxiety that Three Buffaloes would discover them together, he grew quickly aroused, his protests dying on his lips.

A moment later, she crawled on top of him, and he placed his hands on the silky skin of her thighs, caressing with his thumbs, then placed his hands on the russet orbs of her small, firm breasts swaying above him as she moved, sighing and murmuring . . . sighing and murmuring.

The passion built to a crescendo, until she stiffened and threw back her head, and Prophet, climbing out of his own hot bliss, reached up and clapped a hand over her mouth, stifling her scream.

They fell sideways together, rolling and snorting with muffled laughter. A few minutes later, the girl rose and dressed as Prophet watched. He grew aroused all over again as the lithe cinnamon nymph collected her hide dress and pulled it up her legs and belly, covering the lovely breasts with their still-jutting nipples.

Without so much as a good-bye or even glancing at him, she tossed her hair out from her neck and ducked through the flap, gone.

Prophet fell back, his guilt no longer tempered by the delight of the girl writhing beneath him. He'd frolicked with a girl whose father had only a few hours ago become his friend, while Louisa Bonaventure lay fighting for her life in a tepee only a few yards away.

"Law, law, Prophet," he sighed to himself, using his mother's old expression of pained exasperation. "You're lower than a backwater crawdad."

When he was dressed, he went out and looked sheepishly around for Three but saw only one of the wives fanning the cook fire to life with her apron. Relieved, he went into Louisa's lodge. The crone was sitting beside her, legs crossed, singing softly with her head thrown back, eyes closed.

Ignoring the woman, Prophet dropped to a knee and studied Louisa, who was sweating like she'd been running across a hot desert. Her heartbeat was still strong, however.

Having taken more than his own share of bullets, Prophet knew it could be days before the fever broke.

He went out, fed and watered his horses, and returned to the encampment where Three was enjoying a morning cup of coffee near the breakfast fire, around which all the women had now gathered. The old Indian hailed Lou heartily and insisted he join him for coffee while the women prepared their meal. Avoiding the old man's gaze, and more than a little worried about how the old man might react if he found out Prophet had diddled his daughter—even if it had been Sunshine's idea—the bounty hunter manufactured a cheerful grin and extended his hand for the cup.

"How did you sleep?" Three asked when Prophet had taken a seat.

Prophet's body heated from the center of his back to the top of his head. "Very well," he choked. "Very well . . . thanks very much." He couldn't look at the man; only at the fire over which bread was frying and more of the buck was cooking.

"And the girl . . . did she treat you well?"

Prophet jerked a look at the old man staring at him. Three's eyes were utterly without malice, waiting. Then Prophet saw the girl standing behind her father, her hands gently kneading the old man's shoulders and eyeing the uncomfortable Prophet smokily.

The bounty hunter's tongue was stuck to the roof of his mouth, and his throat was sandy. He knew his face was brick red.

"It is the Indian way," Three explained with a smile, "to offer our women to our guests. Sunshine has welcomed many of our visitors with special, man-pleasing methods taught her by my wives."

Prophet had heard of the Indian custom, but still his voice was locked deep in his throat.

"If you wish visits from any of the others," Three said, extending his hand at the women chattering around the breakfast fire, "please remember, Prophet—my women are yours."

Prophet glanced at the others. One of them turned to

him and cackled, opening her toothless mouth and jiggling her enormous, sagging bosom, igniting the others, as well as the old man and Sunshine, to uproarious laughter.

"Thanks, Three," Prophet said, his ears still scalding but finding his voice at last, though he doubted it was audible above the convulsions. "I'll keep that in mind."

But the only one he kept in mind was Sunshine, who visited his lodge again that night, the next night, and the next, and who after sweating and grunting with him for several hours each visit, left without so much as a parting word or nod in the morning.

And she never so much as looked at him during the day.

Prophet became so enraptured by the nightly visits that he had to admit he was in no real hurry to leave the encampment. Rarely had he ever experienced such bewitching, otherworldly charms without the usual complications the next day.

It was enough to turn him into an Indian.

But then Louisa's fever broke, and she regained consciousness. She healed for another week, moving around the camp to rebuild her strength, and resolutely declared herself fit to resume tracking Handsome Dave Duvall.

"Who?" Prophet said. He and Louisa had just returned to the camp after taking their horses out for a light run. Her left arm was in a rawhide sling.

Louisa stared at him, aghast. "Who!"

Prophet jerked in his saddle, startled out of his reverie of last night's blissful coupling with Sunshine. "Oh, Duvall. Right. Handsome Dave. Sorry, I was just thinking I better help Three grease those wagon hubs."

"I know whose hubs you were thinking about greasing, Lou Prophet," Louisa scolded, turning and gigging the Morgan away. "And you've only got one more night left with your lovely Indian princess, so you better enjoy it!"

Prophet stared after her, his sandy brows hooding his eyes. How in the hell had she found out?

Embarrassed and indignant, he yelled after her, "It's not my fault you went and got yourself ambushed, you silly greenhorn! I should've left you to the wolves!"

The next morning they said good-bye to the Indians—to all except Sunshine, that was, to whom Prophet had bid his own special farewell the night before, half hoping Louisa heard the screams—and pointed their horses toward Bismarck. Duvall was no doubt long gone from the territory by now, but Bismarck would be the best place for sniffing out his trail, however cold.

Prophet knew he should have left Louisa with the Indians and tracked Duvall while his trail was still fresh, but he'd been reluctant to leave the girl with strangers, however benign they'd turned out to be. Besides that, he knew how badly Louisa wanted to be involved in Handsome Dave's capture. If he'd taken the outlaw down alone, he doubted she'd ever forgive him.

Sunshine had had no part in Prophet's decision to stay with Louisa. At least, not a very big part.

They'd ridden half the day when Prophet realized Louisa hadn't said more than three words to him since their conversation about Sunshine the day before.

"How come you're so quiet?" he asked her over a small coffee fire at high noon.

She looked at him testily, wrinkling her pert nose. "Who's saying I'm quiet?"

"You ain't said more'n three words all day."

"Maybe I don't have anything to say to you."

"You're jealous of Sunshine. That's why you've been so damn quiet." He smiled, bemused.

She looked at him dully and tossed her grounds on the

fire. She stood, walked to her horse, stowed her cup in her saddlebags, and mounted up. She reined the Morgan around and headed off at a lope.

When Prophet caught up to her, heeling Mean and Ugly abreast of the cantering Morgan, he said, "If that isn't it, what is it?"

"You disgust me," she said, looking straight ahead, her hat shading her stern face and her chin thong bouncing on her poncho. "Spending every night with that girl. You hardly knew her."

"Three Buffaloes was just trying to make me feel at home, that's all. And so what if I didn't know her? I thought I told you—"

"Yeah, you told me all about how you sold your soul to the devil, and take your pleasure whenever and wherever you can. That's disgusting, too. All of it. You act like nothing means anything. Like there's no use in ever acting right because it's all wrong, anyway, and there's no God that cares about us." Her voice was taut with anger.

"I'm sorry, Louisa," he grumbled. "That's just the way I see it."

Later, he shot a couple of quail near a prairie pothole and roasted them over a fire that night. When it got dark, he checked on the horses, then came back and fished some gray cloth and a whiskey bottle from his saddlebags.

"I best change your bandage," he told Louisa, who sat cross-legged by the fire, holding her coffee cup to her breast.

"It doesn't need changing yet."

"The old woman said to change it every night for the first five days, then every three days after that."

He squatted next to her, but she only continued to stare wanly into the fire, as if she hadn't heard him.

"Come on," he urged.

Finally, she scowled and shrugged her poncho and dress

off her shoulder, grabbing her hair away. While Prophet removed the old bandage and began swabbing the wound clean with the whiskey and cloth, Louisa said grimly, "He's long gone by now, isn't he?"

"Handsome Dave?"

"Of course I mean Handsome Dave," she snapped, still angry at Prophet for his bad moral fiber in general and for sleeping with Sunshine in particular.

"I reckon he's a ways ahead of us, all right, but we'll find him. Someone in Bismarck will have seen him—someone in a saloon or a livery barn or a hotel, say. I'll check around while you relax in a feather bed and get your strength back."

"I've had all the idleness I need, and my strength is back." She winced as the whiskey burned her wound, which was healing nicely. The old lady had stitched her up as well as any sawbones from a big Eastern college. "I'm just worried that snake has slithered away for good."

Prophet splashed more whiskey on the cloth. "He may have slithered away, but a man like Dave Duvall can't hide. He likes attention and commotion. Even if we don't hear from him in the next few weeks, you can bet we will before winter. He'll find another gang and rob a train or shoot a lawman or slash a sporting girl, and the word will get out, and we'll be on him again."

"What if a lawman gets him first? I don't want some badge-toting imbecile to get him. I want to get him. Me." She poked herself in the chest and stared into the flickering fire angrily, gray eyes flashing, hair bouncing on her shoulders.

"You will get him, Louisa," Prophet assured her, a smile brightening his gaze. Angry or not, it was good to have her back to her old, determined self. Even while he was being distracted by Sunshine, he'd missed her.

There was a lull in the conversation while Prophet

bandaged her shoulder. When he was done, he replaced her arm in the leather sling and began to move away. She stopped him with a look.

"What are you going to do after Duvall is dead?"

Prophet grinned again, this time without mirth. "Once Duvall has been taken down and, if at all possible, turned over to the authorities, I'm going to do what I always do at the end of one job: go on a bender, then start looking for another."

"You're going to hell when you die, Lou Prophet."

"I told you ol' Scratch is already waitin' for me."

She shook her head. "Such foolish talk from a grown man."

"If chasing Dave Duvall ain't like chasin' the devil all the way to hell, I don't know what is." Prophet stared pensively off. He sighed and turned to Louisa. "What are you going to do?"

She shrugged and sank back against her saddle. She removed her revolver from the holster beneath the poncho, hefting it in her hand and pondering it. "I haven't given much thought to that."

Prophet poured himself a fresh cup of coffee and sank back against his own saddle. "I suspect you'll go back to where you came from," he said. "You'll settle in with a good family and marry one of them neighbor boys that was sparkin' you before. You'll have a passel of kids and raise some chickens and go to church picnics in the summer. Eventually, you'll forget about all this, and you'll have the kind of life a girl like you was meant to have."

Prophet had been staring into the shadows across the fire. When Louisa did not respond, he turned to where she sat to his right. As if she hadn't heard him, she continued methodically taking her revolver apart and cleaning each part with a white cloth soaked in oil. Her nostrils flared prettily, and her lip curled, but she said nothing.

He sighed and sipped his coffee. A more baffling girl he'd never seen.

"Good night," Prophet said finally, rolling up in his blankets.

"Lou?"

He turned to her. She was running the oily rag down the barrel of her Winchester.

"What?"

"How come . . . how come you've never tried anything with me like you were doing with Sunshine? You know, to satisfy your man's lustful desires." She set the rifle aside and looked at him.

Prophet's brows furrowed, and he felt the heat rise in his neck. "Well," he said haltingly. "Well, 'cause I figured you wouldn't have it."

"Well, I wouldn't, but I was just wondering. You think I'm pretty, don't you?"

Prophet grinned. Squinting one eye, he said, "Louisa Bonny-venture, I hesitate to tell you this out of fear of it going to your head, but I reckon you're the prettiest thing I've ever laid eyes on, and that's a fact."

She stared at him, expressionless. Then she smiled shyly and ground a furrow in the dirt with her boot heel.

"But I figured you'd shoot me if I tried anything."

"Well, I reckon I would at that," Louisa speculated. "So you better mind yourself." She paused, working her heel in the furrow. "But if you got real desperate, at the end of your obviously short tether, you might ask me politely, and I might think about it. Somewhere down the road, that is . . ."

"Somewhere down the road," Prophet said.

"Maybe."

"Maybe."

"That's right."

"Thanks, Louisa. That's mighty generous of you."

"That's all right. Thanks for changing my dressing."

"*De nada*. Good night."

Prophet rolled over and closed his eyes, grinning.

He'd almost drifted off when her voice rose again. "I mean, I've never done it before. But I suppose I should know the experience sometime before I die, and I don't know any man better than I know you. . . ."

Her voice trailed off, and the night sounds lifted.

"You will, Louisa," Prophet assured her, suddenly feeling sad for the girl. "Someday you will."

6

HANDSOME DAVE DUVALL wasn't nearly as handsome today as he normally was.

As he reined his trail-weary paint down a hogback near the Missouri River, a heavy layer of clay-colored dust coated his flat-crowned black hat and black cotton duster. His four-day growth of chestnut beard was dusty and seed flecked, and his peeling, sun-seared face bore the scratches he'd received two days ago when he'd ridden through briars just after ambushing the little bitch who'd been trailing him.

Who was that little minx, anyway? Duvall wondered now as he stopped his horse at the river, releasing the reins so the horse could drink. As the outlaw studied the milky brown water sliding between chalky, eroded buttes, he worked his weary mind over the blonde.

And who in the hell was the man she rode with, the big man on the dun? He had appeared armed for bear with a short-barreled shotgun, a Winchester, and what had looked like a Peacemaker revolver through Duvall's field glasses.

A bounty hunter, no doubt—Duvall had seen no badge—who'd picked up the trail of Duvall's gang in Fargo.

Dave's face and neck warmed with anger and confusion as he thought of the man and remembered the shoot-out—his whole outfit cut down in the darkness, wiped out by the bounty hunter and another man Duvall had never gotten a close look at. Having savvied the trap, Duvall was the sole survivor. If he was going to stay that way, he needed to lose the bounty hunter and get the hell out of the territory.

But first, Dave needed to rest himself and his horse. To that end, he reined the paint away from the river, traced a cut through the buttes, and continued south. He had a destination in mind, and when he reached it later that afternoon, after having followed a circuitous route around Bismarck and Fort Lincoln, he halted the horse on a low hill.

With his field glasses, he studied the buildings beneath him. Flanked by the river, they included an L-shaped log house with a sod roof, a log barn, several sheds, a sawmill, and two corrals. The ragged wheeze of a two-man saw rose to Dave's ears above the breeze rustling the grass and the birds chirping in the cottonwood snag to his left.

A brown-haired young woman appeared on the house's veranda. She stepped off the veranda with a lunch basket and headed across the yard to the mill, cream-colored skirts swishing about her legs. Dave waited, watching, until the woman stepped out of the mill and started back toward the house without the basket.

Watching the woman, Duvall grinned. Tired as he was, lust stirred him. And then he knew he was all right. The bounty hunter and the little blonde bitch might have set him back a bit, but by god, Handsome Dave Duvall was still a force to be reckoned with!

"Giddap, horse!" Duvall yelled, spurring the paint over the ridge and down the hill.

With the last bit of juice left in the horse's tired heart,

the outlaw cantered up to the tie rail before the house and swung out of the saddle, feeling fresher suddenly than he'd felt in days.

After all he'd been through—the ambush and the four-day run from the north—it only took one woman seen from a distance to make Duvall feel spry!

He looped the reins over the tie rack, bounded up the squeaky steps, crossed the porch, and noted the wood shingle hanging on the door in which CLAWSON'S RODEHOUSE had been burned. He grinned, spun the knob, and pushed into the dark, low-ceilinged room, his spurs clinking on the rough, sawdusted planks.

Looking around at the half-dozen tables decked out in red-and-white checked oilcloth, he called softly, "Margie?"

"Be out in a minute. Have a seat anywhere," came a woman's weary voice from another room.

Duvall grinned again, walked to a table, and sat down. His ass was sore from riding, but it still felt good to sit on something besides a saddle or the hard ground. The table was set, and when he'd taken his hat off and run a rough hand through his sweat-matted hair, Duvall thumbed a spoon around the oilcloth while listening to pans clattering in the back.

The saw had grown silent for a while, but its rhythmic rasp resumed now in earnest, deepening as the blade bit deep into a log. Its din nearly covered the drone of the flies against the sack-curtained windows. A fat liver-colored cat sat on a chair not far from Duvall, cutting its keen attention between one of the flies and the newcomer, its eyes big and coppery in the sunlight from the window.

"Here, pussy-puss," Duvall called to the cat.

He patted his thigh but turned when a door opened to his right and the brown-haired girl with vanilla skin entered holding a black coffeepot in one hand, a bluestone mug in the other. Striding toward his table, she said, "Sorry, but I just took a pie out of the oven, and—"

She stopped suddenly as her eyes picked Duvall out of the shadows surrounding his table several feet from the nearest window.

Duvall grinned his trademark Handsome Dave grin, his bristly cheeks dimpling, brown eyes flashing as they dropped to the low-cut, Spanish-style dress with short, puffy sleeves that revealed a good bit of the girl's cleavage. "Hi, Margie."

The girl's chocolate eyes blinked astonishment, her jaw sagging. "Dave? Duvall?"

"Been a while, hasn't it?"

"Why, Dave!" Margie's face flushed as she stood fidgeting, sliding her eyes around self-consciously. "What on earth . . . what on earth are you doing here?"

"Oh, it's a long story, Margie," Duvall said balefully, rubbing his hands over his tired, dusty face, then swiping them through his hair. "A long, awful story, and I really, really need some good food and rest. I remembered your old man bought this place from Childress. I was hopin' I'd find you here."

The girl stared at him with a hard-to-read expression, then gave a start as she regained her wits, and moved to Duvall's table, setting the cup before him and filling it from the pot. "Yeah, Pa died last year. Now—"

Duvall gently took her wrist in his hand. "How long's it been, Margie? Three years? Why, last time I saw you, you were just a girl." Duvall let his smoky eyes run down the young woman's curvaceous figure deliciously clad in the light cotton dress, and back up again, lingering in the valley between her breasts, which was lightly peppered with freckles. "Now, why, you're a full-blown woman. Every inch."

"Dave, I—"

"Come on, Margie, let me look at you," Duvall urged, drawing the girl onto his knee. Stiffly, she obliged him, looking at him askance and quickly sliding her eyes away, appearing only semireluctantly trapped.

"My, my, you are some kinda woman," Duvall said

softly, seductively, as he ran his hand along her neck, lightly fingering the auburn curls hanging over her collar. "You know, since we last parted, I haven't met a girl—a woman—who could do half of what you did for me, Margie. Even back then, when you were just a little girl still cypherin' and readin' out of little yellow books with pictures, you had a stranglehold on my soul. I felt your fire burn all the way down to my toes."

His eyes closed, Duvall lightly nuzzled her neck, making light sniffing sounds and puffing her ringlets. His hands gently kneaded her supple thighs through the dress. She appeared drugged, her head sagging slightly back and to the side, her eyes heavy.

"Oh, nanny, Margie—what you did to me! I still dream about you, 'most every night. And I wake up calling your name in my sleep. . . ."

"Dave, please," she said, halfheartedly attempting to stand. His hands on her thighs, he held her in place, and she swooned back against him as his tongue flicked out and traced a semicircular trail along her neck, just below her ear. His hands held taut to her thighs, his thumbs inching inside, making her squirm.

"Dave, please," she said, breathless. She squirmed around and ran her hands through his thick, wavy hair, then pulled them back quickly, as though from a hot stove. "Dave, things are . . . different now. . . ."

Just then the door opened, laying a prism of afternoon light on the sawdusted floor. A broad, stoop-shouldered man in coveralls and floppy hat stood silhouetted in the doorway, his face cloaked in shadow. Another, shorter man in a cloth cap stood behind him, rising up on his tiptoes to see over the bigger man's shoulder.

"What in the hell's goin' on?" The man's voice grumbled up like oil bubbles from deep in the earth.

Margie yanked away from Duvall's grip and stood,

stumbling over Dave's left boot, then sidestepping away, smiling with embarrassment and nervously smoothing her sweat-damp dress across her thighs.

"Jack!" she said, twittering. "Jack, Dave's here."

There was a silence as the two men stared at each other. Dave's cheeks were still dimpled with his grin, though not as deeply as before. Jack took two slow steps into the room. The man behind him took his place in the doorway, peering in warily.

Jack said, "Dave Duvall?" His deep-set, heavy-browed eyes slitted.

"Hi, Jack. How you been? Long time no see. Didn't expect to find you here." Duvall chuckled. "I mean, I know you was seein' Margie back in Julesburg, but I never knew . . ."

"We got married, Dave," Jack said. He stood about ten feet before Duvall, his high-topped Wellingtons shoulder width apart. His jaw was a straight, grim line.

"Well, that amazes me," Duvall said with another chuckle. "So you took over Margie's old man's sawmill. That it?"

"That's it, Dave. I'm a changed man. I ain't like I was when I rode with you an' the boys. I work an honest job now, cuttin' wood for the steamboats and servin' vittles to folks travelin' the post road yonder. I work hard, and so does Margie. Honest hard. Neither one of us are like we was before." Jack turned to Margie, who was staring at her shoes. "Ain't that right, Margie?"

She jerked her head up and glanced at Dave. Turning her gaze to Jack, she said hurriedly, "That's right. I ain't like I used to be."

Duvall turned to her, said brashly, "You mean, you ain't whorin' anymore, Margie girl?"

Margie turned to him as though startled. "Dave, please . . . I—"

"No, she ain't whorin' no more, Dave. And that's the last time that word will be spoken in my house."

"By who? You?"

"By anyone."

Duvall shook his head with mock exasperation. "Boy, that sure is paintin' with a broad brush, don't you think, Jack?"

"And Margie is off limits."

"There you go again—another damn rule. Next, I s'pose you're gonna tell me when I can sip my coffee and shake the dew from my lily."

Jack didn't say anything. The man in the doorway swallowed so hard that everyone in the room could hear it.

Duvall sighed and canted his head to one side. "You don't understand, Jack. Margie and I had something special. I mean *real* special—like I could feel it before I even met her."

Jack's upper lip curled. "Special, huh?" he snarled.

"*Real* special. Like I think Margie felt it before she met me. Like I think she's been feelin' it every day we been apart. Like I *know* she's feelin' it right now, while she's standin' there listenin' to us talk."

There was a long silence. Then Jack's eyes narrowed and his lips formed a tight circle. "Why, you—"

"It's so special, Jack, what Margie and I feel between us, that there ain't nothin' can keep us apart. Now, whether you like it or not, I'm going to take your wife into your bedroom and diddle the holy hell out of her."

"You *son of a bitch!*"

Duvall gained his feet and swung his duster back from the two matched pistols on his hips. "And you and I both know there ain't one goddamn thing you can do to stop me." He took three steps toward Jack, who didn't move a muscle. "'Cause you and I both know I can beat the holy *hell* out of you!"

Simultaneous with "hell," he rammed his left boot hard into Jack's groin. As Jack doubled over with a guttural cry, Duvall lifted his left knee, which met Jack's face with an audible crack of Jack's nose.

Jack bellowed like a poleaxed bull and tumbled over backward, toppling two chairs and a table. Margie screamed, covering her mouth. Duvall squatted down beside Jack, lifted Jack's head with a fistful of hair, and went to work on Jack's face with his right fist.

With grim determination, he worked on the face for close to a minute. He punched with his clenched, gloved fist, knuckles turned out. He drew the arm back like a piston, then shot it straight forward, over and over, at regularly spaced intervals, opening tear after tear on the already-swollen face of the woodcutter.

When he was satisfied with his work, Duvall stood and stared down at the unconscious Jack Clawson, whose face gleamed with blood. Duvall brought his boot back, then shot it into Jack's ribs. Duvall could tell from the snapping sound that he'd broken at least two.

His chest rising and falling, his eyes round and dark, he turned to the door. The other man was gone.

Duvall turned to Margie, who stood against the wall with her head in her hands, sobbing. "You see, Margie girl," he said, "what we have between us is *powerful!*"

7

"NO, I AIN'T seen Handsome Dave Duvall *lately,*" the bartender said, his dark eyes as big as some of the coins glittering up from the mahogany. "You don't need to describe him for me. I know what he looks like. Was on a stage he held up outta Deadwood a year or so back. He and his boys raped the three women on board: an old lady, a parson's wife, and a twelve-year-old girl. We men had to watch or get shot.

"I got sick and turned away for a second, and got a rifle butt to the back of my head. Cracked my skull. I still have headaches so bad I can't sleep at night."

The barman shook his head, his round face slack and expressionless, eyes filmed with bad memories. "So you don't need to tell me what that devil looks like. If I woulda seen him in here, I'd have recognized him. I woulda peed down my leg, skinned out the back, and hid in the privy." He glanced at the sawed-off ten-gauge hanging by the lanyard down the bounty hunter's back. "I'll tell you this, though. I hope you get him. I don't see how it's likely, but I hope you do, just the same."

Prophet nodded and threw back his whiskey. Tossing a silver dollar on the bar, he said, "I appreciate your story. I'll add it to the others I have in my head and remember it when I take him down."

Prophet pushed through the crowd of day drinkers and pleasure girls, and parted the batwings, halting on the boardwalk beside the wide, rutted street. Damn. That must have been the fifteenth person Prophet had asked about Handsome Dave since he and Louisa had ridden into Bismarck yesterday. He'd talked to bartenders, sporting women, liverymen, and even a few traveling drummers he'd stopped on the street or seen in saloons.

Not one had seen him. And most knew the name, knew who Prophet was talking about. Prophet had seen the consternation and downright fear in their eyes, as though he'd shown them an evil talisman. As though just mentioning the bastard's name had reminded them of their mortality.

Prophet turned left and walked over to Gustaffson's Livery Barn carved into the side of a hill on the south end of town, overlooking the distant blue sweep of the Mighty Mo under a clear Dakota sky. He'd already talked to Gustaffson himself, but the liveryman had told him he might want to speak with the kid who worked on Thursdays and weekends, when Gustaffson went fishing.

Today, Gustaffson was fishing, and Prophet found the freckle-faced livery boy repairing a harness in the stuffy tack room in a lean-to shed. The kid hadn't seen Handsome Dave, either.

"Are you huntin' him, mister?" the kid inquired after Prophet had turned away, confounded.

"That's right."

"Are you a bounty hunter?"

"That's right."

"Oh, boy! If you take down Handsome Dave, will you do me a favor?"

His frown deepening, Prophet turned back to the pudgy lad. "What's that?"

"Cut off one of his ears and give it to me?"

When Prophet just stared at the child, the boy continued. "Willy Crockett has one of Curly Bill Carlson's ears. His pa won it off a drummer in a poker game. The drummer won it off the bounty hunter who took Curly Bill down in Milestown. Willy, he's always showin' off that ear. I sure would like to have a famous outlaw's ear for my ownself—so I can show it around like Willy does Curly Bill's ear, scarin' all the girls."

Prophet grimaced and put his hand on the kid's shoulder. "Son, that's pathetic, you wantin' to show off dead men's ears to get attention. Don't you see that?"

The kid looked up at him dully.

"You should be playin' marbles and snarin' gophers and carrying girls' schoolbooks for them, not worryin' about collectin' the dried-up old ears of dead outlaws to frighten them with. That's disgusting."

The kid stared at him, sullen. "That mean you won't do it?"

Prophet sighed and turned away. Younguns, these days. As he stepped through the barn doors into the afternoon glare, he heard the kid mutter behind him, "Old fart."

Prophet wandered back up to the main drag, heading for the hotel where Louisa was holed up, sleeping off her gunshot fatigue. He stopped suddenly before the window of a ladies' clothing shop. Bonnie Rae's Fine Clothing for Women and Young Ladies, read the shingle over the boardwalk.

Getting an idea, Prophet went in. He came out fifteen minutes later carrying a paper sack. He looked around, then headed up the boardwalk until he came to a mercantile, and turned through the door. A few minutes later, he appeared on the boardwalk again with another, smaller parcel in his other hand.

The hotel in which he and Louisa had taken rooms sat on the corner of Main Street and First Avenue, catty-corner from both the Great Northern depot and a lumberyard. Its chipped green paint had faded to a dingy lime, and the rooms offered little more than lumpy beds, but it was a cheap place to bed down when you didn't know how long you were staying.

A little boy and a girl dressed in homespun farm clothes were chasing a barking yellow mutt in circles at the foot of the porch steps, and Prophet nearly tripped over them as he turned from the deeply rutted street and headed for the lobby.

When he'd fetched his key from the surly gent at the front desk, he climbed the creaky stairs and knocked on the door of room eight. Through the door he heard the click of a gun hammer.

Louisa said, "Who is it?"

"Santy Claus."

Behind the door, bedsprings squawked. Bare feet padded on the floor. The bolt was thrown and the door opened. In only her chemise and pantaloons—she'd stopped feeling shy around Prophet when she'd first been wounded back in Fargo—Louisa stared at him, unamused. Her silver-plated pistol hung slack in her right hand.

Grinning, Prophet lifted the largest of the two parcels. "Ho-ho-ho!"

She canted her head to one side and pursed her lips. "Any sign of Duvall?"

Prophet shook his head. "Not yet. But I've put the word out I'm lookin' for him. In the meantime, get dressed." He shoved the parcel at her. "We're goin' out."

"What's this?"

"Open it."

She looked in the bag, reached in, and pulled out the dress. Dropping the sack, she held the garment up before her, studying it as though it were something Prophet had fished out of a privy hole.

"What, don't you like it?"

She studied it silently, her mouth slackening. "This must've cost a pretty penny."

"Near the last of my poke, but don't worry. The sheriff here should have a reward waitin' for me in his safe, for a couple stage robbers I hauled in a few months back."

Louisa's eyes were still on the dress. "What's it for?"

"A night on the town. You and me. I thought we'd have supper over at the Bismarck Hotel with the civilized folk. I'm told the Bismarck has the best food in the territory. Yankee generals eat there, including Custer—before the Greasy Grass, that was." He chuckled.

Louisa lowered the dress and arched her brows accusingly. "You've been drinking. While you were supposed to be out inquiring of the whereabouts of our quarry, you were throwing back spirituous fire in one of the umpteen saloons in this den of iniquity."

"I'm not drunk . . . yet," Prophet said, shaking his head and grinning. "But I aim to be right soon. I'll go down and have the desk clerk send up water for a bath. Let's meet in the lobby around"—he fished in his pocket for his battered old timepiece and flipped the lid—"say five o'clock? I figured we'd have a couple before-dinner drinks, then—"

"If you're not drunk, you've gone insane. I will not frolic while Handsome Dave is free to rape, maim, and kill!"

"There's nothing to be done till tomorrow, anyway."

"It's not right."

"It is right, and what's more, you're gonna do it. You've been on the blood trail so long, you forgot what it's like to have fun. Tonight, Miss Bonny-venture, you're gonna have fun, if I have to hog-tie you and throw you over my shoulder to do it!"

The desk clerk's voice rose up the stairwell from the first story. "I don't allow no arguing or roughhousing on the premises," the man admonished. "I warned you two before!"

"Sorry," Prophet said, pushing Louisa into the room.

"I knew you two were gonna be trouble," retorted the clerk as Prophet shut the door behind him.

In the room, Louisa crossed her arms over her breasts again, cocked her head suspiciously, and squinted her right eye at the bounty hunter. "Are you trying to romance me, Lou Prophet?"

Staring down at the girl, who held the dress in one hand, his eyes turned thoughtful. Through a smoky grin, he drawled, "I ain't sayin' I am or I ain't, but I will tell you this. I'd give my right arm to see a girl who looks like you in a dress that looks like that."

Louisa stared back at him hard. But then, as his words reached her brain, her expression softened. She blinked as though waking from a daydream, and the lines in her forehead planed out. She parted her lips as if about to speak. She did not speak, however. Instead, she lowered her chin and dropped her befuddled eyes to the floor, her ears and neck turning rosy.

"Well," she murmured at last, giving a little shrug and turning the dress in her hand. "It is a nice dress, and since you bought it for me . . . I guess I could—"

Prophet's grin widened, and he turned to the door. "I'll go down and tell the clerk you want some bathwater," he said, his hand on the knob. "I'm gonna find me a barber with a sharp razor and a hot tub. See you in an hour or so."

He went out and began closing the door, then hesitated and poked his head back in. She still stood there, staring at the dress. "Oh, there's some blue hair ribbons in the sack,"

Prophet said. "The lady at the shop said they'd look good with the dress."

Prophet winked, pulled his head out of the room, and closed the door behind him. Entering his own room next door, he tossed the shotgun on the bed, grabbed his saddlebags, and left the hotel. He found a barbershop ten minutes later, and soaked in water so hot it nearly peeled the skin from his trail-weary bones.

When he'd climbed out of the tub, he donned the relatively clean denims and pin-striped cotton shirt in his saddlebags, then fished the string tie out of the small parcel he'd purchased at the mercantile. In a chipped mirror nailed to a joist, he looped the tie around his neck, and, after a half-dozen missteps, finally worked it into a passable knot.

"There, that should do it," he said, patting the knot flat against his throat but stretching his neck against the restriction. The blood burning in his head, he felt as though he had a noose around his neck. Who in the hell came up with the idea that a man would look tricky wearing a noose around his neck? Probably the Eastern dandy who invented the damn things.

When he'd lost a good half-inch of his straight, sandy hair, and his jaws were scraped clean and scented with tonic water, he paid the barber, bade him good evening, and started back to the hotel. He wore only half-clean trail garb and his scuffed boots, but the string tie, shave, and haircut made him feel spiffy. So spiffy, in fact, that he even caught himself bowing with a flourish to the ladies he met on the street.

When he knocked on Louisa's door, she yelled that she needed a few more minutes, as her hair wasn't dry. Smiling at that—at how much like any ordinary girl she suddenly sounded—Prophet told her he'd meet her downstairs in the lobby, and headed that way.

He'd smoked one and a half cigars before she appeared on the stairs, the folds of the aquamarine dress brushing against her legs. She'd brushed her honey blonde hair back and tied the ribbons in it, and it hung down past her shoulders. Her skin, tan from the trail, fairly gleamed with the recent scrubbing. She smelled good, too, like lavender and sage. Her eyes were bright with a subdued, girlish charm, an expression Prophet had never seen there before.

He was relieved to see it there now. Suddenly, she was just a kid like every other kid her age, feeling fresh and pretty and ready for a night with the boy who'd been sparking her. Only Prophet wasn't sparking her. Or was he? He himself wasn't sure. All he knew was that he wanted to see her in a nice dress for a change—without a gun and a knife on her waist and a murderous light in her eye.

"Why, Miss Louisa, I do declare!" he exclaimed, running his eyes up and down her sweet, supple frame. "You look ravishing."

A girlish blush spread over her face, and Prophet offered his arm. "Shall we?"

With a noncommittal shrug, she said, "Have it your way," and looped her arm through his.

Twenty minutes later, a red-jacketed waiter led them across the Bismarck Hotel's carpeted dining room, through a sea of tables draped with linen and set with silver. Although he doubted he'd know anyone in these venerable digs, Prophet's eyes instinctively swept the room for friend or foe.

The other diners appeared to be wealthy cattlemen or horse buyers from Chicago or farther east. Some were seated with either their wives or painted ladies decked out in the conservative tones and cuts of Libby Custer. Prophet knew for a fact that one such "lady" had a murky past, as he'd wallowed in her murk one blissful night a year ago, in Council Bluffs, Iowa.

She grinned as Prophet and Louisa passed her table, her liquid brown eyes catching the windows' fading light. Prophet gave a discreet nod, then sank into the chair the waiter held out for him, and noticed Louisa's critical gaze across the table.

When the waiter had given them menus and left, Louisa said, "Who's that?"

Prophet pretended to be lost in the menu. "Hmm?"

"The lady who lit up like a Christmas tree when she saw you."

Prophet flushed but kept his eyes on the menu. "Just an old friend," he said, as though bored. He glanced around the room at the drapes and chandeliers and hissing gas jets, and let his eyes fall on Louisa. "So, what do you think?"

Louisa was staring at Prophet's old friend. "I think she's a shameless harlot masquerading as that man's respectable wife. She didn't fool me for a second. I suppose the reprobate's poor wife is back home, cleaning his house and tending his children, while he cavorts with fallen women."

"I meant the digs."

Reluctantly, Louisa tore her eyes from the woman and let her gaze wander the room briefly. Shrugging, she said, "I guess it isn't too bad—for this backwater perdition."

Prophet sighed and returned to his menu. When the waiter returned, Louisa ordered the roast beef with new potatoes and baby peas and carrots. Prophet ordered a T-bone, charred.

"And we'd like a bottle of wine. The best you have for under five dollars."

"I'll have a sarsaparilla," Louisa piped up with a smug set to her mouth, her hands clasped before her on the table.

While the waiter hovered over him nervously, Prophet said, "Louisa, you can't come to a place like this and order sarsaparilla. Tonight, we'll have wine."

"I've told you before, Lou, I do not imbibe." She slid

her eyes to Prophet's "friend" across the room. "Look what the devil's brew has done to her!"

Both Prophet and the waiter glanced at the young lady, who sat holding her long-stemmed wineglass while listening dutifully as her gray-haired companion in a stylish suit and bolo tie gassed over his porterhouse.

To Louisa, Prophet said with a chuckle, "You could do a hell of a lot worse than her, my friend."

"Ha! At the cost of my dignity and self-respect. No, thank you. Sarsaparilla will be great plenty for me."

Prophet looked at the waiter, who returned the look with brows raised expectantly, his eyes vaguely troubled.

"Just bring me a double shot of rye," Prophet grunted. "Sarsaparilla for the girl."

When their food arrived, Prophet set to work hungrily, forgetting his surroundings and reverting to the trail custom of wolfing his food. He was gnawing on the T-bone with the contentment of an old dog under a wagon, when, suddenly feeling self-conscious, he looked around and saw several other diners staring at him.

Prophet froze, then dropped the bone on his plate. Wiping his greasy hands on his cloth napkin, he glanced up at Louisa, who regarded him with amusement, then lifted her sarsaparilla to her lips and drank.

When the waiter had taken their plates and brought apple pie and coffee, Prophet glanced at his companion. Louisa appeared content as she sipped her coffee and ate her pie. Not only that, but she appeared to be enjoying herself, her previous reservations having faded. There was a serene flush in her cheeks and a rare sparkle in her eyes.

She looked like a girl who would go home later, stop on her porch to admire the stars, play a few bars on the piano, kiss her parents good night, and fall blissfully asleep on a soft feather mattress.

Indeed, she looked downright civilized.

Deciding this was as good a time as any to broach the subject he'd been meaning to broach for days, Prophet took the bull by the horns.

"Louisa," he said, then sipped his coffee and cleared his throat. "I think you should stay here in Bismarck while I track Handsome Dave alone."

She regarded him deadpan from across the table.

"Did you hear me?"

As she stared at him, a flush rose up from her neck, painting her cheeks, and an angry light grew in her eyes. "So that's what the dress and the dinner were all about."

Prophet grimaced and looked around, as if for assistance. "No . . . see . . . I only wanted you to see what regular life was like again, so maybe you'd get a taste for it and give up this ugly business."

Before he'd finished the sentence, she was standing and shoving her chair back from the table. "You did, did you? But it wasn't your family murdered by those savages, was it? It wasn't your mother and sister hauled into the tall weeds by the creek!" This last she fairly yelled, and all heads whipped toward them.

"Louisa!"

She'd swung around and was marching across the room toward the lobby. Prophet fumbled with his napkin and tried to stand. He hadn't expected the chair to be so heavy, however, and he nearly lost his balance. When he finally got clear of the chair and was heading after Louisa, the waiter appeared as if from nowhere, looking perturbed.

"Is everything all right, sir?" he asked haughtily.

"Does everything look all right?" Prophet groused, digging in his jeans pocket for his last wad of bills.

Hurriedly unpeeling several greenbacks from the greatly diminished roll, he stuffed the money in the man's vest pocket. "There, that should cover it." He hurried from the room, weaving around tables where the diners sat in hushed silence, staring after him bewilderedly.

Prophet stepped onto the veranda and looked both ways along the street. The light was fading, but he saw Louisa retreating westward along the boardwalk. He descended the steps two at a time and jogged after the girl who was crossing a side street a block ahead, on the left side of Main. She marched stiffly, angrily, hair bouncing on her shoulders.

"Louisa, I just don't want you to become one of *them!*" Prophet beseeched her as his boots thumped the boards.

He was approaching a big surplus grocery warehouse when a man suddenly stepped onto the boardwalk before him from an alley between the buildings. He was a short, stocky hombre in a grimy undershirt, a hide vest, and a shabby bowler. His ruddy face was pinched with grim determination. The golden sunlight flashed on the barrel of the revolver he brought chest high and aimed at Prophet's heart.

The bounty hunter saw the flash and heard the boom before he had time to twitch, much less duck.

8

PROPHET STARED FOR what seemed a long time at the shooter's trembling, smoking gun.

Vaguely surprised to not be feeling the cold burn of a bullet, he stumbled back against the warehouse and whipped a quick glance behind him. Incredibly, the man's hand had been shaking so hard that the bullet had sailed wide and plunked into a clapboard, drilling a splintery hole.

Instantly, Prophet clawed his own hogleg from his hip. But when he swung it forward, clicking the hammer back, his assailant disappeared around the building. Hearing boots pounding the boardwalk behind him, Prophet swung the gun that way. Another man—tall and thin and cow-eyed—was running toward him, yelling, "Bill, you goddamn yella dog!" The man came on, extending a revolver and sighting down the barrel.

Before he could fire, Prophet triggered his Peacemaker, the crack lifting angrily. The man took three more strides and dropped to his knees with a grunt. He held there, gazing stupidly down at the blood blossoming on his chest, then fell forward on his face, grinding his hat into the boardwalk.

Confused, his heart hammering, Prophet whipped forward and ran to the cross street. He stopped at the corner and extended the Peacemaker, peering south. Several horses and a leather-topped buggy were tied before a small tavern. Before the tavern, two old men in business suits stood holding soapy beer mugs and peering at Prophet warily.

"A man run this way?" Prophet called to them.

One of the old men nodded dully and pointed southward down the cross street. "And a girl. What's goin' on, mister?"

Prophet bolted forward, running hard, spurs clinking raucously. When he came to an alley, he stopped and looked left, then right. The alley was dark, as the sun was nearly gone, but he saw movement in the shadows that way.

"Louisa?" he called, his voice betraying his concern.

He crossed the street and jogged into the alley, stopping when he saw a slender figure approach, skirts swishing.

"Forget it," she snarled, as angry as Prophet had ever seen her. Her voice was shrill with reproach. "He had a horse back there, and he's gone. I could've shot him if I'd had a gun—and I would have had a gun if it hadn't been for you and this dress and this silly, silly night you concocted!"

She brushed past him and marched up the cross street, her back stiff, her arms swinging furiously.

"Be careful," Prophet told her. "There was another one. I shot him, but there could be more."

She stopped abruptly and turned around. Before she could ask the obvious question, Prophet shook his head. "It wasn't Duvall."

"Who, then?"

Prophet shrugged and, gun hanging at his side, walked up the cross street and turned before the warehouse, where the dead man lay facedown on the boardwalk, blood pooling around him. Louisa came up behind Prophet and peered grimly down at the crumpled body.

"Dave's here," she said coldly. "He sent them."

"Not necessarily," Prophet said. "I've got lots of enemies . . . all over."

"It's too much of a coincidence. He's here."

"You there!" someone yelled. "You there; stay where you are and drop your weapon."

Prophet peered back down the boardwalk, wincing. Two men were heading toward him and Louisa. One was short and nattily dressed in a cream Stetson and suit coat over a vest upon which a badge winked in the fading light. Another, larger man tramped along behind him, wielding a shotgun. He, too, wore a badge.

"Shit," Prophet muttered.

"You there!" the short man yelled, stopping on the boardwalk, turning sideways, lifting an arm, and extending a stern finger at the bounty hunter. "I told you to drop that gun!"

"Droppin' it on the boardwalk will raise hell with the action. Sheriff, how 'bout if I just hand it to you butt first?"

The sheriff acquired a pained look and dropped his arm. "Prophet?"

"Yeah, it's me," he said with a fateful sigh.

The sheriff turned to the big, mustachioed deputy who stood behind him, then shook his head and began strolling toward Prophet, his fingers in his vest pockets. He glanced suspiciously between the bounty hunter and the dead man. "Who in the hell did you kill *now*?"

"Didn't tell me his name," Prophet said. "Just aimed that gun at me like he was fixin' to use it, so I offed him. Miss Bonny-venture here will attest to the fact it was either him or me."

"Miss who?"

"Miss Bonny—" Prophet turned to where Louisa had been standing behind him, but she wasn't there. Looking around, he didn't see her anywhere. "Well, I'll be . . . she was right here." Prophet turned and took several steps up the street. "Louisa?"

"Get your ass back here, Prophet," the sheriff ordered. "I won't have any of your foolishness. Now tell me who this man is and why you killed him. If it's a bounty you're after, there sure as hell better be some paper on him."

Prophet was still looking up the street for Louisa. She'd disappeared into thin air, the ungrateful little hellcat.

Scowling, he turned to the sheriff. The deputy was squatted down, going through the dead man's pockets.

"I told you, Sheriff," Prophet said, "it was self-defense. He and a buddy tried layin' me out. The buddy missed and ran off, and this man here came runnin' up behind me, aimin' that thirty-six he's got there. So I shot him. Fair and square. Him or me."

"He dead?" the sheriff asked the deputy.

"Deader'n hell, Sheriff. Shot him right through the brisket. No one I recognize."

The sheriff turned to the dozen or so people who'd heard the commotion and were milling up and down the street, looking this way. Most had come from the taverns and were holding glasses or cigars.

"Anyone see what happened here?" the sheriff asked them, swinging his gaze around.

No one said anything. A few shrugged. A few others wagged their heads. Deciding the excitement was over, several wandered back into their respective saloons, brothels, or restaurants. A fiddler was fiddling in a tavern up the street, and the lively music was a stark contrast to the grim situation on the bloody boardwalk.

The sheriff brought his gaze back to Prophet and extended his hand. "Give me that Peacemaker, Prophet."

"What for? I told you—"

"I know what you told me, but I'm bringin' you in."

Prophet opened his mouth to object, but the sheriff held his hand up, cutting him off. "I'm gonna hold you overnight while Daniel here makes the saloon rounds. Sometimes it takes a few drinks to loosen people's tongues. Someone must have seen what happened here."

"Someone did see what happened here, Sheriff. Louisa Bonny-venture. She's over at—"

"Now I've had enough of that foolishness, Prophet. You're just up to your old tricks, tryin' to make us lawmen look like fools. Well, I won't have it. Now hand over that gun before I charge you with resisting arrest."

Prophet scowled and wagged his head as he lifted the Peacemaker from his holster. Some lawmen he got along with, some he didn't. Sheriff Edward Teal had always been one of the latter, for no good reason Prophet could think of, unless it was the time Prophet had found the bank robber the sheriff and his posse were tracking into the nether regions of the county, in a cathouse right across from the jail. If only Louisa hadn't stalked off and left him here to explain himself. Some way to thank a fellow who only had her best interests in mind! When he saw her again, he had a mind to truss her up like a pig and give her a good old-fashioned tanning.

"You've just been waitin' for this, haven't you, Sheriff?" Prophet groused as he handed over the Peacemaker.

Teal shrugged and shared a snide glance with his deputy. "I don't know what you're talking about, Prophet. That's enough of your smart talk. Now move out. I'm turnin' the key on you!"

And he was going to enjoy every minute of it, Prophet thought as he stalked off toward the jail, feeling his own pistol poke his back. With no satisfaction at all, he also thought how Louisa's trick could backfire on her if Handsome Dave called on her tonight, without Prophet there to help.

9

HANDSOME DAVE DUVALL set the coffee can on the corral post beside the five other cans he'd placed there after gleaning all six cans from the trash heap behind the roadhouse.

He inspected the cans, furling his bushy, auburn brows. Satisfied with their positions, he turned and took several steps back from the fence. He saw Jack Clawson sitting on the roadhouse's porch across the dusty yard and lifted his hand to shield the light of the setting sun from his face.

"Hi, Jack!" Dave called with a friendly wave and a grin that dimpled his handsome cheeks. "How you feelin' this evenin'?"

Jack just stared across the yard at Dave. He sat in a rocking chair, clad in a tattered green robe and hide slippers. His head was swollen and blue, his eyes mere slits in the yellow purple flesh of his beaten face. His chest bulged with the taut bandage Margie had wrapped him in to secure his broken ribs.

Jack didn't say anything. His thin hair slid around in the evening breeze.

Still smiling, Dave shook his head as though at a peculiar and vaguely humorous twist of fate. Then he swung back toward the cans, clawed the pearl-handled revolver from his hand-tooled holster tied low on his thigh, crouched, and fired, fanning the trigger. The gun roared and jerked, roared and jerked. One by one, from left to right, the cans flew off the fence. The last can rose high in the air over the corral. It winked in the salmon light, twisting and turning as it rose to its apex and started back groundward.

Dave removed the second gun from the waistband of his broadcloth breeches, aimed, and fired. The can jerked again, bounding off toward the barn and landing in a sage tuft with a tinny rustle.

Dave turned to Jack, who sat on the porch without moving, dull-eyed. Dave lifted the smoking barrel of his revolver to his lips and blew on it. "Whew! Now that was some shooting, wouldn't you say, Jack?"

Margie appeared in the door, fists on her hips. "Dave, I declare! What are you shootin' at now? You're gonna give me a heart stroke, with all your shootin'!"

"Just stayin' sharp, Margie girl," Dave said affably, shoving the revolver into his waistband.

"You're gonna give me a heart stroke, Dave," Margie scolded, then turned back into the cabin.

"Sorry, Margie," Dave called to her. "I'll make it up to you later." He slid his eyes to Jack, grinning. He couldn't tell from this distance, but he thought the woodcutter's face turned a darker shade of blue.

Dave was lining the cans up on the fence rail again when he heard the slow clomp of horses to the west. Turning, he saw dust rising and the silhouettes of three riders making their way toward the roadhouse. The sun was a pink ball behind them, making their dust look smoky.

Without hesitation, Dave drew his holstered revolver and began loading it quickly from his shell belt. It took his trained fingers only a few seconds to fill all the chambers with brass, and then he was working on his belly gun. He'd just spun its cylinder when the riders came around the cottonwood tree and the woodshed. They rode slowly, sitting lazily in their saddles, rolling with the slow sway of their mounts.

They were all dressed in rough trail gear, but Dave recognized them as the three soldiers who had stopped here yesterday for lunch. They'd gassed with Dave on the porch, though Dave hadn't told them who he was. Harmless boys they were, bored with the army and searching for distractions. Dave was relieved it was only them and not the man who'd been dogging him, or lawmen.

His brows ridged as he cocked his head to the side, wondering why they weren't wearing their uniforms. And why had they returned so soon? Fort Lincoln was a good twenty miles away, on the other side of the river.

Wondering if they'd recognized him and, after gathering their courage, had decided they'd take him down for the reward money on his head, he felt the muscles along his spine tighten. He held the belly gun down low at his side, ready to bring it up fast and ventilate these blue bellies if necessary.

The middle rider, riding a little ahead of the other two, must have recognized the tension in Dave's stance. He raised a placating hand as he checked his army bay down, twenty yards before Duvall.

"Hello, Mr. Duvall."

The other two youngsters rode up beside the first one and gazed at Dave with a mixture of fear and expectation. He noticed that none moved his hand close to the gun on his hip, and that their eyes didn't appear to be too shifty, either. Both good signs. But if they weren't here to take him down—and they'd called him by name—what were they doing here?

Duvall played it cool. "Hello, boys. What brings you back out here so soon? Your sergeant get generous with the day passes, did he?"

The young man on the far left was a soft-faced young man with brown hair and spare muttonchop whiskers. His eyes were emerald green and glittery. "Nah, he didn't," he said with a mild guffaw, sucking at the wedge of chaw in his cheek.

"Shut up, Harold," the kid in the middle said—a thin, muscular lad with blond hair beneath a weathered, narrow-brimmed Stetson. This kid was all rawhide, with a knife slash for a mouth. "I told you I'd do the talkin'."

"I didn't mean nothin', Clyde. I was just—"

"Shut up, Harold!" Clyde admonished, jerking his head wickedly at his friend.

Duvall waited, sliding his eyes from one lad to the next, then back again. The kid on the far right was the largest of the three. He didn't say a word, just stared silently from beneath the brim of his floppy black farm hat, the acorn of which flopped beneath his anvil chin.

Clyde turned to Duvall with a nervous grin that parted his thin lips and squinted his eyes. He chuckled. "I guess you know we know who ye are. It was Danny over there"—he tipped his head to indicate the big, silent lad—"who recognized you. It didn't come to him till we were down the trail a ways. H-he grew up in your hometown of Saint Joseph, Missouri, didn't ye, Danny?"

"You don't say?" Dave said skeptically. "I s'pose you know old Jack Ramey then—the Nigra that runs the ferry."

"I sure do know Jack," Danny said smartly, giving his big chin a self-satisfied dip.

"What's his big, fat wife's name again?" Duvall said, scratching his chin. "I forget. . . ."

Danny smiled. "Peach."

"Peach—that's right," Duvall said, appraising the lad with interest. "So you're from Saint Joe and you know who I am. What does that make you?"

"Well, we kinda figured it might make us amigos," Clyde piped up, leaning forward on his saddle horn. "I'll put it to you honest, Mr. Duvall, we done been tired of the army's bullshit for months now. We don't see goin' into another winter up here, freezin' our peckers off and chasin' Injuns through the snow. We wanna join up with your bunch and do some real ridin' for some real money."

"Yeah, we heard you boys get all the nice-looking girls!"

"Shut up, Harold, for the last time!" Clyde bellowed, swatting Harold with his hat.

Duvall chuckled.

Clyde said, "What do you say, Mr. Duvall. We know we're prob'ly a little green compared to a man like yourself, but we all—even Harold here—have killed people and robbed. I shot a mean ole Colorado farmer when I was just thirteen years old!"

"You did?" Duvall said with mock surprise. "What for?"

"He caught me stealin' potatoes out of his cellar. Said he was gonna cut my balls off. Shot him right through the ticker."

Harold said, "I shot somebody, too, Mr. Duvall. Just last year."

"That don't count, Harold," Clyde said. He looked at Duvall. "He caught a preacher diddlin' his ma at a church picnic and shot him with his pa's old Patterson Colt. Shot him in the ass." Clyde wheezed with laughter, his face turning crimson. "You shot a preacher in the ass, Harold. That don't count!" Clyde guffawed.

"Why don't it count?" Harold wanted to know.

When Clyde only laughed and wagged his head, Harold turned to Duvall. "I'd say that counts, wouldn't you, Mr. Duvall?"

"Well, I don't know," Duvall said, scratching his head with mock consideration. "I guess it would count if you were *aimin'* at his ass. If not"—Duvall shrugged—"I guess I'd have to say no."

Harold frowned.

"See, Harold?" Clyde mocked.

Harold scrunched his face up at Clyde angrily, but before he could say anything, Duvall said, "Hold on, hold on, boys! On the basis of your obviously questionable characters and clear determination to walk a crooked path, wreaking pain and havoc wherever you go, I would indeed make you probationary members of my gang—if I could."

Clyde wrinkled his brow. "If you could?"

"If I could," Dave said. "But I can't. I'm sorry, boys, but as you can see, the rest of the Red River Gang isn't here. Due to circumstances beyond our control, we had to split up for a while. We won't be back together for . . . uh . . . for some time, I'm afraid. And it just wouldn't be right if I brought in new members without giving the others a say in the matter."

Clyde was about to object, but Duvall held up his hand, stopping him. "I'm sorry, Clyde. Truly, I am. But that's the way the Red River Gang operates. Every gang has to have rules, and that's one of our rules. It's inviolable, I'm afraid."

Duvall raised his hands and dropped them with futility and shook his head. The three lads sat the saddles of their fidgeting mounts with grim expressions on their dusty faces. Harold and Danny cut their eyes at Clyde accusingly. Clyde was staring at his saddle horn, sheepish.

"Well, if that's the way it is, I guess that's the way it is," Clyde allowed quietly.

"Goddamn you, Clyde," Danny admonished. "You said for sure he'd let us join."

"Yeah, goddamn you, Clyde," Harold intoned. "Now we're gonna have to go back to the fort."

"We can't go back to the fort, you moron," Danny said. "Not after all that money Clyde stole."

Clyde sighed and began reining his mount toward the east side of the yard. "Yeah, I guess we'll just have to head south. Maybe disappear in the Black Hills for a while."

Duvall's ears had pricked at the mention of money. He'd lost every penny he'd owned when the bounty hunter had surprised his gang at their hideout in the northern part of the territory. He didn't have a cent—beyond the few dollars he intended to take from Jack and Margie, that was—and he desperately needed cash for his long trip south, to the Indian nations, where he intended to hide until the law forgot about him and he could put together another gang.

If he traveled like most men, living off the land, jerked beef, and coffee, he might have gotten by on what he intended to steal from Jack and Margie. But Dave Duvall did not, could not, travel like most men. His previous lifestyle had conditioned him to luxury, which included sporting women and whiskey at the very least, even on the desperation trail.

"What money?" Duvall asked, trying not to sound too eager.

Clyde checked his bay back down and glanced at Duvall over his shoulder. "Oh, we ran into the three fellas that sold remounts to the fort earlier today. I recognized 'em from a distance and got a wild hair up my ass. Next thing we knew, we was sneakin' up on their camp. We shot 'em all as they snoozed around their coffee fire—"

"And made off with pret' near a thousand dollars!" Danny added, lifting his head to the purple sky and giving a grand coyote hoot.

"I know that ain't very much to a man like you, Mr. Duvall," Clyde said. "But that's more money than the three of has ever even dreamed about. I reckon we'll be on the lam for a while. Well, it was nice meetin' you, and maybe we'll run into you again sometime."

"Uh, hold on, boys," Duvall said, feigning a considering air, crossing his arms on his chest and propping one finger against his chin. "Maybe I've been too hasty in my decision."

The boys sawed back on their reins and turned to Duvall expectantly.

"What's that, Mr. Duvall?" Clyde said.

"Yes, well, I was just thinking," Dave said, "I guess the gang could vote on you three *after* we've all gotten together again. I mean, I really wouldn't be bringing you into the gang if I just let you ride with me for a few months."

Clyde shrugged, his eyes growing large. "No, I reckon not."

"We could even look at it as your trial period," Duvall speculated. "If you boys always did as I said and learned what I had to teach you, the gang might just be inclined to welcome you into its fold."

Clyde grinned. "I sure as hell bet they would, Mr. Duvall!"

Duvall nodded objectively, studying the ground as if looking for coins he'd dropped, finger still propped on his chin. "Yes . . . yes. That might work." He looked at the eager lads and smiled. "All right, I'm game to give it a shot. You can bed down in the barn yonder. I'll have Margie haul you out some grub. We're leaving for the Indian nations first thing in the morning. You can switch your army mounts with any of those you see in that corral on the other side of the barn. *Comprende, amigos?*"

All three heartily agreed, and headed off to the barn, thanking Duvall over their shoulders and assuring him he'd made the right decision.

Duvall watched them disappear in the darkness. If they got on his nerves, he could always shoot them and take their money. That wouldn't be any big chore. On the positive side, he now had three more sets of eyes on his back trail. And you couldn't have too many eyes where he was going, into the fiery bowels of the Indian nations, where he'd be only one more desperado on the lam and at odds with others just like him.

"Hi, Jack," he greeted the beaten man now as he stepped onto the porch. He squeezed Jack's shoulder and said with a quiet, mocking air, "Where's your wife?"

Jack rumbled like a volcano, his chair creaking beneath him.

"Oh, I forgot you can't speak on account of your broken jaw," Dave said with an air of understanding. "That's all right. Don't trouble yourself. I'll just go in and find her myself."

He laughed and went inside the cabin.

Behind him, Jack boiled in his chair, red-faced and sweating.

10

"DAVE, I'M A married lady," Margie protested.

"So, what are you sayin'?" Dave asked as he grunted between her knees.

"It ain't . . . it ain't right, Dave, us carryin' on with Jack sittin' right out there on the porch." She sighed and groaned and wagged her head from side to side on the pillow.

"Well, all right, Margie girl," Dave said heavily. "If you want me to stop, I'll stop."

She scissored his back with her legs and threw her arms around his neck. "Don't you dare!"

A few minutes later, a tap sounded on the door.

"Go away!" Dave barked, still at work, sweating between Margie's knees.

Another tap on the door. A throat was cleared. "Dave? It's Bill. Bill Maggs."

Margie lifted her head and jerked an exasperated gaze at the door lit by the lamp on the dresser. "For the love of God, Bill, *go away!*"

"Shut up," Dave scolded Margie, clamping a hand over her mouth. Glancing at the door and raising his voice, he said, "Is he dead?"

"Uh . . ." the man said through the door, tentative. "I don't think so, Dave."

"What!" Duvall exclaimed, rolling angrily off Margie and grabbing his pants from a chair. He hopped into the breeches, cursing, and opened the door.

Bill Maggs stood in the doorway, looking crestfallen and scared. He was Jack Clawson's woodcutting partner—or had been before Dave had beaten Jack senseless. Fearful for his own life, Bill had quickly become Dave's truckling servant. Dave had sent Bill to Bismarck to see if anyone was looking for Dave.

Sure enough, Bill had heard a tall man with a sawed-off shotgun had bean asking around the saloons and brothels. Hearing this, Dave had sent Bill and Bill's stepson, Edgar, to dry-gulch the man. They'd assured Dave they could do it, and Dave reminded the wizened little man of that now, drawing him up by the collar of his grimy undershirt.

"I know, I know. Jeepers, I sure am sorry, Dave, but it wasn't my fault. Edgar—he took the first shot at him and missed!"

"Goddamn, you, Bill!" Dave seethed in the little man's face, tearing the undershirt bunched in his fists.

"I'm sorry, Dave. But it wasn't my fault. It was Edgar's! That boy's just like his mother! Doesn't amount to a speck o' fly shit!"

"Where is he?" Dave said, savagely jerking at Bill's shirt, flecks of spittle flying from his quivering lips.

"Dead," Bill said. "He . . . that bounty hunter shot him."

Dave sighed and released Bill's shirt. "Good," he growled. His angry eyes turned pensive. "So he is a bounty hunter, eh?"

"That's what Muriel Pierce over at the Pink Lady told

me. A Southern bounty hunter, one o' the best in the business."

"What's his name?"

"Prophet, I believe Muriel said. Lou Prophet." Bill smiled. "Rides a big, mean horse, but the girls like him."

Duvall turned away, nervously scratching his jaw. "Prophet, eh? I've heard that name. Lou Prophet. Yeah, I've heard of him a time or two. Damn you, Bill!"

"I sure am sorry, Dave, but like I said—"

"I know, I know. It's not your fault," Duvall groused, grabbing his shirt and shrugging into it. "Go out to the barn and tell them three boys camped out there to get their horses saddled, and one for me—and not that old paint I rode in on. We're pullin' out in fifteen minutes!"

Bill stood in the doorway looking puzzled. "Boys . . . barn?"

"You heard me, you moron. Any one of 'em is more man now than you'll ever be! Move!"

"R-right away, Dave!" Bill said as he dashed for the door.

"Dave, where are you going?" Margie lay nude on the bed, propped on an elbow and curling a wisp of disheveled hair with a finger.

"I gotta go, Margie girl," Dave said breathlessly as he tucked his shirt in his pants. "One thing I learned here tonight is to never send fools to do a man's work."

He found his socks and sat on the bed to pull them on. "I knew I should have gone after that Prophet fella myself, but I didn't want the law to catch me in town. Then I'd *really* be up shit creek. But I'm up shit creek anyway, because now—on account of that dumbass Maggs and his dumbass stepson—Prophet knows I'm around. And no doubt he'll figure out I've been holed up here. Sooner or later. It's just a matter of time for a cussed bounty man like that one there."

"He won't find you here, Dave."

"Won't he?" Dave said as he reached for his boots. "You've had a lot of travelers pass through here the last few days. No tellin' if one or two might've recognized me. My handsome mug's right famous, you know, Margie girl."

"I reckon you got a point there, Dave. Still, though, I sure hate to see you go. I mean, it wasn't right how you treated Jack, but before you came"—Margie rolled her eyes, glancing around the stark room—"it was so *boring* around here."

"I'm sure it was, Margie," Dave said with a laugh, standing and stomping his heels into his boots. He reached for his gun belt coiled around a bedpost and strapped it on, adjusting the holster on his thigh and tying the thong just above his knee. "But I think I can do something to keep things from being quite so boring around here from now on, Margie."

"What do you mean, Dave?"

"I mean, Margie," Dave said, sitting beside her on the bed and regarding her sympathetically, brushing a lock of hair from her face. "I mean, I think I can take the boredom away, for good."

She stared at him, concern growing in her large eyes. "What are you talkin' about, Dave?"

Dave pinched her right breast like he would a melon, checking for ripeness. Then he ran the fingers of his right hand lightly along her plump thigh. Her skin quivered slightly at his touch, goose bumps rising.

"I mean, I sure am sorry I have to do this, Margie, but damn, if you ain't too purty not to shoot."

Slowly, he drew his revolver and clicked back the hammer.

Margie's eyes widened as she pushed up on her elbows, lifting her knees before her. "What? Dave, what are you doing?"

"Thanks for the good time, Margie," Dave said, smiling

with glassy-eyed insanity. "But you know what the preachers always say: good times don't last forever. No, they sure don't. The grim reaper comes callin' sooner or later. It's just a little sooner for you, I'm afraid."

"Dave, no!" Margie pleaded, her eyes on the gun Duvall swung toward her. "No, Dave, please! Why? Oh, my—"

The sharp crack of the forty-five finished the sentence for her. Her head flaw back against the wall, the hole in her forehead gleaming wetly. Slowly, she sagged to the side and lay limp across both pillows.

Dave gave her thigh one last appreciative pat, then donned his hat and walked into the main room, where only one bracket lamp was lit, sending a weak, liquid light wavering over two tables while leaving the rest of the room in semidarkness. He took one step forward and heard a commotion on the porch. He hurried to the porch door and drew his gun.

Turning to his right, he saw the overturned rocking chair and the dark figure of Jack Clawson trying to crawl to the other end of the porch, making hoarse, fearful rasping sounds as he scuttled buglike on his hands and knees, trying to escape his fate.

"Oh, no you don't, Jack," Duvall said with a menacing chuckle. "You ain't goin' nowhere." With that he raised the gun and fired, and Jack fell on his face with a guttural sigh.

Turning toward the barn, Dave saw something move in the darkness about halfway across the yard.

"Bill, that you?" he called.

The figure stood still, on the other side of a horse trough.

"What's all the shootin' about, Dave?"

Dave stepped off the porch and moved fluidly across the yard, toward the stocky, dark, hatted figure of Bill Maggs. "I just shot Margie and Jack," he said matter-of-factly. "And I'm afraid I'm going to have to shoot you, too, Bill."

"Huh? What?" Bill said, frozen there in the shadows.

As Duvall aproached him, he extended his gun and blew a hole in the man's head, just above his left ear. Bill hadn't dropped before Dave had resumed his purposeful stride toward the barn, before which the three lads were standing and staring, looking jittery.

"What's all the shootin' about?" Clyde asked.

"Just tyin' up some loose ends," Duvall said. "You boys have those horses saddled yet?"

"Well, no," Clyde reported. "We heard the shootin' and we—"

"Boys, if you're gonna ride with me, you have to do as you're told, shootin' or no shootin'. Now get those horses saddled before I change my mind about lettin' you throw in with me."

With that, the three young men scurried back into the barn, and Duvall followed them. Ten minutes later, they were all mounted on fresh horses and galloping south toward the buttes along the river.

Behind them, Bill Maggs gurgled and died.

11

LOUISA BONAVENTURE WOKE much later in the morning than she was used to—before she was wounded, that was. Blinking her eyes and lifting her head from her pillow, she saw that full golden sunlight angled through her room's single, fly-specked window. On the street below she heard voices and the squawk and clatter of freight wagons and the whinnies and snorts of the teams.

She reached for her timepiece on the nightstand, and flipped it open. Eight forty-five. She'd slept half the morning away!

She'd decided last night it was time to take the search for Handsome Dave Duvall into her own hands, if only to spite the cunning Prophet. As she got up and started her toilet, she burned at the nerve of the man, trying to sweet-talk her into letting him track Duvall down alone!

Who did Prophet think he was, trying to tell her what to do? It hadn't been his family that maniac had murdered! And to think she'd actually started to trust the big man, and to even rather sort of enjoy his earthy, if uncouth, company!

Harumph! No more! From now on *she* wouldn't let *him* ride with *her!*

She had to smile, though, at the thought of the look that must have been on his face when he'd turned around last night to find her gone. Vanished into thin air! Actually, when she'd seen the sheriff, she'd just slipped off down the side street and made her way back to the hotel via alleys, hoping Prophet got what he deserved for making a fool out of her with that fancy dress and his tricky charms.

A night in the hoosegow. Yes, that's exactly what the man deserved.

Louisa dressed in her trail clothes: her simple gray farm dress and ratty poncho, which concealed her silver-plated, short-barreled revolver and her sheathed knife honed to a razor edge. She snugged her hat on her blonde head, letting the acorn fastener hang beneath her chin. When she'd packed up her saddlebags, she grabbed her Winchester and headed out, halting at Prophet's door to hook the fancy dress he'd bought her over the knob.

She found a simple café run by a buxom old German woman just up the street, and sat down to a meal of eggs, potato pancakes, and bratwurst. When the woman returned to refill Louisa's empty coffee cup, Louisa wiped her mouth with her napkin and said, "Ma'am, may I inquire as to where the worst part of this village might lie? I mean, I know it's all bad, and if all were right with the world the Missouri would swell up and take it all asunder, but I mean the really terrible part of town."

The old woman blinked down at her, baffled, dentures sliding off her gums. *"Vot?"*

"The really *bad* part of Bismarck. I want to know where the really *bad* people stay."

"Vy on ert vould you vont to know dat!"

Yes, why would she? Louisa thought about it, dabbing at her lips again to buy time. "Because I lost my brother last night, and I'm thinking that, after all our time on the farm, with nary a trip to town in two years and our father thumping our heads with his Bible all the time, Hansel's run off to the really *bad* part of town. You know, to cavort with—"

"Yes, I see vot you mean," the old woman rushed in, nervously eyeing her other customers to see if they'd been listening. She bent down and said in Louisa's ear, her breath smelling like rotten cabbage, "The vorst of dis place is vest by da river. A shantytown, it is. *Ach!* Unspeakable filth. I've never been, but I've heard da stories." She sighed, shook her head, and straightened with an audible crack of the bones in her back. "More coffee?"

When Louisa had finished her breakfast, she went over to the livery barn and saddled her horse. Then she fought the freight traffic to the west end of town, following a well-worn trail through the buttes along the river.

She smelled the shantytown before she saw it: the reek of buffalo hides and overfilled latrines. Then the town itself: a few log shacks and tents strewn along the trail, up and down the buttes and shallow ravines.

In one such ravine many horses had been picketed near small, guttering fires around which men of all sizes and colors lounged, alone or in small groups. Many drank from whiskey bottles or stone jugs. Nearby were bundles of buffalo hides over which black clouds of flies hovered.

A hide-hunter's camp.

Louisa had seen one before in southern Iowa, and she'd never wished to see one again. The stench alone had made her ill. And when you threw in the human vermin that populated such places—women as well as men . . .

Yes, this was a place that would attract the likes of Handsome Dave Duvall. Or at the very least, someone here would have seen or heard of him.

Louisa rode over to a dirty white tent whose wood shingle hanging over the open front door deemed it The

National Saloon. Dismounting, she stepped inside. There were four men at one of the three long tables. Three were dressed like freighters. Another wore coveralls and an apron—the barkeep, no doubt.

Not knowing the best way to broach the subject, Louisa decided to dive in headfirst. "Excuse me, gentlemen," she said, having to spit the "gentlemen" out like a sour plum while maintaining a neutral expression, "has anyone seen or heard of the whereabouts of Handsome Dave Duvall?"

All four men cast their gazes her way. She could tell from their expressions—a mix of wary caution and surprise—that they knew who she was talking about. They stared at her for a long time, looking her up and down, taking her measure.

Finally the barkeep said, "What in the hell would a pretty little thing like you want with Handsome Dave Duvall?"

"Personal business."

"Personal, huh?" the barkeep chuffed, glancing at the others. "I bet it's personal."

All four men just stared. Finally, one drawled in a Southern accent, "I ain't seen him. Don't care to, neither."

When the others did not say anything but only kept staring at Louisa, their eyes growing more and more lascivious, she became convinced none really had seen or heard of Dave Duvall's presence here and walked away, leading her Morgan by the reins.

She stopped at another saloon and a dugout cabin before which an Indian woman, probably a hider's wife, was cutting up a buffalo tongue. Getting no reply to her question at either place—neither the Indian nor the lone man sweeping out the second saloon so much as looked at her!—she headed over to another cabin across the road, sitting in a shallow ravine. It was flanked by three more sod-roofed shacks and a corral in which a handful of horses hung their heads and swished their tails at bugs. Several soldiers sat talking on the first cabin's stoop.

Tying the Morgan to the hitching post out front, Louisa walked across the hard-packed yard and mounted the porch. Ignoring the soldiers, who had ceased talking as soon as they saw her and were now staring the way most men of low breeding stared at her, she crossed the porch and knocked on the door. She did not bother asking the soldiers about Duvall, for she knew such men and knew from the smirks on these men's faces that she could not count on the sincerity of their answers.

One of the soldiers laughed. "Door's open, sweetheart. You don't have to knock!" He laughed again, and the other four followed suit.

Louisa lifted the crude leather latch and stepped inside, shutting the door behind her on the laughing voices of the soldiers. The cabin was stuffed to brimming with crude furniture, including several cots and an iron range. Shelves spilled pots and pans and dry goods. Louisa stood where she was, for she knew that to move in such dusky, cramped quarters would probably mean knocking something over.

"Who're you?" came a female voice from the shadows across the cabin.

Squinting and casting her gaze about, Louisa discovered a woman reclining on another cot behind two blankets hanging from a wire, which she had parted with her hand. Her black hair was streaked with gray. She wore only a washworn chemise, it appeared, exposing nearly one whole, sagging breast. A cheroot smoldered in her hand parting the blankets. The air in the place was fetid with unspeakable human secretions.

"My name is Louisa Bonaventure of Sand Creek, Nebraska, and I'm looking for a man called Handsome Dave Duvall. Have you seen or heard of his presence hereabouts in the last few days?"

The woman stared through the parted blankets, expressionless. Finally, she blinked. "Why on earth would you be looking for such a man?" she asked sadly.

"I've personal business with him."

"Personal?" The woman's gaze turned vaguely ironic as she studied Louisa from head to toe and back again. "Let me give you a free piece of sound advice, honey. Dave Duvall might be as handsome as all get out, but he's the devil's filth. Not the man a sweet little thing like you should be chasing all the way from Nebraska or anywhere else."

"You know where he is, don't you?"

The woman sighed and puffed the cheroot. Her face paled. "I heard from someone who thought they seen him over at Jack Clawson's sawmill down the road apiece, south. I hope to hell he isn't, because there's nowhere Dave goes that the people don't suffer in the most horrible ways."

She studied Louisa, whose heart was thudding. "But you just leave him alone. Stay clear of that man, honey."

"South, you said?"

"Listen, honey, you just never mind what I said. You just—"

Louisa didn't hear the rest, for she'd already turned, opened the door, and stepped back onto the porch. She moved toward her horse, but one of the soldiers gathered around the door stepped into her path, smirking.

"Excuse me, sir."

"Excuse me, sweetheart."

"I was heading for my horse."

"Ah, now, what's the hurry?"

Louisa glanced around at the five leering faces. Fear and anger gripped her, but she was no stranger to either emotion. "Kindly remove yourself from my path, sir," she ordered the young, stringbean firebrand standing between her and the Morgan.

"What are you gonna do if I don't?"

Louisa reached into the slit in her poncho and produced the Colt. Extending it, she thumbed back the hammer. "I'll blow a hole in your worthless hide a mile wide."

The firebrand stared at the gun, his eyes widening. "Jesus Christ, boys, look at the cannon this pretty little gal's packin'!"

Suddenly, his left hand slashed at the gun, knocking it out of Louisa's hand before she had time to fire. It went off when it hit the porch floor, the slug tearing into the base of the cabin. Before Louisa knew what was happening, one of the soldiers grabbed her from behind, lifting her off her feet.

"No!" she cried. "No, you vermin . . . *slime!*"

The soldiers hooted and howled. The one holding Louisa dodged her flying fists and kicking feet, and then one of the others grabbed her legs in his arms, pinning them together.

"Eeee-*how,* Jeb!" the stringbean soldier cried. "Take that little polecat in the cabin and go to work! Let me know when you're done, 'cause I'm next!"

"Help me, Jim!" Jeb howled to the man holding Louisa's feet.

"You got it, Jeb!"

One of the other soldiers opened the cabin door, and Jeb and Jim carried the desperately fighting Louisa into the cabin and kicked the door closed behind them.

12

LOU PROPHET WOKE for the second time that morning, to a scratching, sniffing sound. Opening his eyes, he looked around the tiny cell.

Morning light angled through the single, barred window, making visible the single wood table and chair and the rat that was inspecting Prophet's breakfast leavings: stale gruel with weevils the size of raisins.

Prophet reached for his boot, threw it at the rat. The rat gave a surprised screech as it leaped from the table and scuttled down a hole in the floor. Presently, the door to the cell block squawked open, and one of the sheriff's deputies looked in angrily.

"What's the trouble in here?"

"You got more rats than a goddamn Yankee prison camp."

"Hold it down over there, Prophet, or I'll give you a good poke with the butt of my shotgun. In case you don't know it, you ain't one of Sheriff Teal's favorite people."

"He ain't exactly one of mine, either. So why doesn't he just let me go? He must've had time to *investigate the killing,* as he calls it." Glancing around, Prophet saw that there were only three other prisoners in the cell block. "Hell, he's already let the drunks out!"

"Sheriff Teal's enjoying his breakfast over at the Bismarck. He'll get to you when he's damn good and ready."

With that, the deputy retreated, pulling the door closed behind him.

One of the others prisoners chuckled, the laughter echoing along the cell block. "Amigo, if Sheriff Teal don't like you, you gonna be here awhile."

Prophet knew the man was right. Deciding there was no use getting all worked up over something he couldn't control, he lay back down on the cot for another nap. He'd barely nodded off when the door opened again, and boots thumped in the cell block.

Prophet lifted his hat from his eyes. The deputy was turning a key in the door to Prophet's cell.

"You're in luck, Prophet," the turnkey said. "The sheriff's feeling agreeable this morning."

Prophet stomped into his boots in a hurry and followed the deputy out of the cell block, down a flight of stairs, through a short hall, and into the main office of the Burleigh County sheriff. Teal was sitting behind a massive desk, several filing cabinets and a framed map of the county on the wall behind him. He did not look up as Prophet stepped into the room.

"You're damn lucky the man you killed raped a girl from Ambrose two months ago, Prophet. Damn lucky. Now get the hell out of here!"

"I take it the fishing didn't go so well last night." Prophet smirked. He knew he was pushing his luck, but he didn't appreciate spending the night in the hoosegow after defending himself from an assassination attempt. The attempt was a good indication that Duvall was in the area, which meant Louisa was in danger, whether she knew it or not.

The sheriff looked up now, his florid face swelling with anger. "Don't tempt me to throw you back in your cell, you rebel son of a bitch!"

Prophet was openly defiant. "On what charge?"

"Violation of the city ordinance which prohibits discharge of firearms within the corporate limits other than by those empowered to employ same, except upon Fourth of July, Christmas, and New Year's!"

"That's a new one on me."

"You've just never obeyed it!" Teal waved savagely. "Joe, give him his gear and show him the goddamn door!"

"Wait a minute, Sheriff," Prophet said, softening his tone. "I, uh . . . I think you have five hundred dollars of my bounty money."

The sheriff stared at him, scowling.

Prophet grimaced and fidgeted on his feet, as though he were asking the sheriff for his daughter's hand.

"Remember? I brought in the two rascals that held up that express wagon a few months back. When the reward money came in, you were gonna stow it in your safe until—"

"I remember," the sheriff said, a cunning light entering his eyes. "It's gone."

Prophet's jaw dropped. "Gone? What are you talkin' about?"

"It went to pay your fine for not only wearing your gun within the city limits but for firing it in same. What's left will go to the undertaker who's tending the body."

"Five hundred dollars!"

"It's either that or go before the judge. He don't particularly care for Southern bounty hunters any more than I do."

Prophet stared at the pugnacious old cuss, who stared back, eyes gleaming smugly. Finally, deciding he'd been beaten and was now broke, to boot, having spent virtually his last change on Louisa's dress and on the meal at the

Bismarck Hotel, Prophet sighed and donned his hat. He turned to the outside door. The deputy stood beside it, offering Prophet's gun belt, a grin lifting his handlebar mustache.

Prophet grabbed the belt and put his hand on the doorknob. Before he could pull, the deputy said with a self-satisfied grin, "I wouldn't wear that in town no more. Turn it over to your hotel clerk until you leave"— the man winked and bobbed his head—"or we'll be seein' ye again real soon."

Prophet wanted to smack the kid silly, and even considered it until he remembered Louisa. As he opened the door and started outside, the sheriff called once more from his desk.

"Hey, Prophet, what the hell brought you to town, anyway?"

Prophet considered telling the sheriff about Duvall but decided against it. He didn't want Teal or any of his dimwitted deputies involved. In Prophet's experience, bad lawmen were like bad bird dogs, tending to flush their quarry long before it got within shooting range. Besides, he'd probably already received cables that Handsome Dave was in the area and had decided to ignore them as long as he could.

"Just wanted to see you again, Sheriff," Prophet said with a mocking grin. "A pleasure as always."

He donned his hat and left the courthouse. Worried about Louisa, he went straight to his hotel, ignoring the deputy's warning to turn his gun over to the desk clerk. There was no way in heaven or hell he was going to walk around unarmed with Handsome Dave Duvall gunning for him.

When the desk clerk handed over his key, the man gave Prophet a knowing smirk. "Guess you and your, uh, *friend* had a falling out?"

Prophet glowered at the man. "What makes you say that?"

The man adjusted his paper collar and nudged his glasses up his haughty nose. "Well, since she already checked out and all, I just thought . . ."

Prophet's stomach burned with anxiety. "Checked out? Where'd she go?"

The clerk shrugged and spread his soft hands. "Didn't say. Just took off—in rather a hurry, I must say."

Prophet turned fretfully away and mounted the stairs, taking them two at a time. On the second floor, he found the dress he'd bought Louisa hanging on his door.

"Goddamn you, girl," Prophet groused as he unlocked the door and stepped into the room. Tossing the dress on the bed, he said, "If I've said it once, I've said it a thousand times, you're gonna be the death of me yet."

He went to the window and drew the shade. Staring down at the busy street, he wondered where she had disappeared to. She'd obviously gone out on her own to hunt for Dave Duvall. But where was she planning on starting? Prophet himself had covered all the saloons and brothels in Bismarck.

Well, almost all. There was one place he had yet to search.

To that end, he grabbed his gear, tossed his room key to the desk clerk on his way out of the hotel, and headed for the feed barn. As he'd suspected, the Morgan was gone. Prophet saddled Mean and Ugly and trotted west on Main, swerving impatiently around stalled freight wagons and buckboards loaded with farming and ranching supplies. When he was free of the snarled traffic, he gave Mean the spurs and didn't check the dun down until he'd made the buttes along the river.

From atop a sagey knoll, he appraised the handful of shanties and the buffalo camp to the west.

"Prophet, you rebel dog!" one of the hunters called affably from his cook fire. "Where in the hell you been keeping yourself?"

Prophet gigged his horse toward the man in stained buckskins and a tangled beard. A middle-aged half-breed woman sat near nearby, darning a saddle blanket.

"Max, you seen a blonde-headed girl ride through here on a black Morgan?"

Max scratched his head thoughtfully. "Well, yeah, I did. About fifteen, twenty minutes ago. Rode up to the National over there, as I recall." A wide grin broke out on the man's sun-seared cheeks. "What you up to now, Proph, chasin' blonde-headed girls around the territory?"

Prophet didn't take the time to answer. Instead, he reined Mean and Ugly back on the trail, spurring him hard. A minute later, he rode up to the long saloon tent in a cloud of yellow dust. The Morgan wasn't tied to the hitch rack out front, but Prophet inquired within, learning from the barkeep that a pretty blonde had been there a few minutes ago, looking for Handsome Dave Duvall.

Prophet forked leather again and rode along the trail through the heart of the shantytown, looking this way and that for the Morgan. He was nearly to the town's south end when he turned left.

The Morgan was there, tied before a cabin in a shallow ravine.

"He-yaw!" Prophet encouraged his horse.

Mean descended the ravine in two fluid leaps, kicking up dirt and gouts of sod. Prophet leaped from the saddle as the dun approached the Morgan, the black horse sidling away and giving a startled whinny.

Ignoring the soldiers gathered on the porch, Prophet mounted the steps in a hurry, breathing hard, his face flushed with purpose.

"Hey, hey, hey," one of the soldiers objected, moving to block Prophet's approach to the cabin door. "Just where in the hell you think you're goin', bub?"

"Get the *hell* out of my way, old son," Prophet raged,

thumping the soldier's chest with the flat of his hand. "Or I'll drop you like a jug o' bad milk!"

Prophet's blow threw the soldier against the door. Before Prophet could grab the soldier again and throw him out of his way, one of the others stepped behind him and dealt him a glancing blow with the butt of an army-issue forty-four. Losing his hat, Prophet dropped to a knee, wincing against the pain in his head and neck.

Out of the corner of his eye, he saw the soldiers closing around him and heard their curses. One kicked him in the side as he reached for his Peacemaker, and he dropped his right hand to steady himself. He turned to the soldiers swarming around him. One drew his revolver and clicked the hammer back, swinging the barrel toward Prophet's head.

"Hold it right there, boys!"

Prophet couldn't identify the voice, which came from off the porch. The soldiers froze.

"I'm a United States deputy marshal, and you're all dead if you don't toss those irons off the porch and turn around slow."

Tottering slightly, Prophet gained his feet and cast his glance off the end of the porch, where the deputy marshal stood holding a well-oiled revolver at the dumbstruck soldiers. The deputy was a stylish, red-haired young man in his early twenties, wearing a crisp, snuff-colored hat, black frock coat, and polished black boots. His red spade beard did nothing to add years to his freckled, boyish face.

"Well, I'll be goddamned," Prophet muttered, staring at the badge-toting lad. "Where in the hell did you come from, Zeke?"

Ezekial McIlroy kept his eyes on the soldiers. "Rode into Bismarck last night. I was having breakfast when I saw Louisa ride past the café. Followed her here. Figured she was after Duvall. She's inside, Proph."

"I know," the bounty hunter grunted, drawing his gun. He turned to the door and lifted the latch. Locked. Behind it, a girl cursed and glass shattered.

Prophet offered a curse of his own as he kicked the door in, showering splinters from the frame, and stormed inside with his gun held high.

13

PROPHET STEPPED TO the side of the door and raked his eyes across the cramped, dusky room. A dark-haired woman was yelling from behind a blanket curtain, a cigarillo in her right hand. To Prophet's right, a soldier was struggling with Louisa while another lolled back against the wall, clawing at the broken glass embedded in his bloody neck.

Bunching her skirts in her fists, Louisa lifted her leg and brought her foot toe first into the other soldier's groin.

"Ah!" he bellowed. "You bitch!" Holding his groin with one hand, he clawed at his revolver with the other.

"Don't do it, soldier boy!" Prophet warned.

Heedless, the soldier swung around toward Prophet, raising his gun. Prophet's Peacemaker barked, sending the man back against the wall and curling up in the corner as a washtub fell from the wall and crowned him.

"Oh, that's just wonderful! Just wonderful!" the woman scolded from behind her curtain.

Prophet looked at the soldier with the glass embedded

in his neck. He'd fallen onto his butt, his back to the wall. Blood pumped out of him in waves, cascading down his chest and shoulder.

He looked at Prophet dumbly. "Oh . . . boy," he said. His legs and feet twitched, his eyes fluttered, and then he pitched over sideways, shaking until his heart stopped.

Louisa looked at him. She turned to Prophet, brows furrowed with disdain. "He got his due. As for the other, I could've handled him, too." She bent to pick up her hat, snugged it on her head, and brushed past Prophet as she marched to the door.

"Now, who's gonna clean up this mess? I have customers comin' in a few minutes."

Prophet looked at the woman. "That's a good question," he said, as he turned to the door and stepped onto the porch.

Deputy McIlroy was still bearing down on the other soldiers, gun extended in his hand. The soldiers' hands were still raised. The commotion within the cabin had turned their faces stiff and pale.

Louisa elbowed one of the soldiers out of her way as she stooped to retrieve her pistol from the porch floor. She gave it a quick appraisal, dusted it off with her hand, then returned it to the slit in her skirt and descended the porch steps.

"You all right, Proph?" McIlroy asked.

Prophet only vaguely heard him. He was too busy watching Louisa climb aboard the Morgan.

"Where you goin' now?" he asked her.

"I have a job to do," she said, angrily brushing her honey-blonde hair off her shoulders. "It may not be the most appropriate task for a girl, Mr. Prophet, but I've been called upon to do it. And I will accomplish it in spite of your tricks!" She reined the horse around and with an angry "Good day!" heeled it up the bank and onto the road at a gallop.

Prophet scowled after her, grinding his teeth.

"Where's that crazy girl going now?" McIlroy asked.

"That's what I'd like to know," Prophet groused as he headed for his horse.

"She's going after Dave Duvall."

Prophet stopped suddenly and turned to the woman standing in the cabin's doorway. The woman took a deep drag off the cigarillo and glanced toward Louisa's retreating figure.

"Where?" Prophet asked.

"Clawson's sawmill. It's on the trail yonder, about three, four miles. That girl might've been able to handle those two soldiers in there, but if she crosses Handsome Dave all by her lonesome . . ."

Prophet marched to his horse and mounted up.

"Hey, wait a minute, Lou," McIlroy said, looking anxious as he held his revolver on the soldiers. "You have to wait for me. I've been assigned to track Duvall and bring him in."

Prophet looked at him. He didn't normally care for lawmen, namely because they didn't normally care for him. His and McIlroy's relationship hadn't started out on the best terms, but a cameraderie had grown from an uneasy alliance as they'd tracked the Red River Gang from Fargo to their hideout, and now Prophet counted the young deputy marshal as a friend.

He gestured at the soldiers. "What about them?"

McIlroy stared at the soldiers, wincing. "Damn!" he fumed. "Boys, you ever do anything like this again, I'll have you strung up by your thumbs, and I would now if I didn't have more important matters to tend to. Count yourselves lucky!" McIlroy holstered his pistol, told Prophet to wait while he fetched his horse, and ran behind the cabin.

Lowering his hands, one of the soldiers said to Prophet, "Handsome Dave Duvall really in the country?"

Prophet just stared at him, his nostrils flaring with antipathy. It was answer enough for the soldier. "Damn!" he exclaimed, sharing meaningful looks with his friends.

"What I wanna know is who's gonna drag these two dead soldiers out of my house!" the woman said, fists on her hips.

Prophet didn't have time to hear the soldiers' reply to that. McIlroy galloped around the side of the cabin, and the bounty hunter spurred his own horse up the embankment to the road, then south at a gallop, the two men riding abreast, hat brims pasted against their foreheads.

"Nice to see you again, Proph," McIlroy called above the thunder of his horse's pounding hooves.

"I reckon it's nice to see you, too, Zeke, seein' as how I'd be snugglin' snakes if you hadn't shown up when you did," Prophet replied. "I tell you what, we take down Handsome Dave today, the first drink's on me."

"I hope I can take you up on that."

They rode hard for a good mile and a half. Then the trail forked, and they checked their horses down, eyeing each fork with consternation. Both looked relatively well traveled.

"You take the right fork," Prophet said. "I'll take the left. Reckon we'll know which one's right within a mile or so."

"I reckon," McIlroy said. "If yours is the right fork, don't try to take him alone, Proph. I know you've been in the man-hunting business a lot longer than I have, but there's no sense in taking unnecessary chances. Besides that," the deputy added with a dark look in his young eyes, "I want a part of him."

"I'll wait for you if you wait for me."

Prophet spurred Mean down the trail's left fork, riding hard around a grassy butte and into a swale through which a spring runout bubbled over rocks. He splashed across the runout, then galloped through a small cottonwood grove and up a hill. At the hill's crest, he brought Mean to a halt and cast his gaze into the valley below.

A small ranch operation sat in the valley: a dugout cabin, a small, gray barn, and a corral where several ponies milled. One man sat on a stump before the cabin, sunning himself. Another was digging post holes behind the barn.

The trail appeared to dead-end in the hard-packed yard.

"Shit!" Prophet complained, reining Mean around and heading back the way he'd come.

He cut cross-country to the other fork and rode hard again south through several buttes and over a low saddle. The trail cut through a ravine, and when Prophet came out the other side, several buildings opened out before him. They sat in a shallow valley rimmed with buttes. The Missouri River arced around to the west, wide and milky brown in its chalky cut through the short-grass hills spiked with yucca.

Prophet halted his horse and studied the sawmill warily. There was a long, low cabin, its awning supported by posts, and several open sheds filled with firewood, and an empty corral. Zeke McIlroy was near the corral, hunkered down on his haunches and studying the ground. His horse was tied to the open corral gate.

Prophet rode over and reined up. "You were gonna wait for me."

"Didn't see any point. He's gone." McIlroy gestured at what Prophet had already discovered: a dead man lying by a horse trough in the middle of the yard. "There's another man on the porch and a woman inside. In the same shape."

"Louisa?"

McIlroy shook his head in disgust. "She was galloping off just as I rode in. I called to her, but she wouldn't have any of it. Must be following these tracks here—four horses, not including her own."

"Four?"

McIlroy just shrugged.

Prophet sighed and dismounted. He tied Mean to the corral and walked over to the dead man by the horse trough. He'd been shot in the side of the head. Walking to the cabin, Prophet found another man lying dead on the porch in a pool of congealed blood. The man's face was puffed up and purple as an overripe plum.

Shaking his head, Prophet walked into the cabin and found the woman lying nude and dead across a bed. Her skin was already translucent blue. That and the congealed blood here and on the porch told Prophet the killings had happened a good four or five hours ago, which meant Duvall and whoever he was now riding with had a four- or five-hour advantage.

"What do you think?" McIlroy said as Prophet crossed the yard to the corral. "He have about six hours on us?"

Prophet nodded, wincing against the sun glare. "Around that, I reckon."

"Who do you suppose the other three are?"

"Your guess is as good as mine." Prophet stretched the kinks out of his neck as he looked down the trail. He felt discouraged and, he had to admit, a little hopeless. He'd never had this hard a time, been through what he'd been through tracking Dave Duvall. He'd swear the man had nine lives. And wherever he went, he left carnage in his wake.

Which meant he *had* to be stopped . . . and soon.

Adding to Prophet's frustration was Louisa. It was just a matter of time before he found her along the trail with another bullet in her hide or with her throat slit . . . or worse. He knew he should just give up on her, but he couldn't. She meant too much to him for that. He wanted to see her through this alive.

He grabbed the horn and crawled tiredly into the leather. "Looks like that drink will have to wait."

"Looks like," McIlroy agreed, looking as dark and weary as Prophet. He, too, forked leather and reined his horse out of the yard, falling in beside Prophet. "I hate to leave those bodies there for someone else to find."

"If we take time to bury them, there's liable to be a whole lot more where they came from," Prophet said, giving Mean the spurs.

Louisa had not been surprised to find the bodies. She'd been following Duvall and his now-deceased gang far too long for anything—the most abominable of abominations—to surprise her in the least. The carnage didn't really even turn her stomach anymore, a thought she found only vaguely disconcerting. She was too busy with the task at hand: hunting down Handsome Dave Duvall and killing him as he had killed others, including her beloved family.

It would not be pretty, what she intended to do to Duvall. Not pretty at all. And the thought propelled her with a venom she'd never known, had never suspected she would ever know.

She followed the trail of the four horses now, leaning out from her saddle to scour the tracks, careful not to lose them as she'd lost them an hour ago, when the riders had tried to elude trackers by suddenly swinging off the horse trail and traversing a grassy butte.

They were traveling cross-country now—or had been four or five hours ago—riding single file to make the tracking harder, across a long, flat divide between creeks. The sun was high and hot, and gophers poked their heads from holes, chortling. Two hawks screeched as they traced lazy circles in the blue sky over a box-shaped butte quartering in the hazy eastern distance.

This was a vast country, she saw as she glanced around, giving her attention a momentary reprieve from the trail. It was all dun grass and rimrocks and distant buttes, and it was scored by ravines, canyons, and coulees. She gave her eyes back to the horse trail, trying to stem the tide of loneliness she suddenly felt lapping at her consciousness.

Damn him. This loneliness was Prophet's fault. If she hadn't met him and gotten close to him, come to depend on him more than she'd realized . . .

It was his fault she felt not only lonely but doubtful, frightened.

Never again would she come to depend on someone else for her happiness and security. Never. Her family was dead. She had only herself now, and she could survive if she remained strong.

She shook her head to rid herself of the needling doubt and blinked her eyes at the shod hoofprints in the sod. She followed the trail another slow mile, then another, wondering where Duvall was heading. She knew she'd never be able to overtake him unless he slowed considerably or stopped altogether, which eventually he would have to do. He couldn't run forever. Eventually he'd come to a settlement where he'd stop and rest himself and his horse.

That's where she'd find him, and the cat and mouse game would be over at last.

In the late afternoon, she lost the trail in a deep, brushy ravine. She rode up the ravine's other side and back down again, looking for the tracks with a growing desperation. Finally, she turned the Morgan in the direction Duvall had been headed, hoping to pick up the trail again farther south and west.

She rode for an hour without finding it. After another hour, she found herself on a vast, lonely prairie upon which night was closing fast, casting purple shadows among the sage tufts and occasional cottonwoods. The air cooled and dampened and became fragrant. Distant rimrocks stood silhouetted in the west. Stars sparked to life in the east.

Looking around, Louisa realized with a shudder that

she had no idea where she was. She knew she'd come from the north and east, but how far had she traveled? Finding her way back to the ravine in which she'd lost Duvall's trail would be impossible in the darkness. But only there did she have any chance of finding it again.

Looking for the trail would have to wait until morning, and by then it would be a very cold trail indeed.

Whipping her head around and seeing nothing but gathering darkness and hearing nothing but the breeze rustling the grass, she felt panic overtake her. Her heart hammered painfully, and an apple-sized lump swelled in her throat. She was all alone out here, miles from any settlement, with darkness falling fast.

She'd been alone before. She'd camped time after time on a lonely plain. So why now did she feel so frightened?

"Lou," she said, startled by the thin cry that had escaped her lips as if of its own accord.

Craning around in her saddle, casting her worried gaze back the way she'd come, she said it again. "Lou Prophet, where are you?"

14

FIVE MILES SOUTHEAST of Louisa, Prophet squatted on his haunches atop a bluff and stared off across the dark landscape unfolding before him.

He was looking for Duvall's campfire, but he'd known even before he'd climbed the bluff after he and McIlroy had stopped for the day that he would not find any such light. Duvall was too far ahead. Tracking was a slow process, and Prophet and McIlroy were gaining very little ground, if any.

Still, Prophet scanned the dark land crowned with vivid stars, hearing coyotes and distant wolves, a vagrant night breeze rattling the leaves of nearby shrubs. He realized now he wasn't looking only for sign of Duvall's encampment but for sign of Louisa's, too.

He cursed to himself, worrying about her. In spite of how tough she was, if she met up with Duvall before he, Prophet, did . . .

He gave a grunt and, shaking his head, stood. He took one more long look around him, then turned and started down the bluff, picking his path carefully in the darkness, grabbing shrubs to slow his descent.

"It's Prophet," he announced as he neared his and McIlroy's encampment lit by a small cook fire. Stepping into the circle of orange light, he saw McIlroy sitting back against his saddle, smoking a cigar and idly running an oiled rag over his rifle.

"See anything?"

"Stars," Prophet said wryly. "Lots of stars."

"You're worried about the girl."

Prophet picked his tin cup off a rock. Not saying anything, he retrieved the gurgling pot from the fire and filled his cup with the smoking, black brew.

When he'd sat down against a log, McIlroy cleared his throat. "If you'd pardon me for askin', Proph, just what is she to you, anyway—Miss Bonaventure, I mean?"

Prophet sipped his coffee and stared into the fire and did not speak. He had no answer to the question. It was a good one, though. Just what was Louisa to him, anyway?

"Well, like I said," McIlroy said after a while, sliding his rifle into its scabbard, "pardon me for askin'." He stood with the scabbard and donned his hat. "I'll keep the first watch and wake you in a few hours."

Prophet nodded and took another sip of the coffee, feeling the burn down his throat and the comforting warmth in his gut.

McIlroy turned and headed out of the firelight. He'd taken no more than six steps when Prophet heard, "Well, I'll be! Speak of the devil!"

Prophet's hand jerked to his Peacemaker. He relaxed when he noted there had been no fear, only humorous surprise in the deputy's voice. A horse whinnied, and Prophet heard a snort and the fall of a shod hoof.

"Don't shoot, Proph," McIlroy called. "It's her."

The tension eased in Prophet's shoulders, and his stomach

grew light with relief. Thank god. Arranging a casual expression, he waited for her to step into the firelight. Realizing she must have been picketing her horse, he set to work taking his Peacemaker apart and cleaning it, wanting to look casual when she revealed herself.

He heard her footsteps but did not look up as she stepped into the firelight. Seeing her out the corner of his eye, he said, "Well, look what the cat dragged in."

She said nothing as she dropped her saddle and bedroll several yards from his, under a Russian olive, then turned and disappeared again. She returned a moment later, carrying her rifle scabbard and saddlebags.

He looked at her now. Her hat hung from its strap down her back, and trail dust coated her, streaking her face with mud where she'd perspired. Her hair was disheveled. Her face owned a flushed, weary look. Her eyes were wild. She'd been lost. She'd probably lost Duvall's trail and ended up God knows where. She could handle a gun and a knife well enough, but keen tracking skills took time and experience to acquire.

She took a cup from her saddlebags and filled it with coffee. She sat on the other side of the fire, lifting her knees, grinding her heels into the dirt, and sipping from the cup. She did not look at Prophet, only stared into the fire.

As if reading his mind, she said, "All right, I'm not much of a tracker. I got lost. I need to stay with you until we find him."

The statement had the air of a confession offered at great emotional cost. Her pride was so obviously bruised that he felt sorry for her and lost the urge to gloat. He only nodded and ran his oiled rag over the Peacemaker's cylinder.

"There's some biscuits and beans in that pan over there."

She said nothing, but when she'd finished her coffee, she produced a plate from her saddlebags and filled it from the pan. She ate hungrily, staring into the fire. When she was through, she cleaned her plate and cup, returned them to her saddlebags, and rolled up in her blankets, sighing tiredly as she rested her head against her saddle.

Watching her, he put the Peacemaker back together. In a moment, she was asleep, her chest rising and falling. Prophet got up and tended nature, then turned in himself and fell quickly asleep.

He woke sometime later to the sound of whimpering. Believing it had come from some animal in the camp, he reached for his revolver. He looked around the camp only dimly lit by the dying fire and saw nothing out of the ordinary.

The whimper came again, from right behind him.

Startled, he jerked that way. It was Louisa. She lay beside him, her head on her saddle, tossing and turning under her blankets, enmeshed in a dream. A nightmare.

He returned his revolver to its holster, snuggled back down in his blankets, and took the moaning girl in his arms, gently holding her and patting her shoulder while she dreamed.

"It's okay, Louisa," he whispered. "Everything's gonna be just fine."

Two days later, Handsome Dave Duvall and the three deserter soldiers were waiting out a rain squall under a tarpaulin erected between two cottonwood trees. On a spit over a cook fire, a beef tenderloin sizzled and crackled as the skin split and dripped grease into the glowing coals below. Harold and Danny were playing two-handed poker, and Clyde was darning a sock, frowning like an idiot over a McGuffy reader.

Dave was smoking and considering the possibility of killing these yahoos in their sleep later tonight, and stealing their stolen cash.

In Sante Fe, where he'd decided to head after shaking

his trackers in the Indian nations and before disappearing into Mexico for a few years, a thousand dollars would go a long way toward a new wardrobe and plenty of whiskey and women, not to mention song. He'd get him a couple of good horses, too, and knock off a bank or a roadhouse on his way south. You could live for years in Mexico on a handful of greenbacks.

He was tired of the soldiers. They might've done some killing and stealing in their time, but they were tinhorns just the same. And each was annoying in his own particular way. Especially Clyde, who bragged ceaselessly about his sexual conquests. They were all lies, Dave knew. No kid who looked like Clyde—even if he was hung as well as he claimed—could have sacked as many girls as he professed. Why, not even Dave himself, who was about as handsome a devil as he himself had ever known, had bedded that many ladies.

And the story about the president's niece in the broom closet of Omaha's Imperial Inn—that was just puredee nonsense, and not worth the time it had taken the dumb honyonker to tell it. No, that kid needed his throat cut from ear to ear, and left to bleed to death in his soogan.

Duvall thought about that as he took a long, luxurious drag on his quirley, a thin smile breaking out on his unshaven face. He stiffened and lost the smile when he heard the ratchety scrape of a shell levered into a rifle breech.

Turning left, he saw a man dressed like a common drover—battered Stetson, neckerchief, cotton shirt, and chaps—standing on a knoll, facing his way. He held a Winchester saddle gun low across his thighs, not aimed in Duvall's direction but ready to be. He had a face like a coyote, with a thin patch of beard on both cheeks. His gray eyes flashed.

"Enjoying that Rockin' Horse beef, are ye, boys?"

"What the . . . ?" Clyde said, tensing.

"Easy," Duvall told him. He smiled at the cowboy. "Well, I don't know whose beef it is, but it sure does taste good. You're welcome to join us, if you're hungry. There's plenty for all comers."

"No thanks," the cowboy said. "That beef you're roastin' belongs to my boss, Major Donleavy over at the Rockin' Horse Ranch, and he don't cotton to grub liners movin' through and paddin' their bellies on it whenever they please. Accordin' to him and a few other cattlemen in this area, that's rustlin', and you know how we handle rustlers in this neck of the woods?"

Dave glanced at Clyde, then returned his eyes to the cowboy and grinned. "How?"

"Necktie party."

That hadn't come from the cowboy before Duvall. It had come from someone else, behind him. Berating himself for not posting one of these yahoos on watch duty—he had to admit he'd gotten careless—Duvall craned his head around to see two more drovers standing before a cottonwood tree. One carried a beat-up Sharps rifle with a leather lanyard; the other held a rusty Smith & Wesson with the hammer cocked back. Unlike the first cowboy, these two looked edgy and worried, like they weren't used to trouble like this, and they didn't think their thirty a month and found covered it.

"Necktie party, huh?" big Danny said, a testy light entering his gaze. His hand moved toward the iron on his hip.

"Easy," Duvall said. Then, to the gray-eyed cowboy: "We sure are sorry about the beef. We were hungry, you see, and we just figured, with so many here and there about this big country, no one would miss it."

"Yeah, that's what a lot of 'em think. Who are you, anyway, and where you headed?"

Duvall considered his answer. Then he said, "Well, my

name is Dave Duvall. You might have heard of me. Some call me Handsome Dave Duvall." He paused to chuckle humbly. "I don't know where they get that, but anyway . . . these here boys are part of the Red River Gang."

The gray-eyed drover just stared at him, his eyes going flat. The other two didn't say a word, but Duvall could sense their tension. The soldiers glanced at him and grinned.

"You're, uh . . . you're who, did you say?" the gray-eyed cowboy asked. The lines in his forehead had flattened out so that his face looked like a death mask.

"Why, I'm Handsome Dave Duvall, and these three boys are the latest members of the Red River Gang." Duvall patted Clyde's knee affably. "The rest of the gang is on their way here, to this here meetin' place, even as we speak. Shoulda been here by now, as a matter of fact."

One of the cowboys behind him said, "The . . . the *Red River Gang?*"

Duvall was grinning. "You heard of us, I take it. Who might you boys be?"

The gray-eyed cowboy glanced around stiffly, then worked his throat as he swallowed. "We're from the Rockin' Horse over yonder. Been holed up in a line shack with the summer herd . . . watchin' for rustlers an' such."

"Well, you found some, I'll admit that," Duvall said, nodding his head. "The question is"—here his face went flat and serious—"what are you three gonna do about it?"

Clyde laughed through his teeth. Danny and Harold just grinned. Duvall frowned, his shaggy brows hooding his eyes.

"W-watch out now, Ned," one of the drovers behind Duvall said. "If he is who he says he is—and I think he is—he's dangerous."

Ned stood there tensely, holding the rifle across his thighs, not aiming it but thinking about it. Definitely thinking about it.

"What are you worried about, Mickey?" he said as he watched Duvall. "We got the drop on 'em. Hell, there might even be a reward on their heads."

"Yeah, there might be a reward on the whole damn gang," the other drover piped up, "but hell, are you gonna take the whole dang gang in to the law? I say we just let Mr. Duvall enjoy his beef. I'm sure he ain't plannin' on hanging around long. No reason why the major has to know about it."

"You chickenshit," Ned said. "I don't believe none o' that bullshit about the rest of the gang on its way. I say he's bluffin'. I say we kill these three right here and take 'em into town for the reward."

Duvall laughed, tipping his head back and showing his teeth. He laughed long and hard, as though at the funniest joke he'd heard in a long time.

"What's so damn funny?" Ned asked, indignant, inching the barrel of his rifle Duvall's way.

Duvall let his laughter die, and he turned to Ned. "I don't think you can do it."

"What?"

"I don't think you can shoot us. I don't think you can bring yourself to drop your hammers." Duvall paused, smiling smugly. "I've killed pret' near a hundred folks in my life, and at least a fourth of them were even odds. They didn't need to die. They could've shot me instead. But they just couldn't do it. And because they couldn't do it, or spent too much time thinkin' about doin' it, they died."

Ned stared hard at Dave, his face pinkening as he worked it through his head. Dave could see he was reluctant to bring the barrel forward. He lacked confidence. He wasn't sure he wanted to start a firefight. But then, he also knew that if he didn't shoot soon, Dave would. It was a hell of a pickle, and Ned had the shakes. They were getting worse.

As for Dave, he felt Sunday-morning calm, like he'd just been blessed by angels. No one could touch him.

"Boys," he said calmly, "I'm gonna shoot Ned. You turn around and shoot those dumbasses behind us whenever you're ready."

Dave blinked once, then clawed his revolver from his holster. Ned stood frozen, his eyes flashing terror, as Dave lifted the revolver and planted a forty-five slug in the center of his forehead. Ned jumped back, head twisting around with the force of the slug. He staggered, taking mincing steps, then dropped his rifle and sagged to his knees before falling face forward in the grass.

The soldiers laughed as they turned and took aim at the other two cowboys, triggering their pistols. Duvall turned to see the two cowboys running off through the weeds, both men losing their hats in the wind. The soldiers' pistols clattered, and finally one of the cowboys dropped. The other continued running.

Clyde and Danny fired at him, cursing now as they grew frustrated with their aim.

"Oh, for chrissakes!" Duvall groused, lifting his own revolver, sighting down the barrel, and squeezing the trigger. The gun barked, and the second cowboy pitched forward in the grass.

He turned to the three soldiers looking cowed as they stared off at the dead drovers. "Didn't they teach you how to *shoot* in the army?"

15

TWO DAYS LATER, Dave Duvall said, "Damn. There they are."

He sat his horse on the side of a brown bluff, so he wouldn't be outlined against the sky. He stared north through his field glasses as he rolled a foxtail stem between his lips.

He'd slowed his and the soldiers' pace with the intention of finding out whether or not they were still being followed. He thought if the bounty hunter wasn't still pursuing him, he might change his plans and head for Denver, as Denver was as good as any place to disappear for a while.

He'd lay up in a brothel, and if his trail still looked hot, he'd head to Arizona. If marshals or bounty men trailed him *there,* then he'd head to Mexico, but not before. Why fritter away his relative youth in the land of the bean-eaters if he didn't have to?

Now, adjusting the glasses to bring the three riders—two men and the blonde girl—more plainly into view, it looked like he might have to.

"Boys, I need a volunteer," he said to the soldiers gathered around him.

"What do you need a volunteer for, Mr. Duvall?" Clyde asked.

"I need a volunteer to wait here and see if he can ambush those three—at least pin them down and hole up till nightfall. Give us others a chance to regain our lead on them. Whoever does the ambush can light out after us once dark has fallen. Since they won't know he's gone, they'll hole up till morning."

The soldiers looked at each other. Clyde turned to Duvall with a befuddled crease between his eyes. "Why don't we all just ambush them? I mean, hell, there's only three of 'em, right? And didn't you say one's just a girl?" He chuffed a laugh.

"One's just a girl, but that girl's got nine lives," Duvall said as he watched the three riders angle around an old buffalo wallow, keeping a close eye on the relatively fresh horse tracks in the short-grass sod. "And one of the men is a man by the name of Prophet. Rebel bounty hunter. Tricky son of a bitch. Relentless. If we all laid back, he'd smell the trap."

Duvall thought it over, then lowered the glasses to his chest and shook his head. "No. I don't want to tangle with him out here with our ammo runnin' low and our horses tired. But one man—a good man—could kill him . . . if he knew what he was doing and didn't give himself away."

Duvall didn't really think one of these yahoos could ambush the savvy Prophet without getting himself killed, but what the hell? The worst that could happen was that the ambusher would get himself killed while giving Duvall and the other two time to gain some distance. Then Duvall would only have two yahoos to kill later.

Then again, the shooter could always get lucky.

"But the guy who stays has to be foxy," Duvall warned, looking each lad in the eye, like a sergeant on the eve of battle. "He has to be calm under pressure and good with a rifle. He has to be the kind of man I'd want riding by my side through a Comanche war party."

The soldiers looked at each other, squirming a little in their saddles, knowing they were being tested. Clyde looked a little suspicious, but not suspicious enough to call Duvall on his motives. He wanted far too badly to be a bona fide Red River Gang rider for that.

"I'll do it," Danny said finally, not appearing as enthusiastic as his words made him sound. "But you won't have to ride far, 'cause all three of them's gonna be dead long before nightfall."

"That's the spirit!" Duvall said, patting the hefty lad on the back. "What I'd do if I were you is hightail it down to that cut down there. Let 'em get good and close before you show yourself, and lay into 'em. Most likely, you'll get one or even two, and you'll pin the other one down.

"When you have him pinned down and it's good and dark, follow this creek to the Cannonball River, due south of here. Follow the river to the left about five, six miles, and you'll run into an old shack in an elbow canyon. It's easy to find if you're watching for it," Duvall lied, "even in the dark. Me and the gang threw that shack together a couple of years ago and used it for a hideout. Me and Clyde and Harold—we'll stop there for the night."

"No problem," Danny said, reaching back, shucking his Spencer carbine from his saddle boot, and tugging his hat down low over his eyes. "I'll be there; you can bank on that."

With that, he reined his horse toward the ravine. Duvall watched him go, wanting to chuckle and grin for all he was worth, knowing he had one of these fools out of the way. Instead, he yelled, "I'm proud of ye, Danny boy! Mighty proud, indeed!"

He watched the heavyset lad ride away as though watching one of his own ride off to war. Then he turned to Clyde, who was staring at him with a vaguely puzzled expression on his young, belligerent face.

Then Duvall said, "Come on, boys. Time to ride," and he led off at a trot.

Prophet got down on his hands and knees and lowered his canteen into the stream, filling it. He studied the tracks that disappeared into the slow-moving water, then reappeared in the mud, amid several deer and coyote prints, on the opposite bank.

Before him, cattails and saw grass rustled and scratched in the breeze. Behind him, McIlroy and Louisa sat their horses, watching him. Louisa hadn't said more than five words to him since she'd returned to their camp four days ago, and most of those had been "Yes," "No," and "Perhaps."

He guessed he didn't blame her. He shouldn't have tried to trick her into staying in Bismarck while he went after the man who'd murdered her family. She'd been right; it hadn't been his family that had been butchered. She had every right to see Duvall dead. He hoped she didn't die in the process, but he'd decided not to worry about that. She'd been fighting this war long enough to know the risks, and she was old enough in both years and experience to make her own decisions.

He wasn't her father, after all. He wasn't her brother nor even her lover, though he knew now, after the other night when he'd held her to assuage her nightmares, that he wanted to be.

Such thoughts were only a shadow in his mind at the moment, however. Studying the horse prints, he corked his canteen and said, "Their trail keeps getting fresher and fresher."

"They still slowing down?" McIlroy asked.

"Yep."

"Why, do you suppose? Ambush? Get us off their trail once and for all?"

"I can't figure another reason." Prophet turned to the deputy and Louisa, gazing at each directly. "Watch yourselves," he said. "Now more than ever. Remember what they did to those three drovers we found."

Louisa's eyes met Prophet's for an instant, then shuttled away. "I don't see any sense in dawdling here," she said haughtily, tightening her hat thong beneath her chin. "You've filled your canteen. Let's ride."

She gigged her horse into the stream, starting across. Prophet glanced at McIlroy, whose eyes lighted with irony. "Yeah, will you quit dawdling, Proph? We have a job to do, dammit."

Prophet cursed, hung his canteen over his saddle horn, and forked leather. Then he gigged Mean and Ugly into the stream behind McIlroy, mounting the opposite bank a few moments later and gazing around at more of the same country they'd been traversing; rolling hills pocked with bluffs and cut by creeks and deep ravines.

A big, dangerous, silent country, once owned primarily by the Sioux. There were still some Sioux around, but most had been herded onto reservations so that the country west of here—the Black Hills—could be opened for mining. Now there were a few ranches here and there and a few buffalo. But mostly there was wind and occasional thunderstorms and plenty of places for badmen to hide in ambush for those following.

The thought had no sooner crossed Prophet's mind than a rifle cracked in the distance. Involuntarily, he crouched low in his saddle and clawed his Peacemaker from his holster.

McIlroy's horse screamed to his left and slightly behind. Turning quickly, he saw the horse rear jerkily, twisting. Then its front knees buckled, and it rolled over hard, expiring quickly with one grievous blow, a trickle of blood running from a hole near its left ear.

"Zeke!" Prophet yelled as the deputy went down hard.

"Oh, shit!" McIlroy complained as he tried to pull his leg free of the horse's dead weight.

The rifle cracked again, and Prophet heard the bullet whine past him, no more than a foot away. Mean pranced anxiously. Gun drawn, Prophet held a tight grip on the reins as he whipped his head back and forth, trying to get a bead on the gunman's location.

"It came from that way!" Louisa called, pointing straight south. "From that ravine there!" Her gun was drawn, and before Prophet could say anything, she squeezed off two pistol shots in the gunman's direction.

"Keep shooting while I try to get Zeke out from under his horse," Prophet told her, slipping out of his saddle and rushing to the groaning deputy's assistance.

"Goddamn . . . goddamn thing's on my leg, Proph," Zeke cried, his face blanched with pain.

Prophet tried to move the dead horse, but it was no use. Finally, he grabbed Zeke by his shoulders, grinding his heels into the ground beneath him, and pulled till the veins in his forehead bulged and knotted. By now, Louisa had dismounted, grabbed her rifle, and sat on her butt. Using her knees as a gun rest, she fired one round after another, giving Prophet covering fire while he tried to free McIlroy from his horse.

"Oh, *god!*" the deputy cursed as his leg finally slipped free, his boot and sock dangling off his foot.

"You think it's broke?" Prophet said. "Can you ride?"

"I'll make it," Zeke said, nodding. His face was mottled red from the pain. "That son of a bitch!"

Prophet ran to retrieve Mean. When he'd forked leather, he galloped over to McIlroy, got down, and helped the deputy onto the horse. Calling to Louisa to mount the Morgan and follow him, Prophet again forked leather. With an encouraging bellow, he heeled the lineback dun toward a shallow gully quartering about fifty yards east, at the base of a rocky butte.

With Louisa now riding instead of shooting, the shooter had commenced firing again. Prophet heard the bullets stitching the air around him as he approached the gully. He gigged the horse down the bank, then slid out of the saddle.

"Come on, Zeke," he said, reaching for the injured deputy and easing him out of the saddle.

McIlroy limped over to the gully's south-facing bank and ducked down, drawing his revolver. Prophet shucked his Winchester from his rifle boot and hurried over beside McIlroy just as Louisa approached the gully at a gallop, the Morgan leaping over the side in one fluid stride. Louisa slid out of the saddle with her rifle in her hand and crouched down behind the bank, several yards to Prophet's left.

The rifleman had fallen silent, and there was only the sound of the breeze in the grass, the occasional whinny of Mean and the Morgan.

"Did you see how many?" Prophet asked Louisa, sneaking a peak over the lip of the gully's bank.

"Just one," Louisa said, turning to Prophet with a question in her eyes. How were they going to handle this? she seemed to say.

Prophet thought it over. Beside him, Zeke panted against the pain in his 1eg. Prophet turned to the deputy.

"You think it's broke?"

Zeke wagged his head. "No, just twisted good. It'll be okay. But what the hell am I going to do out here without a horse?"

"We're gonna get you a horse," Prophet said.

"Where?" McIlroy laughed.

"Well, he's gotta have a horse, don't he?" Prophet said, gazing back toward the shooter.

McIlroy stared at Prophet thoughtfully, both doubt and optimism flashing across his features. "You sure are a cocky son of a bitch."

"Yep," Prophet said. He turned to Louisa, who watched him expectantly, waiting for him to make the decision.

"You ready to ride, senorita?" Prophet asked her.

Louisa's full lips spread the first grin she'd offered in days. "Are you thinking what I think you're thinking, Mr. Prophet?"

"I think I am, Miss Bonny-venture."

"It's Bonaventure. There's no *y* in it."

"Get your horse, Miss Bonny-venture." To the deputy, Prophet said, "Sit tight, Zeke."

"Jesus Christ, you two are going to get yourselves killed, and I'm going to be all alone out here on a bum leg!"

Louisa had already run, crouching, after her horse. Prophet pushed off the bank, making a beeline for Mean and Ugly, who watched him owlishly, white-eyed, as though he'd read Prophet's thoughts and didn't like them a bit.

"Steady now, Mean," Prophet said as he grabbed the reins and climbed into the leather. Turning to Louisa, he said, "You ready?"

She held her revolver in her right gloved hand, and now she thumbed the hammer back and nodded.

"You curve around to the left," Prophet told her. "I'll go in from the right. Ride hard now, and whatever you do, don't give him an easy target."

"Okay, okay," Louisa said, impatient. "Let's do it!"

"Let's do it," Prophet said, tickling Mean with his spurs.

With that, the horse bounded out of the gully and onto the tableland, hooves drumming on the short-grass turf. As

Prophet urged the horse forward to even more speed, he crouched low over Mean's neck and saw Louisa gallop away to his left, paralleling him as they raced toward the shooter.

Smoke puffed before them, down low against the ground, about fifty yards ahead. Prophet heard the rifle crack and the bullet stitch the air over his right shoulder.

"Come on, Mean, you candy ass," Prophet urged. "Let's *go!*"

More smoke puffed; the rifle cracked again. This time the man had fired at Louisa. Prophet eyed her apprehensively, but her horse's stride never faltered, and she made no sign she'd been hit.

"Come on, Mean! Ride, old son!"

Prophet grabbed his revolver from his holster. As he approached the gully, he thumbed back the hammer and commenced firing across Mean's neck as he rode, one shot after another, spaced about two seconds apart. Louisa had commenced likewise, and it was working; the shooter was pinned down, unable to shoot, no longer showing himself above the lip of the ravine.

Prophet and Louisa were closing on the ravine now, arcing back toward each other, tearing up gouts of sod and dirt as they rode. Prophet closed first, and as he fired the last shell in his cylinder, he directed Mean to the notch in the ravine from which the shooter had fired. The horse leaped over the side of the ravine, and as he did, Prophet saw the gunman—a beefy lad with a Spencer carbine—look up at the horse's belly, mouth agape.

Mean landed with a loud thump and a blow, leather squeaking, saddlebags flapping. Prophet twisted around in the saddle as he brought up the Richards sawed-off. The beefy kid had raised his rifle and was aiming down the barrel at Prophet with a vicious glare in his dark eyes.

"No!" Louisa cried.

At the same time, she fired her pistol as the Morgan went airborne over the ravine's wall. The beefy kid jerked as the bullet took him in the neck. The rifle cracked, the slug flying wide. The kid cursed as he dropped his rifle and staggered sideways, grabbing his bloody neck.

"Ah, you bastards!" he bellowed, staggering and clawing the revolver from his hip. Before he could raise the gun at Louisa, Prophet slipped out of his saddle and leveled the Richards, nearly cutting the kid in half with ten-gauge buckshot.

The kid went down screaming before he died and lay still.

A few minutes later, Prophet and Louisa walked their mounts back toward McIlroy. Prophet was leading the bay behind Mean and Ugly.

He grinned as he called, "Here's that horse I was talkin' about, Zeke!"

16

PROPHET BROKE THE sign of the other three riders about fifteen minutes after he and Louisa had shot the dry-gulcher. They followed the trail along a creek bottom, over a divide, and into another watershed, gradually tracing a southeastern route toward water-scored country that lay like toothy shadows before them.

McIlroy rode the bay easily. He claimed his leg felt fine, but Prophet could tell by the occasional flush in his cheeks that he was lying. As Zeke had pointed out, the leg probably wasn't broken, but sometimes a severe sprain or a twist could hurt just as bad.

"Thanks for shooting that varmint when you did," Prophet told Louisa when they'd stopped to rest their horses in a small box canyon shaded by cottonwoods. McIlroy was sitting with his back to the rock wall, eyes closed, resting his leg, a dozen yards away.

Louisa looked at Prophet as though she hadn't understood what he'd said.

"You know—the fat kid with the Spencer repeater," he

said. "If you hadn't shot him when you did, I'd be wolf bait 'bout now."

She turned her hat over and wiped the moisture from the sweatband with a lacy white handkerchief trimmed with green leaves—an heirloom, no doubt. "You would have done the same for me, wouldn't you?"

"Of course."

"Well, what's the point in thanking me, then, Mr. Prophet?"

"Hey, what's all this Mr. Prophet stuff? I thought we were friends."

Louisa shrugged and set the hat on her head, shaking her hair back from her shoulders. "I guess you could say I've been reevaluating our relationship," she said with characteristic presumption. "We're partners, yes, but friends—well, I haven't decided if I want to be your friend any longer, after the trickery you pulled in Bismarck."

"Is that a fact?" Prophet said, staring at her with anger flushing his cheeks.

Finally, he grabbed her, pulled her to him brusquely, and kissed her. It wasn't a slow kiss, but it wasn't fast, either. He let his lips linger for about two seconds, noting how she'd stiffened in his arms after giving a sudden gasp of surprise.

But she didn't resist him.

When he eased her away from him, he found himself wanting more. So that's how those full lips felt . . . tasted. He'd never kissed lips so soft and sweet and pliable . . . so utterly delicious. They were like the softest peach he'd ever tasted in his Georgia boyhood.

Why, he wondered, as he stared at her, trying for something to say, had he been resisting her for so long? Why had he been trying for so long to keep his distance?

Two reasons occurred to him. One: she was just a kid. Two: he was a rapscallion, born and bred.

Besides, it was just better—easier—to keep things simple.

But as much he wanted them to be, things just weren't that simple anymore. And he knew from the way she'd screamed when she'd thought the beefy kid was going to plug him with the Spencer that she felt the same way.

Finding no words, he just stared at her, flushed and grim and confused, for another couple of seconds. She stared back, flushed and befuddled. Then he sighed and turned toward his horse.

"Come on," he said gruffly, trying to cover his emotions. "They're not far ahead of us. Let's ride."

They rode for another hour. As the sun was setting, Prophet reined his horse to a stop. He looked around, smelling the air like a dog.

"What is it?" McIlroy said, gazing around cautiously.

"I thought I smelled woodsmoke. Lost it now."

Louisa said, "I smelled it, too."

Prophet sat the dun for nearly a minute, sniffing the air and looking around apprehensively, his rifle resting across the pommel of his saddle. Finally, he said, "Come on, but be careful."

They rode along a narrow, meandering river for another half mile. It was full dark when Prophet, smelling the woodsmoke again, stopped his horse and slipped out of the saddle.

"Wait here," he told the deputy and Louisa.

He handed his reins to McIlroy, then walked around a bend in the river, staying near the woods and moving slowly. Behind him, Louisa and McIlroy watched him until he disappeared in the darkness. Five minutes later, they watched him return from the trees, walking quickly but softly, with a grace odd for a man his size. The sliver of moon rising in the east winked light off Prophet's Winchester.

"What is it?" Zeke asked.

"A cabin," Prophet said. "Smoke coming from the chimney."

"You kidding?"

Prophet shook his head. "It has to be a trap. I want you two to stay right here with your guns out and cocked. I'm going to check around the woods real good, see if they've laid a snare for us. Keep your eyes and ears peeled for anything."

"There he goes, telling me what to do again—me a deputy United States marshal," Zeke complained to Louisa.

"Yes, he likes telling people what to do," Louisa remarked as Prophet slipped away, quickly disappearing in the darkness.

The bounty hunter made a careful reconnaissance of the woods before the cabin, moving slowly, taking his time to stop and wait and watch before moving on, ready for anything. When he was certain no traps had been set before the cabin, he made a wide sweep around it, at one point making noise enough to attract would-be attackers.

Nothing happened. The only sounds were owls and coyotes and burrowing night critters. The cabin itself was dark and silent, though Prophet could see a thin column of smoke rising from its tin chimney pipe.

Why hadn't Duvall posted a night watch? Could he actually believe Prophet hadn't been able to follow his trail? And where were the riders' horses? In his reconnaissance, Prophet had seen no sign of the mounts.

The bounty hunter hunkered down behind a cottonwood and stared at the boxlike cabin that had been erected at the base of a high bluff, with brush and trees nearly concealing it from the view of anyone passing along the river. Discontentedly, he rubbed his jaw. He didn't like it. This was too easy. He felt as though he'd been led here, and if that were true, he'd been led into a trap, sure enough.

Unless Duvall only wanted him to believe it was a trap, as a way to befuddle and confound. While Prophet was standing around here, wondering if he'd been snookered into a fox trap, Duvall could be hightailing it down the trail, pushing for the Indian nations or wherever the hell else he aimed to disappear.

The way Prophet saw it, he had two options. He, McIlroy, and Louisa could storm the cabin and risk getting caught in a trap, or they could wait around out here a few hours and see what happened. The second option meant losing a few hours' trail time, but . . .

Prophet's thoughts were stifled by the sound of the cabin door opening. He watched as a figure appeared on the narrow stoop. The man made a coughing sound as he hacked phlegm up from his lungs. He stopped at the edge of the stoop, a wiry, youthful-looking figure clad in only short summer underwear and socks, his longish hair in disarray. The kid fumbled with his fly, then stood there as Prophet heard the tinny trickle of urine hitting the ground.

Prophet lifted his rifle, uncertain what to do. If he took this kid out now, that would leave only Duvall and one other man in the cabin. But if he waited until later, when all would probably be asleep, he, McIlroy, and Louisa could take them all by surprise.

Deciding to wait, Prophet watched the kid tuck himself back into his underwear, turn with a weary grumble, spit once more, and disappear back inside the cabin.

"Well, I'll be goddamned," Prophet said under his breath. "They really are inside the cabin."

He looked around, wondering again if he could have walked into a trap. But the only sound was a cricket and a light stir of leaves at the very top of a nearby tree. If this were a trap, surely Duvall or the other rider would have sprung it by now.

Doubt lingered in Prophet's mind as he made his way back to Zeke and Louisa.

"What did you find?" Zeke asked as Prophet approached.

"As far as I can tell, they're all in the cabin."

"They didn't post a watch?" Louisa asked.

"Not as far as I can tell, and I scoured every inch around the place. I don't like how it sounds, but I say we go in."

Zeke nodded and gripped his rifle. "Sounds good to me."

"Sounds too good to me," Louisa said darkly, lost in thought.

"Something don't seem right to me, either," Prophet said. "But I knew when I started out in this trade there'd be risks involved. I don't feel like waiting around till daylight. What do you two think?"

"I say we take them now," Zeke said.

Louisa nodded. "I agree. It's time. It's long been time."

Prophet turned to his horse, which Zeke had tied to a tree with the other two. He slid his Winchester into the saddle boot, as this looked like a close-range operation, and retrieved his Richards from the saddle horn. He slung the lanyard around his neck, holding the short-barreled barn blaster under his arm as he headed out toward the trees and the cabin.

Zeke and Louisa followed, stepping carefully, making little noise as they walked through the darkness of the woods. The only light was that shed by the crescent moon and a few stars not obstructed by clouds.

Several times, Prophet stopped, as did the others, and they crouched and listened. Satisfied they were alone, they moved out again, Prophet in the lead, gripping the Richards before him.

When they finally approached the bluff behind the cabin, they stopped once more to listen. Then Prophet said softly, "The cabin's about fifty yards on the other side of this bluff. We'll skirt around the base of the bluff and approach the cabin from the right rear side. Zeke, you go around behind the cabin to the left. Louisa and I will take the right—after I've stopped up their stovepipe."

"Smoke 'em out?" Zeke asked.

Prophet nodded. "We'll meet at the front door."

"You got it," Zeke whispered.

"Let's do it," Prophet said, moving forward, around the rocky base of the bluff, pushing quietly through the shrubs.

When Prophet saw the dark outline of the cabin before him, something moved to his right, screeching. Giving a start, he brought the Richards up, his thumb ready to pull the rabbit-eared hammers back. Then he heard the wind of the beating wings.

"Owl," he said to Louisa and the deputy. "Just an owl."

Behind him, Zeke gave a relieved sigh.

Prophet watched the giant owl wing out across the stars and lose itself in the darkness around the butte.

The three continued on to the cabin. Prophet could hear snores resounding within. Still unable to believe Duvall's carelessness and hoping he'd tracked the right trio of riders—he'd been sure the hoofprints had matched those of Duvall's gang—he tore up a handful of grass and motioned to Zeke for a lift.

The deputy crouched, lacing his hands together. Prophet set his boot in the deputy's makeshift step, stretched, and grabbed the overhang as Zeke heaved him onto the roof from below.

Quietly, Prophet crawled forward on hands and knees, testing the weight of the roof lest it should collapse beneath him, which had happened, to his everlasting chagrin, while trying to surprise a group similar to Duvall's. He'd lived to tell the tale, but things had gotten a mite hairy after he'd plummeted into the badmen's lair, waking the sleeping crew, and he doubted the good Lord would help him out of another cockamamy jam like that one.

When he reached the stovepipe from which smoke issued, he quietly stopped it up with the grass, packing it good until not even a hairlike thread of smoke escaped the pipe. Then he carefully crawled back to the rear of the cabin and lowered himself over the side, dropping to the ground with an unavoidable thump. Crouching, he made a face as he listened to the sounds within. One of the snores ceased for a moment, then continued.

Prophet breathed a sigh of relief and turned to Louisa, who stood at the cabin's corner with her revolver raised.

"In a few minutes, the smoke should get pretty thick in there," he whispered with a smirk, brushing past Louisa toward the front door.

He, Zeke, and Louisa had stood around the front door, backs pressed to the cabin, for nearly two minutes before one of the snorers sputtered. "Hey," he said. "What's goin' on?"

Another snorer ceased snoring and gave a sigh. "What . . . what the . . . what the hell's all the smoke about?"

He coughed. "Goddamn—my eyes! Open the damn door for chrissakes!"

"Open the door?" the other man said. "Hell, let's get the hell *outta* here. Somethin's burnin'!"

"Grab your gun, Howard! It could be a trap!"

Feet pounded the board floor, shaking the walls. The door burst open, and two men ran out in a gauzy shroud of eye-watering smoke.

"Hold it there!" Prophet and Zeke yelled at nearly the same time.

The two men heard the yells, but they did not heed the warning. They twisted around, revolvers in their hands, but before either could fire, Prophet cut one down with the Richards, and Zeke fired two rounds into the other with his Winchester.

Prophet's man was dead before he hit the ground.

Zeke's man rolled around, groaning and kicking his legs.

Surprised and confounded to see only two men, and neither one Duvall, Louisa bounded into the cabin a second before Prophet had the same idea. He stepped in behind her, gazing through the smoke.

"How could he not be here?" Louisa said, cupping her mouth and nose with her left hand as she peered through the smoke wafting from the sheet-iron stove in the room's center.

"Well, that explains the missing horses," Prophet said.

He turned and went out. Zeke was standing over the wounded rider. Prophet walked over and crouched down.

"Where's Duvall?" he asked the wiry lad with two holes in his chest.

The kid only spat curses, fuming as blood spurted from his wounds.

"You're dyin'. Might as well come clean and give us Duvall," Prophet urged.

The kid fell silent, and a befuddled expression arranged itself on his face as he slid his eyes around as if looking for something . . . someone. Then a thought appeared to dawn on the lad, and he cursed once more.

"That son . . . that son of a . . . bitch," he said, and died.

Prophet and Zeke looked around. Louisa stood by the smoky front door, doing likewise.

"What do you think?" the deputy asked Prophet after a while.

"I think he gave us all the slip, his partners here included," Prophet said. "Made off with all three horses."

"Shit."

"Yeah, I'll say shit," Prophet agreed. "Three horses means he can ride all day and all night. He's probably got a good three hours on us, to boot."

"We'll never catch him now," Louisa said thinly, staring at the ground. "We'll never catch him now."

Prophet looked at her. "Yes, we will." Then he gazed off through the smoke billowing against the stars.

"Yes, we will," he repeated, though it sounded hollow even to himself.

17

DUVALL RODE HIS three horses hard through Nebraska and into Kansas, avoiding settlements where someone might recognize him. He slept only three hours a night and kept his cook fires small. That's how badly he wanted to lose the pursuers.

He'd never seen such a formidible trio of trackers in his life. Not only had they wiped out his entire gang, they'd tracked him relentlessly from up near the Canadian border, even rooting him out of Jack Clawson's sawmill south of Bismarck.

He knew why the lawman wanted him, and he supposed the bounty man wanted the reward money several express companies had offered for his head. But what about the girl? Why in the hell was she after him, for chrissakes? He usually got along with women.

Duvall didn't know if the three trackers were still on his trail. He hadn't slowed up enough since deserting Clyde and Harold in the shack to find out. He didn't really want to know, because he had a feeling they were back there, all three of them sniffing out his scent like supernatural hounds straight from the devil's hell.

He just hoped he could finally get shed of them once and for all in the Indian nations. If not, he'd have to head to Mexico, and he really didn't want to head to Mexico. He was still young, and he had several good, hell-raising years left in the States—if those three would leave him be, that was.

Goddamn them, anyway! If it hadn't been for them, he and his gang would be living high on the hog about now. He wouldn't be out here alone, running for his life and having to possibly fritter his best years away south of the border.

His was a long, hard ride through some of the emptiest country he'd ever seen, crossing one river after another: the Missouri, the Niobrara, the Platte, and the Republican. He had to laugh in spite of his trouble, however, whenever he thought of how he'd duped Clyde and Harold that night in the hideout cabin, telling them he'd keep the first watch while they got some shut-eye. He'd wake one of them in a couple hours, he'd said. Instead, he'd swiped their thousand dollars from Clyde's saddlebags and lit out with their horses, leaving them sound asleep in their bunks!

Duvall grinned as he rode now, pondering the look that must have been on that big-talking Clyde's mug when the bounty hunter had poked his gun in his sleepy face, and Clyde had realized he'd been duped.

If that little, no-account kid had diddled the president's niece in Omaha, Dave Duvall was a monkey's uncle. No siree, it hadn't happened. Couldn't have . . . no way.

Duvall was six days into his journey from the cabin and was deep into Kansas—or so he reckoned from the amount of country he'd covered. He crossed a shallow stream, splashed up the opposite bank, and decided it was time to camp. The sun was nearly down, and all three horses were lathered and hanging their heads.

After picketing the horses in deep grass in willows near

the stream, Duvall threw down his tack and bedroll and gathered kindling for a fire. He'd shot a jackrabbit earlier, and he skinned the animal now as the fire took and his coffee began to sputter and steam.

The rabbit was roasting on the spit when his horse whinnied. Duvall was sitting back away from the fire, to preserve his night vision. He reached for his rifle and shucked a shell in the chamber, his heart beating rhythmically against his chest. He heaved himself to his feet and stepped into the willows, hunkering low and looking out through the spindly branches.

His horse whinnied several more times and danced around in the grass, pulling against its rope. Finally, Duvall heard the clomp of a hoof on his right, from somewhere upstream. He waited. More hoof clomps grew until a man called, "Hello the camp. Harlan Doolittle here, just a harmless old preacher lookin' for a brother and fellow Christian to break bread with."

Duvall frowned, wary. "Come on in," he said finally, turning his rifle toward the sound of the hoof clomps. "I have a rabbit on the spit."

"Thank you, friend. Don't mind if I do."

The mouse-brown, blaze-faced horse appeared at the edge of the firelight. A dark-clad figure sat the saddle, the white preacher's collar glowing against the wrinkled, leathery neck. The man wore a round-brimmed, bullet-crowned hat. His face was long, with a goosey nose and deep-set eyes capped with bushy, gray brows.

The man sawed back on the horse's reins and glanced around. "Brother? I say, brother?"

Duvall scanned the area, making sure no one was behind this man who called himself a preacher, and no one was approaching from behind Duvall. You didn't get far in Duvall's business by overly trusting anyone, even men of the cloth.

"Step down from the leather, Reverend," Duvall called. "Call me skittish, but a man can't be too careful in these parts. I just wanna make sure you're not a road agent bent on robbin' poor saddle tramps like myself."

"Ah, I see," Reverend Doolittle said with a reasonable nod. Stiffly, he climbed out of the saddle.

"Now, would you mind throwing both tails of your coat back?" Duvall called.

"Certainly," the preacher agreed, doing as instructed. He wasn't carrying a gun. It didn't look like he was even packing a rifle on his saddle. Doolittle stared at the rabbit roasting on the spit, turning a succulent golden brown. "That varmint you got there sure looks tasty."

Satisfied the man was harmless and alone, Duvall stepped out of the willows, holding his rifle across his chest. He grinned. "Sorry, Preacher, but like I said, a man can't be too careful in these parts." He extended his hand. "Name's Dave."

"Pleasure to meet you, Dave," Doolittle said, accepting Dave's hand with his own, gnarled as an old root. "I don't blame you for being cautious. Why, two nights ago I met up with three fellas that seemed right peaceable when they rode into my camp. I shared my coffee and stew with them and even recited a few words from the Bible. The next morning I woke to three gun barrels poking my face. Those rapscallions took my last two dollars and thirty-five cents, and rode off and left me poor . . . a vagabond."

The old man shook his head sadly, his shoulders sagging wearily. "I don't have a gun to shoot game, so, well, I'd be mighty obliged if you'd share that jack in exchange for a few lines from the Book."

Doolittle looked at Duvall hopefully.

"No problem, Preacher," Duvall said. "You can hold on to your recitation, though."

Doolittle frowned.

"I mean, might as well save it for someone who don't know his Maker as well as I do. Me and the good Lord, we're like this." Grinning, Duvall held up two crossed fingers. He lifted his chin proudly as he recited, " 'Blessed is the man that walketh not in the counsel of the ungodly, nor standeth in the way of sinners, nor sitteth in the seat of the scornful. But his delight is in the law of the Lord; and in his law doth he meditate day and night.' " Duvall raised his voice and his chin about two more notches, shoving his right hand knuckle deep between the buttons of his vest. " 'And he shall not be like a tree planted by the rivers of the water, that bringeth forth his fruit in his season; his leaf also shall not wither; and whatsover he doeth shall prosper. The ungodly are not so: but are like the chaff which the wind driveth away.' " Duvall grinned. "That's from the Book of Psalms, chapter 1, verses one through four."

Doolittle stared agape at Duvall, his old eyes rheumy with emotion. "A God-fearin' man," he said with hushed astonishment. He wagged his head slowly from side to side. "Just when my faith had been tested, my purpose unclear, my destiny in question . . ." Doolittle shook his head again and choked back a sob. "You don't know how refreshing it is to find a man like you, Dave."

"Oh, likewise, Preacher," Duvall said. "Believe me, I feel just as refreshed as you do! Why don't you go picket your horse next to mine over there and fill your plate. That jack's about done."

"Thank you, Brother Dave. Thank you."

"No, thank you, Reverend. You don't know how blessed I feel, havin' a man of the cloth ride into my camp, this lonely summer's eve."

The preacher nodded solemnly, then turned and led his horse into the willows. Duvall watched him go, his smile diminishing, his expression turning cold as a January morn.

Later, when the two men were sitting around the fire,

drinking coffee after wolfing down the jack and tossing the bones into the willows, Duvall rolled a smoke. When he'd snapped a lucifer ablaze on his thumbnail and lit the quirley, he blew smoke out the side of his mouth and reclined against his saddle. "So tell me, Preacher, where you headed, anyway?"

The old man blew on his coffee and sipped. In his low, tremulous voice, he told Duvall that he was heading for his new congregation in a small Kansas town named Greenburg, about forty miles south. He'd never been there before, but he'd heard it was a nice, quiet little town, and that the parishioners had recently built their first Lutheran church. They were eager for a full-time preacher instead of the itinerant clerics that happened through only once or twice a month, delivering sermons in the town's only hotel or in the town hall.

"Yes, the good people of Greenburg will be quite happy to see me, and I them. The last town I was in, Coffeyville, was, if you'll pardon the expression, Dave, a hellhole." Doolittle shook his head and stared into his coffee. "Damned place. Truly damned. I was there for five years and couldn't make a dent in that wall of sin they'd built through the heart and soul of that town."

Duvall hadn't heard a word since Doolittle had said he hadn't yet visited Greenburg. "So, you mean, you don't know anyone in the town?" he asked the preacher.

"No," Doolittle said. "But I'm not worried. I've heard from other ministers that it's a nice little place, not at all like Coffeyville. If the citizens are half as eager for a full-time preacher as I am to settle in a God-fearin' town, I know everything will work out fine." He looked at Dave sincerely. "It always does, you know, Dave . . . in the end."

He smiled smugly and tossed back his coffee. Then he tossed his cup aside and rolled up in his blankets. "Well, time for this old sinner to turn in. Good night, Dave, and thanks once again for your warm hospitality."

"No problem, Reverend," Dave said. He was leaning back against his saddle, smoking his cigarette, arms crossed against his chest. He stared at the stars thoughtfully, his mind toiling over a new plan.

He lay there for a long time, staring at the stars but not seeing them. His mind labored over the details of his plan. Finally, a dark grin spread across his lips. He flicked his cigarette stub away and snuggled down in his blankets, satisfied that, like the reverend had said, everything would turn out just fine.

"Yep," he said to himself as Doolittle snored nearby. "Everything's gonna work out just fine . . . for me."

Dave snickered himself to sleep.

The next morning, over a spartan breakfast of coffee and some jerked beef the preacher found in his saddlebags—Duvall needed to find a town where he could buy trail supplies, he realized—Dave talked with the old man.

He feigned only a desultory interest in the preacher's life, as though there really wasn't much else to talk about, so why not talk about the reverend's hopes and dreams for the future? Every once in a while, he threw in a few lies about his own life to balance the exchange.

In reality, in his characteristically cunning fashion, Duvall was pumping the old man for information about Greenburg: logistical details like whom the old man intended to see when he got to town and where he was going to stay, and so on. The old man gave the information freely, innocently, thoroughly buffaloed and grateful to have someone to talk with after his several lonely days on the trail from Coffeyville.

When Duvall was satisfied he'd wrung the old preacher

dry, he stretched, yawned, said it was time to answer nature's call, and moseyed into the willows. By the stream, he found a stout driftwood branch and carried it back to the camp, where the preacher was rolling his soogan.

Duvall walked up behind the old man, who was whistling "How Great Thou Art," and swung the branch hard against the old minister's head. The old man jerked to the side and stiffened.

Duvall swung the branch again, making a cracking, thumping sound as the branch connected with the preacher's head. The old man gave a guttural cry and slumped forward. Duvall stepped toward the old man, his mouth a savage slash across his face.

"Ah . . . mercy . . . mercy . . ." the parson sighed, his left cheek in the dirt, eyes fluttering.

"You know who taught me those Bible verses I recited?" he asked the old man tightly, breathing hard through his nose, his face crimson with rage. "A preacher just like yourself." Again, Dave smashed the branch against the preacher's head.

The old man gave another grunt. His eyes fluttered some more, the light in them weakening.

"Yep," Dave said as he lifted the branch once again, "and I finally learned it after the old bastard horsewhipped near all the hide off my back." Dave swung the club down hard against the back of the old man's head, breaking the branch in two.

The preacher's head jerked, his eyes fluttered and closed, and a long, final sigh escaped his lips. He jerked for a while, then lay still.

"Go with God, Reverend."

Duvall sat down on a rock, squeezing his hands together as he tried to get his nerves and anger under control. He didn't know what happened to him sometimes. It was almost like he filled with hate and anger the way a hot teapot filled with steam, until he couldn't control it anymore, and he had to let out some of that wrath.

A laugh escaped him as his eyes slid back to the old preacher lying slumped on the ground. Duvall wrung his hands together, gave a shake to calm himself at last, and stood.

He stared at the old preacher.

"Yeah, you're about my size," he said, as he knelt to remove the old man's clothes. "Maybe a little taller and thinner, but the good ladies of Greenburg'll be more than happy to fix my duds."

Duvall laughed uncontrollably, his shoulders jerking as he worked the old man's tunic up over his head. "Yeah, they'll be more than happy to offer their services to the new preacher in town!"

That started another fit of laughter that did not completely die down until he'd dumped the preacher's body in a deep ravine, scared off his own three horses, and mounted the preacher's mouse-brown mare. Dressed in the dark coat and white collar and black hat of the preacher himself, he jogged the mare toward Greenburg.

What better way to escape his pursuers than in the identity of another man?

As he rode, Duvall whistled an old hymn he'd learned a long time ago at considerable cost to his hide.

18

PROPHET TROTTED HIS horse back to Louisa and McIlroy, who'd been waiting for him along a creek bank while he'd surveyed the terrain from a butte top. The sky was lead gray. It had rained all night, and the low areas were filled with water.

"Okay," he said with the air of grim confession. "I'm lost. Not only do I not know where in God's green earth Handsome Dave Duvall is, I don't even know where *we* are."

"Ha!" Louisa scolded. "I knew it. Some tracker you are!"

"If you think you can do any better," Prophet retorted, his face red, "it's all yours. Lead the way, Miss Fancy Britches!"

"Okay, okay, calm down," Zeke said, holding up a placating hand. "I think Proph has done one hell of a job, considering who we're tracking and all this rain. So we're lost. Arguing about it isn't gonna get us unlost."

The deputy looked at the frustrated Prophet, who sat scowling at Louisa, who scowled back at him with her own unique brand of scorn and defiance. Zeke said, "Well, do you at least know what *territory* we're in?"

Prophet scrubbed his chin with his gloved hand and glanced around thoughtfully. "I'd say we're still in Kansas." He thought about that for a few seconds, then thought about it again. "But hell, we might've slipped into Oklahoma by now. How in the hell would I know? I been scouring the ground for hoofprints. You two should've been keeping an eye on what direction we were headin'."

"Oh, now it's our fault," Louisa said with a caustic grunt.

Before Prophet could launch a counterattack, McIlroy said, "I said that was enough, Miss Bonaventure!"

Louisa whipped her head at the deputy. "And who are you to tell me what's enough? You think that tin badge you're wearing gives you the authority to—"

She stopped when she saw that both men were no longer paying attention to her. Their gazes had been drawn to the west. Turning that way herself, she saw a weathered-gray box wagon meandering across the prairie, pulled by a pair of mismatched horses. The driver was a slight man in coveralls. A medium-sized dog sat atop the hay piled in the box.

"Well, maybe that farmer can tell us what country we're in, anyway," Prophet grumbled, gigging his horse down the slope.

Zeke and Louisa followed as Prophet cantered Mean down the hill, across a natural levee, and onto an intersecting route with the wagon. When the driver saw them, he planted his high-topped, lace-up boots on the footboard and sawed back on the reins, jerking the horses to an abrupt halt.

Reins held tight in his hands, he watched with wary curiosity as the singular trio—two men and a pretty, long-haired blonde—approached from across the undulating sod. Prophet hoped that Louisa's presence along with

Zeke's badge would put the man at ease, keep him from reaching for a shotgun.

The dog scrambled to the side of the box and barked, planting its front feet on the side boards, wrinkling its long, pointed snoot, and stiffening its tail.

Prophet raised a friendly hand as he checked Mean down alongside the driver. "Good day to you, friend," he greeted.

The man said nothing, just slid his gray, cautious gaze from stranger to stranger. His eyes lingered longest on Louisa, curious lines etched in their corners. The dog growled deep in its throat.

"We were just wondering," Prophet continued, fidgeting around with embarrassment, "where in the hell we are."

"Where ye are?" the man said, drawing his upper lip back from a flat wedge of chew on his gum. "What do you mean where ye are?"

"Well, for starters," Louisa piped up sarcastically, "we'd like to know what territory we're in. Then maybe you could tell us what part of that territory—east or west, or north or south."

"And the way to the nearest town," McIlroy added. "We're low on trail supplies, and we could all use some real food for a change, and a couple nights in a bed."

The farmer scratched the back of his head and squinted at the strangers bewilderedly. "Well, you're in Kansas, I reckon. The south-central part of the territory." He turned to the growling dog and told it to hush. "Nearest town is Greenburg." He nodded to the west. "Straight that way about six miles, just over that divide yonder."

"Greenburg, eh?" Prophet said.

"Yep, that's the place. It's small, but it's grown, by jingo. There's a hotel and a couple saloons and a school. Even got us a new church a few weeks back. I helped put it up myself. We been waitin' on a preacher." The old man's lips stretched into a proud grin, chew juice dribbling out his mouth.

"You don't say," Prophet said with only mild interest.

"How 'bout a sheriff?" Zeke asked. "There any law in town?"

The man's eyes dropped to McIlroy's deputy marshal's badge. "Why, sure, we have us a sheriff. Elmer Tate's his name. Say, if you don't mind me askin', what are the three of you up to in these parts, anyway?"

"We're hunting a degenerate by the name of Handsome Dave Duvall," Louisa said. "You haven't seen him, by any chance, have you? A handsome devil in spiffy duds trailing two horses on a lead line?" She cast an accusatory glance at Prophet. "We lost his trail a few days back."

"It wasn't that long ago," Prophet said defensively, wondering what had ever compelled him to kiss the little polecat. What he felt for her now was nothing close to affection.

"No, I ain't seen no man leadin' two horses," the farmer said. "Ain't seen no one today but you and the man I bought this hay from this mornin'."

"Much obliged, then," Prophet said, tipping his hat to the man and reining his horse westward. When Zeke caught up to him, he said, "Well, I guess we'll check out Greenburg. If Dave's there or passed through, the sheriff will probably know it, it bein' a small town and all."

"I reckon," Zeke said. "And I can wire a report to Yankton."

"Kind of out of your territory by now, aren't you?"

McIlroy shook his head. "There's no way I'm heading back north until I know Handsome Dave's out of commission, once and for all. I'll remove my badge, if I have to."

"Maybe you should exchange it for a compass," Louisa carped as she spurred the Morgan into a gallop, passing Prophet and McIlroy in a dust cloud.

The two men looked at each other as they held their mounts at a leisurely walk. "That girl's as nettling as she is pretty," Zeke remarked.

"Yes, she needs a stern hand. I think when all this is over, you should marry her, Zeke."

"Me? Why the hell should I marry that minx?"

"Well, you said yourself she's pretty. Underneath it all, she's even civilized. You could give her a nice, comfortable life in Yankton."

Prophet halfway meant it. He certainly wasn't the man for her, no matter how much her beauty attracted him. What she needed, sooner or later, was a husband closer to her own age. If Prophet knew one thing about himself it was that he would never in any stage of his life be a suitable husband to any woman worth marrying. He was a bounty hunter, and he would die a bounty hunter, a free man of the mountains and plains, his closest ally his horse, no matter how mean and ugly that horse might be.

A steady woman just didn't fit into those plans.

"Nah," Zeke said as they rode, squinting off through Louisa's thinning dust. "You're the one she wants."

"How's that?"

"Haven't you ever seen the way she looks at you, Proph? Well, I have. That girl's smitten. She doesn't want to be. In fact, she fights it and even hates it in herself. But she's gone for you. Plumb gone."

Prophet sighed, scowling, staring at the diminishing speck that was Louisa.

"And you know what else I know?" McIlroy said.

"I suppose I'm going to hear it whether I want to or not," Prophet groused.

"You feel the same way about her."

Prophet jerked his gaze at the red-haired deputy, who was grinning at him knowingly. Prophet scowled, flushing, working his mouth around a retort that never formed.

"Come on," he said finally, spurring Mean into a gallop. "Let's ride before you bore the tallow right off my bones!"

They caught up to Louisa a mile from the town, and rode abreast through the outskirts of tar paper shacks and log cabins where small children played, chickens scratched, and dogs barked. Greenburg sat on a high bench, with a grand view of the Kansas prairie stretched out around it, tawny and green in the sun that peeked through the tattering clouds.

The trio passed the school and the new church, whose fresh paint gleamed brightly in the kindling afternoon sun, and continued on to the town's small business section. McIlroy reined up to the sheriff's office, and Prophet and Louisa followed suit.

A thickset man with a shock of salt-and-pepper hair sat on a bench before the window. He wore a five-pointed star on his cowhide vest. A little boy of six or seven sat to his right, watching as the man slashed at a chunk of wood with a pocket knife.

"Well, hello there," the sheriff said. "What can I do for you three?"

"Afternoon, Sheriff," Zeke greeted the man. "Tate, isn't it?"

"I'm Elmer Tate," the sheriff said, letting his hands relax in his lap. He tilted his head to the boy beside him. "And this is my grandson, Sam. He's home from school today on account of he's got a tummyache." The sheriff winked, indicating the lad was really just playing hooky for one reason or another.

"Ah, I see," Zeke said. "Most likely just growing pains."

"That's probably all it is," Sheriff Tate agreed with a smile. His eyes found the marshal's badge on Zeke's vest. "I see you're sportin' a badge of your own."

"I'm a U.S. deputy marshal," Zeke said with a nod. "I'm looking for an outlaw by the name of Handsome Dave Duvall. Tracked him all the way from north of Bismarck, as a matter of fact."

"You don't say," the sheriff said soberly. "Handsome Dave Duvall's in these parts, is he?" The man, who appeared to be fifty or a little older, glanced up and down the street, as if half-expecting the badman to be riding into town at that very moment. "I have a couple wanted dodgers on him in the office. I posted them, but I sure never expected—or I should say I hoped—I'd never run into him. It's usually pretty quiet around here. Heck, I rarely even carry a gun unless them cowboys is up from Texas."

"Then you haven't seen him," Prophet said.

"Nope," the sheriff said, shaking his head and pursing his lips. "And I can't say as I'm sorry, neither." He looked at Zeke, squinting an eye against the sunlight. "You're kind of out of your territory, aren't you?"

"I reckon so," Zeke said with a sigh. "I plan to cable the marshal's office in Yankton as soon as I can find a telegraph office. But, with orders or without, I don't intend on going home until Duvall's either dead or behind bars. That's how bad he is. We three have seen it with our own eyes."

"You three are together, then?" the sheriff said, his eyes sliding to Louisa, who met them boldly with her own.

"That's right—for one reason or another," Zeke said. "This is Lou Prophet and Louisa Bonaventure. Mr. Prophet's a bounty hunter."

"I've heard of Mr. Prophet," the sheriff said with a nod at the bounty man, who smiled affably and touched his hat brim. "I reckon if anyone can catch Handsome Dave, it's you two."

Louisa gave a caustic grunt and turned away. Apparently, the sheriff didn't notice. He said, "But if you need any help, you just let me know. If you find him in Greenburg, why, I reckon this is my jurisdiction . . ."

Prophet could tell the sheriff wanted nothing to do with the outlaw, and he didn't blame him. Tate had probably been a cowboy or a farmer most of his life and had taken the Greenburg sheriff's job because he'd thought it would give him time with his grandkids. He hadn't planned on having to hunt killers like Duvall. Not for twenty dollars a month, a free beer in the saloons now and then, and a cut on his house rent.

Apparently, Zeke had read the same thing in the sheriff's demeanor. "Much obliged," he said. "I'll call you if we need you, Sheriff, but I think Prophet and I can take care of it."

"With a little help from the lady," Louisa cut in with customary sarcasm.

Zeke looked at her with annoyance, then flashed a discomfitted grin at Tate. "She's a . . . an unofficial deputy, you might say," he explained to the sheriff, who only nodded, puzzled lines etched across his forehead.

"Yeah, that's what she is," Prophet wryly agreed as he reined his horse away from the sheriff's office. Under his breath he added, "And an official pain in the ass."

"You'll find the telegraph office up the street a block," the sheriff called.

"Much obliged, Sheriff," Zeke said with a wave. "Good day to you, sir."

"And don't forget," the sheriff returned, his halfhearted voice faltering a little, "you need any help with ole Duvall . . ."

"We'll send for you," Zeke said as he, Prophet, and Louisa walked their horses down the street.

Only the occasional farm or ranch wagon passed. A handful of ranch ponies milled before saloons. While boasting a few ladies in sunbonnets, the boardwalks were fairly uncluttered, as well.

"Looks like a nice town to hole up for a few days, listen to the wind for word of Duvall," Prophet said.

Zeke nodded. "My tired ass isn't going to know what to make of a feather bed."

The town's only hotel, the Kansas House, sat in the middle of the main drag, flanked by a tinware shop and an apothecary. Zeke continued on to the telegraph office while Prophet and Louisa tied their mounts to the hitchrack before the hotel and walked inside.

The front desk sat to the left of the lobby, opposite the stairs and the door to the adjoining café. Prophet and Louisa headed to the desk, where the clerk was talking with a tall man dressed in black holding saddlebags and a rifle boot.

"Well, I'm very sorry to hear you're leaving us, Reverend," the clerk said. "But the Rumisheks are a good, God-fearin' family. I'm sure you'll be more comfortable there. That Mrs. Rumishek and her daughter Marliss, they're about the best cooks in the county, don't ye know?"

"That's what I've heard, that's what I've heard," the reverend sang back to the clerk. "Thank you mighty kindly, Mr. Haskell. Your accommodations have been more than adequate, but it's time I joined my flock. Good day to you, sir, and God bless."

"God bless, Reverend," the clerk said as the reverend turned away.

When the preacher saw Prophet and Louisa waiting behind him, he bowed graciously. "Good day, brother. Good day, sister."

"Good day, Reverend," Prophet replied automatically, only glancing at the man's collar before stepping up to the desk and asking the clerk for some rooms.

19

DUVALL'S HEART WAS pounding as he stepped onto the boardwalk. He shuffled to the side of the door and pressed his back to the wall, his stomach churning with fear and excitement.

They'd seen him. Both the bounty hunter and the girl had looked him in the eye. Had they recognized him?

No, they couldn't have, or they'd all be flinging lead every which way. Although a side arm did not go with Duvall's preacher's attire, he still had his rifle—for hunting, he'd explained to the curious. He'd strapped a hideout pistol to his right ankle, just in case.

Duvall grinned with delight. No, they hadn't recognized him. They'd looked at him directly, but they hadn't recognized him. He'd started growing a beard after he'd killed Doolittle, but he figured the main reason he hadn't been recognized was the preacher's costume. Duvall had suspected that what most people saw when they saw a preacher was the black wool tunic, black coat, and white collar, not the man himself.

And what had just transpired—or not transpired—in the hotel lobby proved his theory. The disguise had worked. His plan was perfect.

All he had to do now was continue the preacher masquerade for a few more weeks, until the bounty hunter and the law and the girl finally gave up on him. Then he could ride on, free as a tumbleweed, under a different guise, of course, and a different name. He'd have to lie low for a few months, but then, hell, he'd be back on his high horse in no time!

Duvall felt so cocky all of a sudden, he was tempted to make another little stroll through the lobby, dare Prophet and the girl with another peek at his face. He suppressed the idea, however. Pushing his luck would be stupid.

No, he didn't want to give them any more chances than necessary to realize who he was. He doubted he had much to worry about. The bounty hunter and the kill-crazy blonde weren't likely to spend much time around Duvall's new place of employment, the First Lutheran Church of Greenburg.

The preacher snickered again, shaking his head with delight at his new ruse. Not only had he pulled the wool over his pursuers' eyes, he'd pulled it over a whole town! And what a lovely town it was, he thought now as the image of Marliss Rumishek flashed in his mind.

The buxom daughter of the God-fearing family who'd offered him quarters until a parsonage could be built was only fourteen years old, but in mind only. She had the curves of a woman twice her age, as well as the yearnings. Duvall had sensed her desires the first time he'd laid eyes on the chestnut-haired little vixen.

Marliss was one exception to the rule that most people saw only a preacher's attire. Marliss had seen Dave's devilishly handsome mug and had fallen head over heels in lust with the parson. Dave was as certain of that as he was of the bankruptcy of his own soul.

Standing with his back to the hotel, he snickered again.

"Good afternoon, Parson."

Dave jerked his head up quickly, an embarrassed flush replacing his grin in a hurry. Before him stood the middle-aged wife of the banker, in a bright orange dress adorned with gold buttons and lace and a wide collar flattened across her mannishly wide shoulders. The tony veil of her black hat fluttered in the fresh-smelling breeze.

"Uh . . . good afternoon, Mrs. Winkleman," Duvall said, trying to come up with a fast excuse for standing around grinning and snickering like an idiot.

The woman stared at him puzzledly, a thin smile yanking on her flat lips. "You seem to be very pleased about something," she pleasantly chirped.

"Oh, yes . . . well, you know, I was just walking out of the hotel when, out of the blue, the Good Lord whispered the final lines to Sunday's sermon in my ear. You know, I've been struggling for days with that ending, and just now, when I wasn't even thinking about it, He gave it to me ever so gently—bestowed it upon me, I should say—like a feather from a dove's wing." Duvall called up a laugh from deep in his chest—a pious old parson's laugh, he hoped. "Now, isn't that something? Wasn't that merciful of Him to bless me with that, so out of the blue, Mrs. Winkleman?"

"Oh, that's marvelous, Reverend," the lady said, clapping her gloved hands together with delight. "Just marvelous. I guess it just goes to show that even a man of the cloth isn't above His help now and then."

"It certainly does, Mrs. Winkleman. It certainly does."

"What a lovely story, Reverend. I'm going to share it with Mr. Winkleman as soon as he comes home for supper." The old biddy squeezed Duvall's hand as she started off with a smile, flashing her yellow teeth. "Adieu, Reverend, adieu. And welcome once again to our humble little town."

"Thank you ever so much, dear lady," Duvall called with a pious bow of his head.

When she'd turned away at last, Duvall gave a deep sigh of relief and admonished himself to be careful. He couldn't go wandering around town acting like a halfwit if he didn't want to endanger the whole charade.

And another thing he had to be careful about was Marliss Rumishek. He had to keep as far from her as possible, lest that tasty little morsel compel him into an impious act. He could dream about her all he wanted, in the privacy of his own room in her family's little house, but . . . *Dammit man, you have to stay away from that tart!*

Needing three fingers in a rain barrel as badly as he'd ever needed them, Duvall shifted the saddlebags on his shoulder and headed for the saloon across the street. He hadn't stepped inside any such establishment since entering the good little town of Greenburg. After all, ministers weren't supposed to frequent saloons. But just this once, since the town was quiet and the taverns relatively empty, he concocted a little plan.

As he walked into the Smokehouse, he saw only two others in the place, not counting the barkeep, partaking of the free meat and cheese. They looked up curiously as the reverend entered. Dave tipped his hat to the customers and smiled, then stepped up to the bar.

"Good day, Reverend," the barkeep said—a short, stout little man with bushy gray muttonchops and a raspy voice. "What can I do you for this afternoon?"

Dave concocted a pained expression and gave a tight cough, pressing his fist against his chest. "Well," he said, making another face and conjuring a rasp in his voice. "I was wondering if I could get a little whiskey. Don't normally care for the stuff, but the doctor recommended a teaspoon before bed. Said it might loosen up my chest and help me breathe. Seem to have come down with a little frog after the rainstorm."

"Oh, certainly, Reverend. I use it all the time myself . . .

for purely medicinal purpose, of course." The barman chuckled and glanced at the two other customers in the shadows. "I'll fix you right up with a pint of good Kentucky bourbon."

"Uh"—Dave coughed into his fist—"better make it a quart. I need to have my speaking voice back by Sunday. My first sermon, you know."

"A quart . . . well, you betcha, Reverend. A quart it is. There you go. That'll be two dollars and twenty-five cents. Thank you kindly, Reverend. Hope you're better soon."

"Amen, brother," Dave said, stuffing the bottle in his coat pocket and turning for the door. "Amen."

He went outside and turned east, heading for the little house of his temporary benefactors, the Rumishek family. He figured he'd have a couple nips from the bottle and then get to work on his sermon. He'd never written a sermon before, and he knew he had to make the first one as good as he possibly could. First impressions and all that. He wasn't too worried. What were sermons, anyway, but thunder and lightning and quotes from the Book about how we were all going to hell in a handbasket if we didn't straighten up and surrender our souls?

Yeah, that's all they were. He'd make his harangue just as nasty and scary as he possibly could. He'd breathe some fire, get the women gasping, the children bawling, and the men sweating in their suits. The bourbon would lubricate him, help him blow the flames onto the page.

But then again, he couldn't drink *too* much at the risk of losing control of himself around young Marliss.

Jesus, just her name filled his head with impure thoughts! Lord help! He should've stayed in the hotel, but what excuse would he have given the Rumisheks, who'd insisted he stay with them?

Their house was a two-and-a-half-story affair with clapboard siding in need of paint. There was an add-on shed that hadn't yet been painted, though it looked as though it had been added on about two years ago. A small barn and chicken coop shared the big, weedy lot with the house, and chickens and two pesky pigs had the run of the place during the day. So did a dozen cats, mostly kittens, which didn't make them any more attractive to Dave, who'd always considered the only good cat a dead one.

Dave strolled into the yard with the whiskey secure in his coat pocket and headed for the front door. As he did so, he heard a smacking sound from the right side of the house, by a large cottonwood and the privy. Looking that way, he saw Marliss. With a broom she was beating a rug draped over a low tree branch. Her back was to him, and Dave hoped she wouldn't see him before he could get inside. He didn't want to have to look at her lovely face with its lustrous, girlish brown eyes.

No such luck.

"Hello, Reverend," she called, turning toward him.

She wore a shabby straw hat and a simple blue gingham dress. She was barefoot. Her dark brown hair fell smoothly to her shoulders, ruffled a little by the breeze. Her face was smooth as vanilla frosting, and her chin was dimpled and dainty.

"Oh, hello, Miss Marliss. I didn't see you over there."

"Are you really moving in with us, Reverend?"

"Well, I reckon so. A poor man of the cloth can't turn down the offer of free quarters. It sure was nice of your mammy and pap to turn one of your bedrooms over to me. I hope it won't be too much of an inconvenience."

"Oh, it's not an inconvenience at all, Reverend!" the girl intoned, casting a serious, beseeching look at Duvall. She was starstruck, utterly love-struck. Dave dropped his eyes to her heaving young bosom, caught himself, and returned them to her eyes with a patrician's smile.

"Well, lovely then, Miss Marliss." He wanted to go

inside and have a drink, but her eyes held him. This girl stirred him deeply, so that he was afraid of her and himself, but for the life of him he couldn't move.

Go inside the house, Dave. Get your ass inside!

"Yes, it will be lovely, Reverend," the girl said with a cherubic smile, cocking one hip and poking the toes of one bare foot at the grass. "I mean, having a man of the cloth around. It'll be like . . . well, it'll be like the house is blessed all the time, every night and every day."

As she dragged her toes through the grass, the hem of her dress slid up her slender calf.

"Yes, well . . ."

"And Grandma will especially enjoy it, seein' as how she's so sick an' all."

"Yes, well . . ."

"Do you think you can tell me things about the Bible, Reverend? I mean, I go to church, but I've never studied the Good Book like Grandma always says I should. I try sometimes, but I swear, I just can't make heads or tails out of the things it says."

"Well, we can certainly arrange something, Miss Marliss. You have to understand, though, I do have quite a lot of work to do—you know, writin' sermons and buyin' wine for communion and such. Visiting sick folks like your grandma."

"Oh, I know, Reverend! And if there's anything I can do to help, please let me know. I'd love so much to help you any way I can—I mean, since you're so new here and everything. I can show you where all the sick folks live."

"That would be most kind of you, Marliss, and I'll keep that in mind. In the meantime"—his eyes bounced off her bosom once more—"I think I'll take a short nap, then get to work on my sermon."

"Okay, Reverend. Momma's gone to the mercantile to sell chickens, so if you need anything, just give a call out your window up yonder. I'll be happy to fetch whatever you need." She glanced at the dormer window in the second story, overlooking the cottonwood tree.

"Thank you mighty kindly, my dear," Dave said, grinding his molars as he turned inside the house.

He quickly mounted the narrow stairs to his room, which, incidentally, lay right across the hall from Marliss's. He was going to have to start working late at the church, that's all. Either that or end up giving in to temptation and getting run out of town on a long, greased pole.

His room was spartan, with a simple cot furnished with a quilt and a feather pillow, a small desk, a chair, a wardrobe, and a porcelain thunder mug. The single window was open, and a breeze fluttered the curtains. The rhythmic sound of Marliss beating the rug rose from the yard below. Dave found himself edging over to the window and peeking out at the barefoot, straw-hatted girl.

He allowed himself a short stare. Her feet were so delicate, the ankles so fine, the toes so pink and plump. Grinding his molars again, he tossed his hat onto the desk, set his saddlebags and rifle on the chair, and sat himself down on the bed. He produced the bottle from his pocket, uncorked it, and took a long pull, then another.

Then, listening to the girl smack the broom against the rug, he took another and another.

20

LOUISA STEPPED OUT of the hotel and cast her gaze across the street, at the Smokehouse Saloon before which three ranch horses stood, noses to the hitchrail. Distractedly, she watched a farm wagon with six sullen kids of all ages riding in the box, and gave a thoughtful sigh.

She, Prophet, and Zeke McIlroy had been holed up in Greenburg for three days now, and they'd seen no sign of Duvall. While Zeke had been keeping in close contact with the town's sheriff and the local telegrapher, the deputy hadn't heard any news about Duvall, either.

His home office had ordered him back to Yankton, Dakota Territory, but the deputy had no intention of returning until Duvall was out of commission. He'd decided to tell his boss that for one reason or another he'd never received the telegram. It was a believable lie. Communication was problematic on the frontier, rarely reliable. But even if his job was on the line, McIlroy was determined to see the hunt for Duvall through to its conclusion.

To that end, he, Prophet, and Louisa had decided to remain in Greenburg until they heard something of Duvall's whereabouts. They could ride circles around the West and get nothing for their trouble but saddle sores and exhausted mounts.

It was the right decision, Louisa knew, but the inactivity was driving her crazy. That's why she stepped off the boardwalk now and crossed the street. Before the Smokehouse, she paused to read the hand-printed placard in the window: Serving Girl Wanted, Apply Inside.

Louisa had never worked in a tavern before. In fact, she'd never had any kind of job before. But she had to do something, and she needed money. Also, by working in a saloon she might possibly overhear news of Duvall. Greenburg lay on a prominent cattle trail, and salesmen and cattlemen from all across the territory stopped here on their way to other places.

What's more, if Duvall was still in this region—and Louisa sensed he was—he might stop to refresh himself in Greenburg. If so, the town's main saloon would attract him like a magnet. And then Louisa would drill a forty-five slug through that devil's skull without batting an eye.

But first she'd shoot his knees, and then his elbows, and then . . .

She wagged her head, not wanting to get ahead of herself—she didn't even have the job yet—and pushed through the Smokehouse's batwings.

She let her eyes rove the saloon's dark interior, where three cowboys played a lazy game of cards back near the piano. The smell of fresh sawdust lay heavy in the air, covering the smell of stale beer and the tobacco the cowboys smoked. The bartender was slicing cheese onto a large tin plate beside another plate heaped with smoked sandwich meat.

"Hello, there, missy. If you're lookin' for your daddy,

I haven't seen him." The bartender smiled at the cowboys, who had turned to regard Louisa with interest. They chuckled at the barman's joke.

"I'm not looking for my father," Louisa said, stepping up to the bar. "I'm here to apply for the job you advertised in the window."

The bartender, a stocky man with a hoarse voice and gray muttonchops, stopped slicing the cheese and took Louisa's measure with a discerning frown, looking her up and down.

"How old are you?"

"Nineteen," she lied. She didn't know if there was any certain age she needed to be, but she decided to add a couple years, just in case.

The barman ran his eyes over her body and pursed his lips. Apparently deciding she was telling the truth, he said, "Well, you can't wear that," gesturing to indicate the poncho and black, bullet-crowned hat.

"Does that mean I have the job?"

"Well, no one else has applied for it. You'll do, but, like I said—"

"I know, I know, I can't wear the poncho. What exactly do I need to wear? I've never done this sort of thing before."

The barman sent a smirk toward the cowboys, who were still listening to the conversation as they played cards.

"What do you boys think this gal should wear to sling drinks in my joint?"

"As little as possible," one of the cowboys replied as he slapped a card onto the felt. He grinned; the others snickered.

"I think she'd look good in something pink," another man said.

"And low cut," added another.

"And she'll have to have a very short skirt, or by god,

we'll take our business over to the Raging Lion. By god, when I go to a saloon, I expect to see some skin on the girl serving the strychnine."

"Hey, I don't serve any of that crap in here, Collie!" the barman snapped with offense. "Don't you dare say I do."

The cowboys elbowed each other and laughed. "Collie's just tryin' to get your goat, Ford," said the nicest-looking one of the three. He wore trail garb but it wasn't as ratty or dusty as what the other two wore. His hat was a crisp, clay-colored Stetson with silver conchos tooled into the band. His eyes bespoke more intelligence and character than what you'd normally find in a thirty-a-month trail waddy. "He's just bored an' waitin' for roundup, like the rest of us."

He cast his handsome face at Louisa. "Say, what's your name, miss?"

Louisa wasn't ready for the question. She didn't normally talk to strange men unless there was something in it for her. She was about to ignore him and get on with her business with the bartender, whom she assumed was also the owner.

But something made her look again at the handsome young drover in the crisp Stetson, with a red neckerchief knotted around his neck. She realized he probably wasn't much older than she; maybe a couple years was all. His face was clean-shaven, and he looked like he took a bath once in a while.

"Louisa," she found herself saying.

"Louisa what?"

"Bonaventure."

She turned to the barman and was about to speak when the nice-looking cowboy said, "What brings you to Greenburg, Miss Bonaventure?"

Louisa turned to him again, vaguely annoyed but for some reason feeling compelled to answer his question. She decided to do so with a lie, however, as the truth was a little more than most civilized folks could handle. And, despite the company the young man kept, he did look civilized.

"I'm just . . . passing through," she said haltingly, her mind suddenly too sluggish to come up with a detailed fib.

"Well, why would a pretty girl like you, just passin' through, want a job in a little nowhere saloon like this?" Before the barman could object, the cowboy added placatingly, "No offense, Ford! For bein' out in the middle of nowhere, you still serve the best whiskey and free eats in the territory."

"Harumph," the barman growled, crossing his stubby arms over his vest.

"I need the money," Louisa told the cowboy. "And I saw the placard in the window there, so I thought I'd give it a try." Turning finally to the barman, she asked, "What do you pay, Mr. . . ."

"Fargo. Ford Fargo. You get paid in the tips you receive from boys like these." He flicked a hand to indicate the drovers. "So, if you're sportin' a nice figure under all those clothes, and you appear to be, you should make out just fine. If not . . . well, in this business it don't pay to be hit with the ugly stick, and I mean that literal." He snorted a laugh.

"Yeah, like that last girl you had workin'," the tallest drover said, his back to the bar and sucking a quirley. "That girl pret' near starved to death before she finally got savvy and applied over at the mercantile for an hourly wage."

He chuckled, as did the others. "Blackjack," the handsome one called.

This started a mild argument, and Louisa looked at the barman. "I don't intend to dress like a hussy," she intoned. "But I do need the money, so I don't mind wearing a dress a tad less conservative than what I would normally wear. Where, if you please, can I find one?"

The handsome young cowboy cleared his throat meaningfully as he stuffed a wad of winnings into his pocket and rose from his chair. He strode to Louisa and offered his arm with gentlemanly flair. "Allow me the honor of introducing you to Mrs. Lonigan at the Ladies' Fashion Emporium."

Louisa looked at the cowboy skeptically. His smile and demeanor, with his clear green eyes and dimpled chin, were so engaging that she found herself reaching for his arm. "I guess . . . as long as you are a gentleman," she said.

"Oh, my mother raised me to be a right and proper gentleman indeed," he assured her, flashing a toothy smile and ignoring the hoots and chortles of his friends.

The two other waddies laughed and hooted them through the batwings and onto the boardwalk. "Miss, you can start this afternoon at four!" the barman called after them.

"Right this way, Miss Bonaventure," the cowboy said, directing Louisa left along the boardwalk and tipping his hat at two passing matrons in bonnets and long dresses, who smiled at him affably, indicating to Louisa that he had a sound reputation.

"I told you my name," she said, still not sure why she was allowing this young man as much latitude as she was. "What's yours? And as soon as you've told me that, you can tell me why you're being so friendly. It's not that I don't appreciate the help, being unfamiliar with the town, but you can understand how a young lady can't be too careful."

"Name's Riley Nugent," the young man said. "My father is Thomas Nugent, owner and operator of the Sweetwater Ranch just over them western hills, about twenty miles. Me and the two other men I'm with—Collie and

TJ—we're waitin' on a string of horses Pa bought from a horseman east of here. We're not sure what day the man and his horses are due to arrive, so Pa sent me and the other two to town to wait him out. This is our second day. I 'spect he'll be here tomorrow or the day after. If not, Collie and TJ aren't gonna have enough money for a cup of soup by the time we head home."

The young man chuckled, but it was not a cunning chuckle. It was an affable chuckle, with no real mockery in it.

"A gambling man, are you?" Louisa said.

"Oh, now and then, when my old man's not around," Riley Nugent admitted. "He won't put up with it—neither him nor Ma. But Pa sent me out to the bunkhouse when I turned sixteen, to live and work with the range riders, to turn me into the men they are. Well, I reckon it worked. Maybe a little less than he would've liked in some ways, maybe a little more than he would have liked in others."

Louisa stopped on the street corner and turned to him. "You answered only part of my question."

Riley scratched his head. "What was the other part again?"

"Why are you being so friendly and helpful to me, a total stranger?"

"Well, because you're pretty, of course!" He made the exclamation as though the question were the silliest he'd heard. "I have to tell you, Miss Bonaventure, you're about the prettiest girl I've seen in this country in a long, long time."

His penetrating smile disarmed her, and her face heated. She dropped her eyes to the boardwalk. "Thank you."

"But that's not the only reason," Riley rushed to admit, the confidence in his voice flickering. "I mean, you just seem . . . I don't know, kind of alone and lost in a way. You just seemed like a person who could use a friend."

Louisa measured him against the countless other men

she had run into on the frontier, and her tally came up in young Riley's favor. He seemed like a truly decent sort. And his voice had quickly lost its bravado, once he'd gotten away from his friends.

He returned her look with a sincere one of his own. "I'd like to apologize for the behavior of Collie and TJ—and myself, for that matter. They haven't been to town in a while, and neither have I, and we do tend to entertain each other a bit in the Smokehouse. We're harmless, though, I assure you."

Louisa found herself smiling over a blush and returning her eyes once more to her shoes. "You're forgiven. I appreciate the help. You're right; I don't know my way around here, and . . ."

"Pardon for stickin' my nose in," Riley said, "but you don't seem like the kind of girl who'd apply for a job in the Smokehouse or any other saloon."

Louisa returned her eyes to his. "I appreciate your help, Mr. Riley," she said softly, "but that's all the questions I'd like to answer for one day. No offense."

"None taken," Riley said, holding out his hands appeasingly. He swung around and pointed to a store sitting catty-corner across the street. "That there is the Ladies' Fashion Emporium, as you can tell by the sign. It might not look like much, but Mrs. Lonigan's filled her shelves with all the latest Eastern fashions, or so Ma says, anyway."

"Your mother shops there?" Louisa asked as she and Riley crossed the intersection.

"Whenever she can get away from the ranch."

"You must come from a family of means, Riley Nugent." Louisa's voice was affably jeering.

"Oh, I s'pect we're about the richest hereabouts, Miss Louisa," the young man returned without irony. "It ain't what it's all cracked up to be, though. Plenty look up to us, but plenty more envy us, and you know what the man says about envy: 'Pride, envy, and avarice spark hearts afire.' "

"Who said that?"

"I believe it was a guy named Dante."

They were before the dress shop now. Louisa looked up at young Nugent's face and said, "I thought you sounded more educated than you looked."

Riley shrugged self-effacingly. "Pa has a whole library of books in his study, and since there's nothing much else to do winters, I look through them now and then." He opened the door and gestured for her to enter. "Shall we?"

Louisa looked at him, still shocked by the name Dante escaping the young drover's lips. She, too, had read the works of Dante Alighieri, but she'd never expected to run into anyone else who had—especially out here.

With a thin, incredulous smile, warming to this young Riley more every minute, she stepped into the store and listened to the comforting sound of his boots clomping in behind her.

When they walked out a half hour later, Louisa carried a narrow, rectangular box in her arm. "And you're sure," she was asking Riley, "that it isn't too revealing? I mean, like you said, it does have to reveal a little, or I might as well apply at the mercantile. But I don't want anyone to get the wrong idea about me."

Riley Nugent was flustered and tongue-tied. After all, he'd examined the several dresses the lovely Louisa had tried on, and he was certain the experience was one he'd remember on his deathbed. His ears were warm. His heart spun.

"No," he said, swallowing, trying to steady himself. "It's not near as revealing as the first two you tried on. I think . . . I think it's a good compromise."

"Thank you so much for your help, Riley," Louisa said, smiling warmly and clasping his wrist in her hand. "And thanks even more for buying this for me. I promise I'll pay you back as soon as I can."

"I wish you'd just see it as a gift," Riley complained.

"Never," Louisa said, shaking her head. "But thanks again. Maybe I'll see you around?"

"You certainly will, Miss Louisa," he said, his eyes burning at her, his brain reeling. Then, realizing how presumptuous that must have sounded, he added, "I mean, I'll probably be at the Smokehouse when you start at four. If the man and his horses don't show up, that is."

"I'll see you then," Louisa said. Turning, she headed for the bathhouse Riley had told her about.

Riley watched her march down the boardwalk, honey-blonde hair bouncing on her shoulders. He hoped against hope the horses he was waiting for didn't show up for at least a month.

21

THE AFTERNOON SHADOWS were long when Prophet gigged his horse up the bench toward Greenburg.

He stopped when he saw another rider cantering to his right, heading his way through the golden prairie grass touched with salmon. Prophet could tell by the horse and the rider's posture it was McIlroy, heading back to town after he, like Prophet, had been scouting the country for news of Dave Duvall.

"Anything?" Prophet asked as the deputy pulled up to him.

"Not a thing. Yourself?"

Prophet shook his head and sleeved sweat from his forehead. "I talked to four farmers and three ranchers, several cowboys. Nothing. No one's seen a thing."

"He might have ridden on out of here."

"Probably," Prophet said. "But you know, Zeke—and I don't have anything but my rebel gut to back this up—but I don't think so. I just don't think ole Dave is one to run unless he's bein' chased. And he must know by now that he lost us."

"Well, where could he be?"

Prophet gazed around thoughtfully. The breeze was dying. The air cooled as the sun sank, but it was still hot here on the southern Kansas plains. Humid, too. Prophet had gotten used to the drier climate up north.

"I don't know," he said after a while. "But I say we hunker down here a few more days, see what turns up."

"Well, I don't have a better plan," Zeke said. "So I reckon for the time being, I'm going to head into town and get a bath and round up some supper."

"I'm forgoing the bath for a drink," Prophet said, gigging Mean along the trail toward Greenburg looming on the crest of the bench. "Then I sure could use a woman. Zeke, you see any fallen doves around?"

"Can't say as I have," Zeke said as they rode. "There must be some somewhere, even in a town Greenburg's size. Unless that new minister they have has driven them all out. Those Lutherans can be a bit persnickety, you know."

"I reckon," Prophet replied with a sigh. "But by god, after I've had a few drinks and a steak, I'm goin' on the prowl. It's been a while for me. Don't forget, I sold my soul to the devil, so I might as we'll be takin' advantage of the situation."

The deputy chuckled. "What about Miss Louisa?"

Prophet's return was as dry as the sage their mounts dusted as they passed. "What about her?"

Zeke looked at him, then turned back to the trail and shook his head.

It was Friday night, and the town's main saloon, the Smokehouse, was hopping. Ranch horses were tied along the street, and a couple buckboards sat at the end of the block.

When Prophet had stabled Mean and Ugly, he parted the batwings and headed for the bar. It took him several minutes to find a place near the zinc, and a couple more to get a drink.

"Busy tonight," he said when the barman, Ford Fargo, finally set a shot glass of sour mash before his elbows. Fargo shook his head as he collected Prophet's coins. "Yeah, weekends in the summers can get pretty woolly around here. That's why I finally hired a girl to work nights."

Prophet turned to glance at the girl making her way through the crowd behind him with a tray of drinks. "Good-looking girl," Prophet said. "Nothing like a pretty serving girl to keep your customers—"

He stopped and wheeled back around to give the girl another look. She'd turned sideways, and Prophet studied the rich, honey-blonde hair and the clean, delicately carved profile of her face. She wore a lovely, low-cut, formfitting dress, and her hair had been fashionably piled atop her head and secured with a whalebone pin.

She looked so different that Prophet blinked his eyes. It could have been Louisa's older, town-born sister working there, a little uncertain with the tray but holding her own as she collected coins and cash and set the drinks on the tables. Meanwhile, the grinning customers consumed her youthfully pert bosom, a good third of which was revealed by the low dress, with their eyes.

Yeah, it could've been Louisa's older sister, but it wasn't. It was Louisa herself, revealing considerably more flesh than Prophet even knew she had.

"Louisa!" Prophet called across the room.

The girl couldn't hear him above the din.

Prophet called again, slammed down his drink, and barreled toward her, pushing through the crowd and heaving several chairs out of his way, ignoring the indignant protests. When he finally got to Louisa, he grabbed her arm and jerked her around. Fortunately, her tray was now empty.

"Louisa, what on earth do you think you're doing?"

"Ow! Lou, let me go. I've got a job to do."

"Job? What do you mean, job?" He gazed at her dumbly, thoroughly befuddled. What in the hell was she up to, slinging drinks in a saloon like any common serving girl? And what in the hell was she doing in a dress that revealed—he lowered his eyes to her smooth, white cleavage—more of her than most decent women displayed to their own husbands in a lifetime?

She jerked her arm loose and returned his angry glare. "I applied today. I need money. And if Duvall ever shows up in town, this'll be the first place he heads. Now let me go. I have orders to fill!"

She swung away, her skirt swirling. Wisps of loose hair fluttered around her face, which was alluringly damp and pink with perspiration.

"Yeah, let her go, mister. We're thirsty," someone complained behind Prophet.

He didn't turn to reply. He just stood near the silent piano and watched Louisa wend her way through the crowd, plant her tray on the bar, and shout her drink order to the harried Ford Fargo.

Prophet was amazed. She'd just started today, and already she looked as though she'd been doing such work for years. Leave it to Louisa. That girl had a will on her that Prophet had seen on only a few he-coons high in the Georgia hills.

He fought his way back to the mahogany. She was right. If Duvall showed in town, he'd show here first thing. News of him might be discussed by travelers here, as well.

Prophet had another drink at the bar. When McIlroy showed up looking freshly bathed, his hair trimmed and pomaded, his spade beard combed and his coat brushed, they took a corner table. It took McIlroy several minutes to realize the serving girl was Louisa.

"It's her, all right," Prophet answered the deputy's exclamation.

"What in the hell is she up to *now?*"

Prophet only chuckled and shook his head as he watched Louisa work, unable to suppress the stirring in his loins. That was one sharp dress, and it displayed her figure in the most ravishing way possible. Her shoulders were lovely, her arms long and not overly delicate but more like those of a girl who'd spent the last year on the vengeance trail, wrestling the reins of a black Morgan.

Ford told her to take a fifteen-minute break around eleven o'clock, when the drink orders had died down and the crowd had thinned a little. Prophet expected Louisa to join him and McIlroy. Instead, she removed her apron and headed to a table near the piano, which was being played unexpectedly well by an old cowboy in a battered cream sombrero.

"Where in the hell is she going?" Zeke asked.

Prophet didn't say anything. He watched Louisa accept the chair held out for her by a nice-looking young cowboy in a crisp Stetson and clean trail clothes. A burning started in Prophet's gut as he watched the two talking across the table. Louisa sipped her sarsaparilla and smiled occasionally, brightly, now and then tipping her head back and laughing. The burning in Prophet's gut grew, and he wasn't sure of its source.

Yes, he was.

The cowboy was a nice-looking kid, anyway. Closer to Louisa's age than Prophet was. Looked like he'd been raised well. Might even have a little money, as his duds were store-bought and the lucre that hat and pistol belt came from didn't grow on trees.

Prophet and McIlroy had another few drinks. They didn't talk, just watched and listened to the crowd that thinned considerably after midnight. Finally, Prophet stubbed his cigarette butt out in the tobacco-stained sawdust and climbed unsteadily to his feet.

"Ah hell, I'm gettin' the hell out of here, Zeke."

The deputy drained his beer mug. "Me, too. Time to crawl into the sack."

On the way to the hotel, neither man mentioned anything about Louisa. In the hall, they bade each other a solemn good night, and retreated to their rooms. Prophet shucked off his hat and shirt and washed at the basin. He kicked off his boots and lay on the bed, his head propped against the brass frame.

He had a drink from his bottle, smoked another cigarette, and nodded off. He didn't know how long he'd slept when someone tapped on his door.

"Who is it?" he said, snapping his eyes open and reaching for the revolver hung from the bedpost.

Louisa said, "Me."

Prophet left the gun in its holster and opened the door. She stood in the hall, a light shawl draped over her shoulders.

"What time is it?" he asked, sleepily blinking his eyes.

"Two or two-thirty."

"Kinda late, ain't it?"

"Riley and I went walking by the creek."

"Riley and you, eh?" Prophet hated the jealousy he heard in his voice. "Well, what do you want with me?"

Louisa reached out a hand and shoved him back into the room. She stepped forward and closed the door.

"What's goin' on?"

Louisa looked up at him, the orange lamplight flickering in her eyes and across the clean lines of her face. Her lips were slightly parted. Her bosom rose and fell heavily. She dropped the shawl.

"Kiss me," she said.

Prophet didn't know what to make of that. But she stirred him. Oh, how she stirred him, standing there in that dress, her shoulders and neck revealed, her tender breasts snugged down in that soft, orange, lace-edged silk! Her eyes sparkled. She lifted her chin, parting her lips even more. A sheen of sweat formed above her left brow.

Without even thinking about it—he wasn't able to think about anything—Prophet grabbed her shoulders in his big, trail-roughened hands, pulled her to him, and closed his mouth hungrily over hers. Lifting onto her toes, she wrapped her arms around his neck and turned to the side, snuggling against his shoulder as he kissed her, surrendering herself to his hungry tongue and lips, to his powerful arms.

Finally, he removed his lips from hers, swallowing, barely able to contain his want and need for her, and gently held her away. He looked her up and down, as if seeing her for the first time. He looked into her eyes, deep pools of reflected lamplight boring into him.

Seeing that she wanted him as badly as he wanted her—not knowing or caring why, unable to think about why or any repercussions—Prophet slid her dress slowly off her shoulders. He slid it down her arms. Slowly, her bosom slipped free, and her tender breasts bobbed gently as the cotton slipped over the nipples and down her flat belly.

Prophet sighed.

He picked the girl up and carried her to the bed. He lay her gently on the mussed quilt and ran his hands down her slender arms, cupped her breasts in his hands and kissed them, rolling his tongue across the nipples that quickly stirred to his caress.

She lay back on the pillow and sighed, roughly running her hands through his hair.

"Lou," she said in a voice thin and brittle with desire. "Show me . . . show me everything."

He lifted his head and looked into her eyes. He nodded soberly. "I will."

He removed her shoes and underclothes, slid the dress

down the rest of her body, revealing the long, willowy legs and the downy patch between her thighs.

She lay quietly, the lamp's amber glow upon her skin, and watched him undress. He shrugged out of his undershirt, tossed it aside, and kicked free of his jeans. Naked, his swollen member jutting, he moved to her. She ran both her hands over it curiously, a peculiar smile etched on her lips.

Then she opened her legs as he lowered himself between them.

In a few minutes they were rocking together, silhouetted by the lamplight. Her legs were wrapped around his back, her arms around his neck. The bedsprings sang quietly, the two front posts tapping gently against the wall.

22

PROPHET WOKE THE next morning to Louisa massaging his dong.

"Go away," he said, exhausted.

Crouched over it, she worked all the harder. "I want to do it again."

"No."

She chuckled as the member responded of its own accord.

"Jesus, there any skin left on it?" he asked, his arm thrown over his eyes. They'd made love for at least two hours before they'd each collapsed from exhaustion.

"I want to try it this way," she said, climbing on top. He opened his eyes to her lovely, pale breasts in his face, pink in the dawn light penetrating the window.

"We tried it that way—about three times," he reminded her.

"Oh," she said, squirming around on top of him, her hair caressing his chest. "We did it so many ways, I guess I lost track." After a minute, she said, "There . . . that's it."

"Oh, Jesus," Prophet carped, running his hands up and down her smooth thighs as she rose and fell atop him. "If I said it once, I said it a thousand times; you're gonna be the death of me yet."

"Not a bad way to go, is it?"

He looked up at her lovely face shrouded by her hair. How fresh and inviting she looked. In spite of himself, he grinned. "No, it sure isn't."

They came together with a shudder, trying to keep their voices down. Prophet remembered there was an elderly couple in the room next door.

Louisa fell forward on his chest, snuggled her chin in his neck. They dozed together, Prophet's hands on her butt, until she jerked her head up suddenly.

"What is it?" he asked.

"Oh, my gosh!" She scrambled off the bed and splashed water into the washbasin.

"What is it?"

"Riley's picking me up for a buggy ride."

Prophet suddenly came alive, indignant, bolting straight up in the bed. *"Riley?"*

"Sure."

Prophet just stared as she washed and dressed. "I have to get back to my own room and brush my hair," she said, going to the door and throwing Prophet a kiss.

"Louisa," he said, astounded he was even having to give voice to such sentiment, "we made love last night. And now, this morning, you're walking out for a buggy ride with another guy?"

"And what grand lovemaking it was, too, Lou. You see, I wanted you to be the first. I knew, after all your experience, that you'd be the best teacher a girl could ever have." She returned to the bed, leaned down, and kissed him hungrily on the lips. "Besides, I wanted you to be the one for sentimental reasons, I guess. And because, while I know I'll always love you and you'll always love me, it's all we'll ever really have—us being who we are."

She canted her head slightly as she stared into his eyes. Then she kissed him again, got up from the bed, and straightened her dress. "Thank you for the best night of my entire life, Lou Prophet."

She went out.

Prophet lay there, still flabbergasted and feeling more than a little hurt. His pride was bruised. After dwelling on it for a while, he realized what really nettled him was that she'd turned the tables on him. He was the one who usually left first, after blowing a kiss from the door.

He got up and washed. But she'd been right. He shook his head, smiling sadly as he lathered his cheeks. In spite of their love for each other, a fleeting night of blissful coupling was all they could ever really have between them. After all, he wasn't the marrying kind. He knew that as well as he knew anything.

Louisa needed someone like that handsome cowboy.

He heard the squeak and clatter of a buggy in the street below. He went to the window, peered behind the shade. A leather-covered two-seater sat before the hotel, the handsome young cowboy at the reins.

He dismounted when Louisa walked out, and helped her aboard. A minute later, he tossed the reins, and they clattered off.

Prophet couldn't help feeling sad and more than a twinge of jealousy. But he felt hopeful for Louisa, too.

"Reverend, I just have to tell you"—the overwrought woman in a lemon-green dress took a deep breath and tucked a stray tuft of hair under her feathered straw hat—"that was, indeed, the most exalted discourse I've ever heard uttered by human lips."

Duvall smiled modestly, dabbed sweat from his forehead with a hanky, and placed both hands on the Bible he held before him. "I'd like to take responsibility, Mrs. Cantlinson. I really would. But I'm afraid that sermon and all my orations are the work of the Good Lord. He speaks through me. I'm only the vessel, you see. I am, as you are, as are we all, just another poor sinner begging to be saved."

"Just the same, Reverend, I've never been privy to such wisdom. It was even better than the sermon you gave earlier this morning, in church."

It was early Sunday afternoon, and the congregation of Duvall's First Lutheran Church was enjoying a picnic along the banks of Little Otter Creek, about two miles east of Greenburg. Duvall's blessing, which he'd started when the spitted turkey was deemed ready to serve with all the salads and fresh breads the women had trundled out from town in their wicker hampers, had blossomed into a full-blown sermon.

Dave, aka Reverend Doolittle, hadn't been able to contain his zeal. He'd started out mumbling a few solemn words of thanks to the great Jehovah, and, before he knew it, he was strutting around, shaking his Bible over his head and spewing verbal fire as the sweat ran down his face like rain from a cloudburst.

He'd found sermonizing at once stimulating and addicting. Especially when Dave saw all the fear-blanched faces surrounding him. Men as well as women and children appeared truly awestruck and frightened when he really got tanked up to full pressure, and that fueled his fire all the more. There was nothing like seeing men of authority—the mayor, the sheriff, the sheriff's deputy, wealthy ranchers, and even the banker—recoiling like naughty boys when Dave swung toward them, his admonishing finger scolding them for their most secret sins, their most devious trespasses.

Head bowed and nodding gravely, Dave said, "I thank you, ma'am, for your kindness. We both thank you, the Great One and I."

"I just hope Homer was listening."

Homer was Mrs. Cantlinson's husband, a bookkeeper and infamous carouser.

"Oh, he was listening, ma'am," Dave said. "I assure you of that."

"Do you think it had any effect?" she asked, stepping toward the venerated parson to speak privately. "I mean, do you think it will stop him from . . .?" She couldn't continue, so ghastly was the thought.

"From frequenting fallen women?" Dave helped. "I believe so, ma'am. And there's one other thing you might try."

She looked at him, arching her dark eyebrows beneath the brim of her straw hat. "Oh, please, Reverend. Please, what? I'll do anything to keep Homer from . . . from . . ."

Dave draped an arm over the beefy woman's shoulders, glanced around to make sure the other picnickers were a safe distance away, and whispered in Mrs. Cantlinson's ear, "You might try spreading your hairy old legs for him now and then."

The woman's jaw dropped as she gasped and jerked her eyes to his. Her gaze was filled with incredulity—had she heard right?—then revulsion and horror. She lifted her hand to her mouth, biting her knuckles, her jowls quivering.

"Reverend, I—!"

Dave was a little shocked himself. The words had slipped out, as though mouthed by an inner demon. He stuttered, trying to explain. But the woman was far too shocked to listen.

Giving up, he merely patted her back. "Well, I seem to have gotten a little too much sun," he said. "I think I'll take a little stroll in the woods. Good day, Mrs. Cantlinson. Enjoy the meal. Smells good, very good indeed."

The woman staring in horror after him, Dave strolled across the meadow, nodding at the frolicking picnickers, pausing to tousle a boy's hair and to admire, under the guise of a beneficent smile, the forms of two young maidens crouching to spread a blanket, drawing their bright gingham dresses taut against their asses.

When Dave reached the woods, he followed a game trail into the dark recesses smelling of mushrooms and moist earth and fresh, green cottonwood leaves. He paused and stole a look behind him. Deciding he was alone, he produced the small, hide-covered flask from a pocket of his coat and guzzled nearly half.

Then he walked on, trying to get as far as he could from the picnicking Christians with their mindless smiles and vacuous conversation. Where were the lions when you needed them? He'd enjoyed his charade for the two weeks he'd been in Greenburg. He had especially enjoyed the sermons. But he had to admit he was beginning to feel bored. He wondered if he'd be able to keep the act up for another two or three weeks like he'd planned.

It was working, though. Prophet, the blonde, and the U.S. deputy marshal, whose name, Dave had discovered, was Zeke McIlroy, had been thoroughly outwitted. They were not in the least aware that Handsome Dave Duvall was right under their noses in the guise of Greenburg's new parson, the venerable Reverend Doolittle.

No doubt in a day or two, they would move on. And, a few weeks later, Dave himself would disappear, don another guise until he could locate another gang with whom he could ride and wreak havoc.

"Oh, hi, Reverend."

Dave had been tipping back the flask again, when the

voice rose behind him. He snapped the flask down, the whiskey shooting back up his throat. Coughing, he quickly capped the flask and stuffed it into his coat.

Wiping his mouth with his hand, he turned to see Marliss Rumishek sitting on a long, gray log jutting into the creek. Her red-checked dress was drawn up her thighs as she slowly kicked her bare feet in the milky-brown water. The dress was wet. Soaked. It lay flat against her skin, like the thinnest of cotton veneers, molding to and highlighting her nubile curves deliciously.

Her nipples protruded like thimbles.

Dave cleared the whiskey from his throat, tried to keep the hunger from his voice. "Hi, Marliss. What are you up to, young lady?"

"Me and some friends were wading along the creek, and I fell in. The rest went back to eat. I'm waiting to dry off, so Ma won't know. This is my only Sunday dress."

"Oh. I see." Dave took the sandy trail down to the shore.

"You won't tell her, will you, Reverend? I mean, not telling her—that ain't a sin or anything, is it?"

"Nah, that ain't a sin," Dave said, chuckling. "I'll tell you what is a sin, though, Marliss, is how you look in that dress—all wet and everything."

The girl cast her gaze at her breasts, then lifted her arms to cover them. "Oh. I'm sorry, Reverend."

"Are you really, Marliss?"

"Huh?"

"Are you really sorry, or did you want me to see you in that wet dress?"

She stared at him, her cheeks flushing.

"I mean, you've been wanting me to watch you, haven't you? Isn't that why you're always playing outside my window and taking baths in your room, where I can see you through the cracks in the door?"

She started to deny it, then fell silent and dropped her

chagrined gaze to the water. Her bare legs hung still, sunlit water beading on them. "I guess so. I'm sorry, Reverend. It's just that . . . I guess I just wanted you to like me. I didn't mean no harm by it."

"I do like you, Marliss. Why don't you slip out of that dress, and I'll show you how much I like you."

She jerked her head up, shocked. "Reverend . . .?"

"You're not just teasing me, are you, Marliss? Because that wouldn't be very nice, teasing a man of the cloth and all."

"Reverend, I . . ." She slowly shook her head from side to side, fear growing in her eyes.

"Come on, Marliss. Get over here and get out of that dress. Let me see you good and proper, before I give you what you been wantin'." He reached behind and retrieved the short-bladed, bone-handled knife he carried under his belt. He flashed it at her. "Come over here, Marliss. And don't think about screaming, because you'll be dead before anybody can get here. Come on over here and get out of that dress, and let me have a good, long look at you. That's what you been wantin', ain't it?"

She was crying now, her lips trembling, tears rolling down her cheeks.

"I said get over here!"

She jumped, slid off the log, and waded slowly to the shore, eyeing him like a wounded doe with wolves circling.

"There. That's better." Duvall grinned. He sat down in the sand, reclined on an elbow. "Now get out of that dress like I told you, and lay down here with the preacher."

"I . . . I don't . . . want . . . to," the girl sobbed.

"Yeah, but you're going to," Duvall assured her, his lips spreading in a knowing grin. "'Cause if you don't, I'm gonna cut out your tongue, run a thong through it, and wear it around my neck." He took a drink from the flask and patted the ground again. "Come on now. I don't got all afternoon."

The sobbing girl stood trembling and staring, horrified. Then, slowly, her shaking hands went to work on the buttons of her dress.

And soon the dress lay in a wet heap about her feet.

"Come on down here," Duvall coaxed, chuckling crazily as his flat eyes stared. "I don't bite. Not hard, anyway."

23

DUVALL STEPPED OUT of the woods a little while later, feeling nauseated and disgusted with himself. He wanted a drink, but the flask was empty. He'd had enough anyway, he argued to himself.

That damn whiskey! If he hadn't started drinking, he might not have attacked the girl. But now that he had—now that he'd snapped her neck like dry kindling so she couldn't tell anyone about what he'd done to her—he had to get the hell out of here.

"Fool!" he inwardly raged, trying to wring some wit out of his whiskey-addled brain. "Now you've done it, Dave! Now you've really done it! Everything was going so well. You could have stayed here indefinitely, but now . . . shit, several people saw you enter the woods, and when they find Marliss's body in there, they might put two and two together, and not even your handsome mug will get you out of that one."

Oh, it might, he reconsidered, running a hand down his bearded face. But he was too damn worked up to chance it.

When the town got wind of a killer on the loose, it was going to start looking very carefully at its citizens, even the new preacher. Duvall doubted he could hold up to that kind of scrutiny, especially with that damn bounty hunter in town.

A little wobbly on his feet but trying to look natural, he made his way across the meadow. He painted a preacherly, celestial smile on his face but did his best to avoid eye contact with anyone. He wanted to climb into the phaeton which the banker, Orton Winkleman, had loaned the new parson indefinitely, drive back to the Rumisheks' house, pack up his few things, and hightail it the hell out of here.

"Where you going, Reverend?" someone asked him. "You haven't eaten yet, and that turkey sure is good!"

Startled, Dave whirled to see Mr. Rumishek himself, smoking a cigar under a cottonwood with several other men dressed in their Sunday finest. Rumishek was a blacksmith, and he had the dark, brawny physique normally associated with his profession. Arms like young oaks, a nose as big as a wheel hub.

"I seem to have acquired a headache," Dave said, his heart thudding. He had only the knife on him, and if Rumishek and his buddies found out what he'd done to the blacksmith's daughter, he'd probably be drawn and quartered and pummeled before they hung him from the nearest tree.

"Oh, I'm sorry to hear that, Parson," Rumishek said, taking a puff from his cigar. "I hope you're feelin' better real soon."

"I'm sure an hour's nap will have me back on my feet," Dave said, nervously touching his hat brim, then wheeling and heading for his phaeton, which was parked in the shade with a dozen other wheeled rigs.

When he arrived at the Rumishek house, he parked the buggy on the street, ran inside, and hurriedly threw his few personal articles into his saddlebags. He left the house with the saddlebags and his rifle, mounted the phaeton, and turned it toward the livery barn, where he'd stabled Doolittle's mare.

He didn't want to ride the heavy-footed old horse, however, so after turning the phaeton over to the hostler, he rented a good saddle horse, a high-stepping Appaloosa with a speckled rump. The hostler assured the parson that the Appaloosa was the fastest horse in his remuda, although he couldn't help wondering why the reverend would need such a mount.

"Just decided to go for a good, old-fashioned, hell-for-leather ride in the country, Jimmy," Duvall said as he threw his saddlebags over the Appaloosa's back and tied the rifle boot to the saddle. As he climbed into the leather, he added, "Even we men of the cloth like to air it out now and then."

"When can I expect you back, Reverend?" Jimmy asked as he threw open the big front doors.

"Oh, I don't know, Jimmy," Dave said as he gigged the horse out of the barn and into the street. "Don't be so goddamned fussy, for chrissakes!"

With that, Dave heeled the mount into a gallop. The hostler stared after him, scrunching up his eyes and scratching his head. "Now, parsons," he muttered to himself. "I don't think they're supposed to swear, are they?"

Prophet sat on the boardwalk outside the Smokehouse Saloon, his chair tipped back against the wall, his booted feet dangling about three inches off the puncheons. Two old geezers sat beside him. They'd talked his ear off for nearly two hours before the beer and the free lunch finally knocked them out. Both men's chins sagged against their chests, and guttural snores bubbled up from deep in their bowels to ruffle their lips.

"I have to get out of this town," Prophet grumbled to himself as he tipped back his soapy beer mug.

He and Zeke McIlroy had decided yesterday that they'd pull out of town tomorrow, as it looked like Duvall was not going to show. It also looked like they weren't going to hear about him, either. Prophet had decided that he and Zeke should split up, one go south and one go west and keep in touch via the telegraph wires.

As for what Louisa would do, Prophet wasn't sure. He hadn't yet told her that he and Zeke were pulling out. She'd been seeing her handsome young cowboy, Riley Nugent, nearly every day they'd been in Greenburg. Prophet couldn't help feeling jealous of young Nugent's youth and promise as well as his ability to paint a happy glow on Louisa's otherwise solemn features, but he nevertheless hoped the girl from Nebraska had found true love at last, and a refuge from a life of violence like Prophet's.

He'd resigned himself to the fact that she wouldn't rest until Duvall was found, but maybe afterward, if she lived through it, she'd settle down and live the kind of life she was meant for. Life on a prosperous ranch wouldn't be bad at all. And if the Nugents had as much money as Prophet had heard they had, why, it would be a better life than most.

Commotion to Prophet's right attracted his gaze. A man in a Sunday suit was running down the boardwalk, holding his bowler on his head with one hand. As the man crossed the side street and mounted the boardwalk before the Smokehouse, Prophet lowered his chair with a thump and said, "Where's the fire, amigo?" His voice had been thickened from the four beers he'd consumed this slow Sunday afternoon.

The portly man slowed, catching his breath as he approached Prophet and the old-timers. "A little girl, the Rumishek girl, was killed during the church picnic! Someone snapped her neck and threw her in the creek. Even cut off a couple of her toes. Oh, it's awful, just awful. The family is so torn up! I have to get the undertaker."

With that, the man sprinted off down the boardwalk and hung a left at the corner, disappearing down the side street.

"Good Lord," one of the old codgers exclaimed beside him. Apparently, both men had heard the news and snapped awake. "The Rumishek girl? Who on earth would do such a thing?"

"Cut off a couple of her toes?" the other one added distastefully. "Who'd do such a ghastly thing as that?"

Prophet thought it over. Finally, he turned to the codgers. "She was missing some toes? Is that what that man really said, or was I hearing things?"

"No, that's what he said, all right," one of the codgers assured Prophet sadly. "My hearin's bad, but I'm sure that's what he said."

Thoughtfully, Prophet rubbed his jaw. After a few minutes, he got up and headed across the street. "Where you goin', young fella?" one of the codgers called behind him.

Prophet didn't hear. He was lost in thought, his heart thudding in his chest. When he got to the hotel, he pushed through the door, climbed the stairs, and knocked on McIlroy's door.

"Zeke, it's me. Open up."

There was a groan and a squawk of bedsprings. The door opened, and young McIlroy stood there, his red hair and his clothes mussed from an afternoon nap.

"What's happening?" he said, reading trouble in Prophet's eyes.

"A girl was killed at the church picnic. Someone snapped her neck and threw her in the creek."

"The hell! In Greenburg?"

"That's not all. A couple of her toes were cut off."

The deputy stared at him. "What are you thinking?"

"I'm thinking, who do we know capable of something that hideous?"

McIlroy thought about it. His eyes grew large as his sleep

left him, replaced by a cold awareness. He nodded and said, "Let me grab my hat and gun. I'm right behind you."

Prophet slipped into his own room for his sawed-off two-bore, slipped the lanyard around his neck. On his way out, he considered Louisa's door. She'd want to know about this, but she was off somewhere with Riley Nugent, as she usually was this time of the day before she started slinging drinks at the Smokehouse.

McIlroy stepped out of his room, shrugging into his frock coat, and he and Prophet headed outside, angling across the street toward the livery barn. They saddled their mounts and asked the Sunday hostler where the church picnic was held, then rode east from town at a gallop. As they headed for the creek, they passed the undertaker driving a box wagon, a teenage boy, probably his son, riding on the seat beside him.

It wasn't hard to locate the picnic. Prophet and McIlroy just followed the line of buggies and wagons pulling away from the same place along the narrow strip of woods. The families inside appeared pale and bewildered, several of the women and girls sniffling into handkerchiefs.

Only a few buggies and saddle horses remained tied to the trees at the edge of the woods when Prophet and McIlroy arrived. The two men tied their horses with the others, then strode through the woods to the clearing bordered on the east side by the creek.

They stopped when they saw several people gathered around a blanketed figure in the grass. Prophet recognized the sheriff and his deputy, the town mayor, and one of the Main Street businessmen. Two others, a big man and the bawling woman in his arms, he did not know but assumed they were the girl's parents.

Prophet glanced at McIlroy, who returned the dark look, then crossed the meadow to the men standing over the blanket-draped body.

"What happened here, Sheriff?" Zeke asked.

"Well, that's what we'd like to know," Elmer Tate said. He was dressed in a cheap brown suit with a string tie hanging askew, and a matching bowler. He didn't look at all comfortable in the getup. "This girl's friend found her floating in the creek."

Overhearing, the bawling woman bawled even harder, shaking and bashing her head against her husband's shoulder. The man whispered something to her, glanced at the sheriff, then led the woman several more yards away, where she wouldn't overhear the conversation.

"That's a shame," Zeke said solemly. "What happened?"

"Someone abused her and snapped her neck," the mayor put in. He was smoking a cigar, but his face looked stricken.

"I heard she had a couple toes missing," Prophet said, trying to put it as delicately as possible. Most folks in small towns were not used to their citizens being murdered, and he knew he had to tread softly when speaking about the particulars.

The sheriff looked at Prophet as though the bounty hunter had just sworn in church. With a ragged sigh, he said, "That's right. Some creepy bastard even . . . even did that to her."

"Can we have a look?" Zeke asked.

The sheriff glanced at the mayor, who only shrugged. Then Tate looked over at the girl's grieving parents, but they weren't looking this way. Tate shrugged and nodded.

Zeke hunkered on his haunches and lifted the blanket. Prophet crouched, running his gaze over the pale, blue form of the naked girl. Her face and arms were badly bruised, and her lips were swollen, as though she'd been hit several times. There was a cut above her left eye. Her head lay canted at an unnatural angle, her damp hair sprayed across her forehead.

There were more bruises on her thighs, and, as had been reported, two toes were missing from her right foot, leaving bloody stubs.

"Was she with anyone in the woods?" Prophet asked the sheriff.

"She was off wading with some other kids," the sheriff said, "but they said she was alone for a while after that. They said she fell in and got her dress wet, and she was waiting to dry off before she returned to the picnic."

"The reverend was the last one to walk out of them woods before we found Marliss," the father of the dead girl said over his sobbing wife's head. "He was actin' strange, said he had a headache and was headin' home for a nap. Thought I smelled whiskey on his breath, too. I didn't think anything about it at the time, but . . ."

"You don't think the new preacher did this, do you, Frank?" the mayor asked, shocked.

Rumishek shrugged, but a fierce light flashed in his eyes. "All I know is he's got some explainin' to do, a man of the cloth or not. It wasn't the first time I seen him actin' funny. I've smelled whiskey on his breath before."

Prophet stared at the agitated father. "The new reverend, huh?" he said, chewing his lip.

In his mind he saw an image of the parson in the hotel lobby when he, Zeke, and Louisa had first ridden into town. He hadn't looked straight at the man's face, but as he took a second look at the image in his memory, he realized the man had been about Duvall's size, with similar features.

Could it have been Handsome Dave himself? Could Prophet have been that close to the man without recognizing him?

What better way to hide than in plain sight?

The sheriff was speaking, but Prophet talked over him, directing his question at Frank Rumishek. "Where'd you say he went, this new preacher?"

"He's livin' with us till the parsonage gets built. That's where he went."

"Direct me."

"South end of town, across from that abandoned cabin. There's a chicken coop sitting catty-corner and a big cottonwood right beside it."

To McIlroy, Prophet said, "Let's go," and headed back across the meadow at a purposeful gait.

Zeke jogged to catch up to him. "What do you have on your mind, Lou? You think the preacher did it?"

"No," Prophet said, pushing through the low-hanging tree branches when he got to the woods. "I think Duvall did it."

The deputy stopped and looked at him, befuddled. "Then why are we going after the preacher?"

"Mount up," Prophet said as he untied Mean and Ugly and climbed into the leather. "I'll tell you on the way."

24

RILEY NUGENT WHEELED the buggy along the swale and climbed a low, tawny butte upon which one lone box elder stood, a sentinel over the hogbacks swelling in all directions.

Beside Riley in the two-seater, Louisa looked around and formed a smile. "What a lovely afternoon."

"Sure is," Riley agreed. "Why don't we get down and take a walk?"

"Why not?" Louisa said.

She took his hand as he helped her to the ground. With the other hand, she held up the high-waisted skirt of the second dress Riley had bought her at the same shop he'd bought her the first one. This was a midnight-blue gown, simply and conservatively cut but formfitting, with a white lace collar. It wasn't the most comfortable dress Louisa had ever worn, but when she saw the look on Riley's face when she tried it on, she knew she had to have it—with the assurance that she'd pay him back as soon as she could, of course.

She wasn't sure what was happening between her and

Riley. It was a little disconcerting, really—this affection she felt for him, this pleasure she took in his company. Especially when she was also in love with Lou.

Could she love two men?

Oh, for heaven's sakes—she didn't have time to love even one! What was she doing here, anyway, when she should have been in Greenburg on the lookout for Dave Duvall?

"Thank you," she told Riley when her high button shoes were planted firmly on the ground. Riley had bought her the shoes when he'd bought the dress.

He must have seen the pensive look in her eyes. "Are you okay, Louisa?"

She smiled and looked at his handsome, young, clean-shaven face. He was dressed in a white silk shirt, black cutaway coat, and crisp black hat. He'd gone home when his father's horses had arrived, but he'd returned to Greenburg nearly every other day to see Louisa. He'd been planning to take her to church earlier this morning, but his ranch chores had held him up, so they'd enjoyed an afternoon lunch at the hotel, then hopped into the two-seater for a leisurely ride in the country south of Greenburg.

"I'm fine," she said, feigning a carefree smile. "Shall we?"

Riley offered his elbow, and she took it. "We shall."

They strolled a little ways down the hill. Louisa stopped when she saw something move across one of the hogbacks before them, to the east. It was a horseback rider dressed entirely in black. The horse's legs were stretched out nearly parallel with the ground, at a hell-for-leather gallop. The man crouched low over the horse's neck, and his elbows flapped like wings.

"He's sure in a hurry," Louisa remarked. She and Riley followed the rider with their eyes.

"Sure is. I wonder who it is."

"You can't tell?"

"Not from here. Looks like an Appaloosa. Norman Lewis rides an Appaloosa, but he wouldn't be out here on a Sunday. Quaker, you know. He better slow up, though, or he's liable to lose that horse in a gopher hole—and himself, to boot!"

"He sure is."

"Well," Riley said, gesturing for them to continue their walk when the rider had disappeared over a distant hogback.

He and Louisa walked down the hill and over another, smaller one. When they came to a winding ravine choked with shrubs and small trees, Riley led Louisa along a deer path. Louisa enjoyed the walk. In spite of its clinging, she even enjoyed wearing the dress. It reminded her of happier days. Days of church picnics, summertime walks, and afternoon swims in Sand Creek.

Birds chirped in the shrubs. A porcupine ambled toward her and Riley around a bend in the ravine. Seeing the two interlopers, it turned sharply into the brush and made a thrashing noise before it stopped, hiding.

Tempering her complete enjoyment of the afternoon, however, was the angst Louisa sensed in Riley, who hadn't said a word since they'd stopped to watch the galloping rider. Louisa knew he was pondering a problem, and she wondered what it was.

Was he getting up his nerve to kiss her? If so, she wished he'd just get it over with so they could chat naturally like they'd been doing since they'd met. His easy, honest way of speaking was one of the things she liked most about the young rancher's son. It reminded her a little of Lou, but without the bounty hunter's irony and guile.

"Riley, please tell me what's on your mind," Louisa said at last, stopping to face the young man.

"What makes you think something's bothering me?" he said, feigning a look of innocence. When she merely raised an eyebrow at him, he relented. "Okay, I guess it was rather obvious, eh? Well, two things really. First, I was wondering if I could kiss you?"

"Sure."

"Really?"

Louisa shrugged. "I don't see why not. As long as you don't try anything else, I guess a kiss wouldn't hurt. It might even be nice. I'll let you know." She smiled to indicate she was teasing.

Riley sighed. "Okay, then. Here goes." He removed his hat and kissed her softly. He pulled away, looking at her with a question in his eyes. "How was that?"

She rolled her eyes discerningly and grinned. "Not bad."

"Boy, I was worried. I haven't kissed many girls, and . . ."

"I'm not exactly a woman of experience myself," Louisa said, feeling a twinge of guilt as she remembered her recent night with Lou. She didn't regret the experience, however. It was one she knew she'd remember forever, and one she doubted any other man—even Riley—would ever equal, and not only because Lou had been her first.

Riley hesitated as he faced her. "Here's the other thing. I know we just met and all," he said at last, "but I was wondering if you'd come to dinner out at the ranch sometime this week. I'd like you to meet my parents."

Louisa's stomach tightened. She'd been afraid he was going to propose something like that.

She winced as, dropping her chin, she said, "Riley, we hardly know each other. I mean, you don't know me at all . . ."

"I know there's a lot you don't want to talk about," Riley said. "And that's all right. We'll talk about it when you want. It can't be all that horrible."

"It's pretty horrible," Louisa allowed.

Riley thought about this, his hands on her shoulders, gazing into her downcast eyes. "You're not . . . you're not on the run from the law or anything, are you?"

She looked at him honestly. "No, I'm not on the run from the law. As a matter of fact, I'm not running from anything. It's what . . ." She wanted to say it was what she was chasing, but decided against it.

"It's what?" Riley urged, gently squeezing her shoulders.

She shook her head, wishing she could explain but not wanting to relive the horror. Not yet. Maybe later she would tell him the whole story, if she remained here much longer—or when Duvall was dead—but not yet.

"I can't go into it, Riley. I'm sorry. And"—her face acquired a pained expression—"I don't think it would be a good idea for me to visit your parents. You see, Riley, what we have right here and now is all we can expect. We shouldn't look ahead. I stopped looking very far ahead a long time ago."

"Are you saying we don't have a chance for a future?"

"I'm saying we can't expect one."

She knew she was being frustratingly complicated, and she felt sorry for the young cowboy, but how could she make any promises to him when she didn't know if she'd be alive tomorrow? She could run into Duvall any time, and while she fully intended to kill him with the utmost impunity, she couldn't be sure he wouldn't kill her first. Even if she lived, she didn't know what kind of person she would be after Duvall was dead.

How does one go back to a normal life after what she'd seen done to her family, and after fifteen months of tracking and killing the culprits?

Looking confounded, he started to form another question, and she stopped him by placing her finger on his lips. "Sometime I'll tell you why, but right now let's just enjoy the day. Okay?"

Reluctantly, he nodded. "Okay."

"Let's keep walking," she urged. "It's such a beautiful afternoon."

They walked for another hundred yards, talking about simple, everyday things, about Riley's family and his future. His father planned for him to take over the ranch when Mr. Nugent retired, and Riley guessed that's what would happen, although he harbored a secret desire to attend medical school in Saint Louis. He didn't have any brothers, however, just two sisters, so his future was pretty well set. That was all right, he assured Louisa. He liked ranching, and he loved Kansas. He'd never really feel at home anywhere else.

"Yes, your homeland means a lot," Louisa said as they neared the buggy at the top of the hill, in the shade of the lone box elder. "I'd like to return to Nebraska someday."

"Uh-huh!" Riley intoned. "You're from Nebraska. At least I got that much out of you."

Louisa blushed and was about to say something when again movement in the east caught her eye. About a hundred yards away, two riders were galloping southward.

"Looks like that bounty hunter and U.S. marshal that's been hangin' around town," Riley said. "Where do you suppose they're headed in such a hurry? They're riding as fast as that other fella."

"They're heading in the same direction, too," Louisa observed, her mind beginning to race and her pulse to quicken. She watched Prophet and the deputy disappear in a crease in the hogbacks, and turned to Riley sharply. "Riley, take me back to town, please."

She turned and, lifting her skirt, marched toward the buggy.

Riley ran up behind her. "What's wrong, Louisa?"

"Just hurry, please, Riley. I have to get back to town as fast as possible."

"Well, at least tell me why!"

She wheeled to him, trying to remain calm. "Riley, I know I'm being impossible, but please don't ask me any more questions. Just get me back to town—fast!"

"Okay, okay," Riley said with a sigh, untying the sorrel from the tree and climbing into the buggy beside Louisa. Shaking his head, he wheeled the horse around and urged it into a run.

They made it back to Greenburg in twenty minutes, the buggy's wheels churning the powdery dust on Main Street as Riley eased back on the sweating sorrel's reins.

"Where to?" he asked Louisa.

"The hotel."

Still confounded but resigned, the young cowboy steered the buggy to the hotel and stopped before the hitchrack. Louisa climbed down before Riley could make it around to help her.

She said, "Will you please do me one more favor, Riley? Will you have my horse at the livery barn saddled, and bring him here? It's a black Morgan. The hostler will know which one."

Hoarsely, as though at the end of his tether, Riley exclaimed, "Your horse? Why? Where you goin'?"

Louisa felt deeply guilty about keeping the affable young man in the dark like this, but she simply had no choice. Prophet and McIlroy had been riding as though the hounds of hell were on their heels, and they were following the same trail as the man before them—the man in black. That could mean several things, one of which was that the man in black was Dave Duvall.

She had to find out for sure, and if she wanted to catch up to them, she had no time to waste explaining her motives to Riley Nugent.

"Riley, please!" she begged, tugging on the young man's arm.

"All right, all right," he said, throwing up his hands and reboarding the buggy. "I'll get your horse," he groused under his breath, "but I sure would like to know what in the hell is going on around here."

Before he'd wheeled the buggy around, Louisa ran into the hotel. She came out a few minutes later, dressed in her trail garb—gray skirt, poncho, and black hat—just as Riley was leading the Morgan toward the hotel. She ran out to meet them. Riley eyed the Winchester rifle she slid into the saddle boot.

"You're packin' a *rifle?*"

He stood in the street looking shocked as Louisa took his shoulder and kissed him quickly on the cheek. She grabbed the horse's reins and climbed gracefully into the leather.

"Thanks, Riley. I'm sorry about the intrigue. I hope I can make it up to you sometime. You deserve so much better." She reined the horse around and as she started off, she looked behind her at the young cowboy watching her go. "Thanks so much for the dresses and the wonderful time. I promise I'll pay you back . . . somehow."

She turned and heeled the Morgan into a trot.

"When will I see you again, Louisa?" Riley called.

"I don't know," Louisa returned, not looking back.

Then she turned the corner around the tobacco shop and was gone in a cloud of dust.

25

THAT NIGHT, PROPHET dropped a chunk of wood on the cook fire, sending sparks rising toward the near-dark sky.

"I just can't believe that son of a bitch was right there in Greenburg, under our noses all the time."

"What I want to know is why no one questioned who he was," McIlroy said.

He was hunkered on his haunches, staring angrily into the fire, a cup of coffee in his freckled hands. His hat was off, and his red hair was sweat-matted to his head. They'd endured a long, hard ride from Greenburg and had stopped only when it got too dark for tracking. They figured Duvall was at least an hour ahead of them.

So close, yet so far.

"He must've killed the real preacher somewhere outside of town and donned his clothes. The church must've hired the poor man sight unseen. Desperate for a parson, I guess."

McIlroy cursed and gritted his teeth. "Wormy son of a

bitch. Cagey bastard. I bet Duvall was laughing at us all the while."

Prophet reached for his canteen. "I just wish we could have gotten on to him before he killed that girl."

"How many more is he gonna kill before we finally catch him, Proph?"

"None, if I can help it," Prophet said, lifting the canteen to his lips.

The deputy looked at him, his eyes wide and dark even with the flames dancing in them. "I just want you to know, I'm not taking him alive. It goes completely against all I was taught and the morals I was raised with, but I just don't see any reason why that hellcat should stand trial."

"Glad to hear you say that," Prophet said. "Because I've been plannin' on beefing that bastard ever since he ambushed Louisa." The bounty man shook his head. "That ain't normally my way. In this job it just can't be, or you turn into what you're chasing. But this . . . this here's different. You and me, we're that son of a bitch's judge, jury, and executioner."

"Me, too," someone said from the shrubs.

In an instant, Prophet and McIlroy had their revolvers in their hands, ratcheting back the hammers and jerking their heads toward the voice.

"Don't shoot—it's me," Louisa said, pushing through the brush, her figure taking shape in the fire's dancing glow.

"Jesus Christ," Prophet complained, depressing the hammer and slipping the Peacemaker back in his holster.

"You two make enough noise to wake the dead. You're lucky I'm not Duvall."

"Are we?" McIlroy said with a wry curl of his upper lip. "I'm not so sure."

"Where in the hell did you come from?" Prophet glared

at her, embarrassed by being snuck up on like that, by a girl, of all people, and by her most of all.

"My tracking skills are improving," she boasted, tossing down her saddlebags and bedroll, fanning the fire. She slipped into the bushes again and returned with her rifle sheath and saddle. "Riley and I were out for a Sunday ride in the country when we saw you two chasing the man in black. Who is he?"

"Duvall," Prophet said.

She looked at him, her eyes wide and expectant. "Really?"

"Who did you think we were chasing, the tooth fairy?" Prophet grunted. "Where's Riley?"

"I left him in Greenburg."

"That poor son of a bitch," Prophet chuckled to McIlroy. "He must feel like a hog's supper, chewed up and shit out the other end."

"Did you expect me to forget about Duvall?" Louisa said as she knelt to retrieve a tin cup from her saddlebags. "You should know me better than that by now."

"No, but I was hoping," Prophet admitted. In spite of a slight, needling jealousy, he would have liked nothing better than for her to have stayed in Greenburg with Riley Nugent, safe and sound and building a new life for herself. Like she said, he should have known better.

When Louisa had poured a cup of coffee, she sat down against her saddle and nibbled a strip of jerked beef. "So tell me where you found Duvall. Did he finally show up in town?"

"Yeah, he showed up, all right," McIlroy said. "But not finally."

Louisa gazed at him, one eyebrow raised.

Prophet told her all about it. By the time he was finished, Louisa was looking around as though for a hog to kick, her face flushed, nostrils wide with exasperation. "That son of a—"

"Yeah, he'd be good buzzard bait if a buzzard could stomach him," Prophet said.

"You sure you haven't lost him?" Louisa asked.

Prophet stared at her, indignant. "Two things that rankle me the most is being left afoot and cheeky women."

With that, he stood and grabbed his rifle. Stalking off through the brush, he grumbled, "I'll take the first watch."

Dave Duvall halted his horse on the wagon road and stared ahead through the dark, where buttery light shone in the night. He studied the light for a few minutes, then gigged the dusty, sweaty Appaloosa foward.

He was tired, and his ass was sore. It didn't take much sitting to get one's seat unaccustomed to riding.

As the lights neared, they separated, becoming two windows in a square, two-story log cabin. Nearby, a log barn loomed darkly against the starry sky.

Duvall gigged his horse into the yard, his horse fiddle-footing when the cabin door squeaked open. A man appeared on the narrow stoop, silhouetted by the doorway. He was a tall man but thin in the shoulders. He appeared to be wearing an undershirt and suspenders, the sleeves rolled to his elbows.

He hefted a shotgun in his arms and swung the barrel toward Duvall.

"Stop right where you are," he called. "State your name and business."

Duvall stopped the Appaloosa about twenty yards from the stoop. "Hello, neighbor," he called more loudly than he needed to, for it was a quiet night with only the chirping crickets. "My name is Brother Doolittle. I'm a messenger of the Good Lord. I was just passin' through, and I saw your light. I don't s'pose you'd have a morsel to spare, and possibly a bed? A straw pile in the barn would more than serve. I'd be happy to help out with chores in the mornin', as a way of repaying your kindness."

Seeing the white collar, the man lowered his shotgun. "Sorry, Parson," he said. "I've been havin' trouble with rustlers lately. Can't be too careful."

He turned to yell through the door, "Maggie, we have any vittles to spare for a travelin' preacher?"

A woman replied, but the sound was too faint for Duvall to hear what it was.

The man turned back to Duvall. "The wife says we always have vittles to spare for a man of the cloth, Reverend. You can stable your horse in the barn yonder, and come inside. We have an extra bed since Maggie's pa died."

"That would be most kind of you, my good man," Duvall said, turning his horse toward the barn. Smiling to himself, a devilish plan forming in his mind, he added, "Most kind of you, indeed. Bless you."

Prophet, McIlroy, and Louisa rolled out of their soogans before daylight and were mounted and following Duvall's trail southeast as dawn pearled the eastern sky. They rode for two hours before they stopped to water their horses at a stream. Continuing, they picked up a wagon trail.

They followed the trail to a fork.

"Shit," Prophet said. "Another damn fork in the road."

"Can't you tell which one he took?" McIlroy asked.

Prophet shook his head. "There've been a couple riders through here in the past few hours, on both forks. He's done a good job of making his tracks blend with theirs."

"We'll split up, then," Louisa said, impatience in her voice. "I'll take the right fork."

"I'll go with her," Prophet said. "Don't take any chances, Zeke."

"I'll wait for you if you wait for me."

"Deal," Prophet said, spurring Mean after Louisa, who was already a good ways down the trail's right fork.

McIlroy gigged his chestnut down the left fork. A half hour later, he came to a cross trail. One set of fresh horse tracks gouged the dirt, and as far as the young deputy could tell, the shoe prints had the markings of Duvall's horse.

Releasing the thong over his revolver, McIlroy turned his horse onto the intersecting trail. He'd ridden twenty minutes when he saw a cabin, barn, and corral in a wooded crease in the buttes before him.

The house was shaded by several poplars and ash. Cows milled about the place, grazing the rich bluestem. What brought McIlroy to a halt, however, was a commotion by a big tree by the barn. From this distance, he couldn't tell what it was, but it looked damn peculiar.

He reined the chestnut into the brush and dismounted. He tied the horse to a sapling, retrieved his field glasses from his saddlebags, then climbed a butte, keeping the right shoulder of the bluff between him and the ranch. Halfway to the top, he hunkered down and raised his field glasses over the butte's sloping shoulder, focusing on the ranch yard.

When he brought the scene into focus, he stiffened, his breath freezing in his lungs.

A woman in a long skirt and torn blouse stood under the tree. Her hair was disheveled and her face was bruised and smudged with dirt. On her shoulders stood a young boy of around seven or eight. The woman was balancing the boy on her shoulders, wavering from side to side with the burden. She couldn't waver too much, however, for there was a hangman's noose around the boy's neck, and the end of the noose was tied to a branch of the tree. The boy's hands were tied behind his back. If the woman gave way beneath him, the boy would strangle.

The woman was crying. So was the boy, his face contorted with terror.

Not far away from them, a man lay facedown on the ground, blood staining his shirt. Three horses stood with their heads over the corral, staring and twitching their ears curiously at the woman and the boy.

Bringing his glasses back to the woman, McIlroy saw her knees buckling, giving and stiffening, giving and stiffening, her hands desperately gripping the boy's black shoes atop her shoulders.

"Oh, my god!" McIlroy said to himself, his gut filling with bile. It could have been a trap, but he didn't care. He had to save the boy.

Lowering his glasses, he ran back to his horse, dropped the glasses in his saddlebags, mounted up, and gigged the chestnut into a gallop. He drew his revolver as he approached the yard, clicking back the hammer and looking around for Duvall. He didn't see anything but the dead man, the woman, and the boy. Seeing McIlroy, the woman's crying grew louder.

"Help me . . . please!" she wailed. "Oh, god, *help me!*"

McIlroy steered the horse toward her. As he approached the tree, he reined the chestnut to a stop and retrieved his barlow knife from the small sheath on his belt. Reaching up with his left hand, he cut the rope above the boy's head.

As the boy fell into the woman's arms, a shot rang out. McIlroy felt the icy burn in his shoulder as the impact of the bullet knocked him sideways from the saddle.

"Run!" he yelled to the woman as he hit the ground.

The woman grabbed the boy, and they ran, screaming, behind the barn.

McIlroy's horse whinnied as another shot rang out, and galloped off, kicking. The deputy turned toward the cabin. A bearded man in black stood in the doorway, aiming a rifle at McIlroy. The gun cracked, smoke puffing, just as McIlroy raised his revolver.

Duvall's slug tore through McIlroy's other shoulder, and he dropped his gun with a yell.

"*Ah!* Goddamn you, son of a bitch!"

"You're gonna die, lawman," Duvall yelled.

"Maybe, but I'm gonna make sure you're right behind me," McIlroy retorted, reaching for his gun. But before he could get off a shot, Duvall's rifle cracked again, and the bullet plunked into the deputy's thigh.

McIlroy yelled again as he dropped the revolver and writhed in excruciating pain.

He cast his gaze back toward the cabin. Laughing, Duvall shucked another shell in the rifle's chamber and moved in for the kill.

26

WHEN HE AND Louisa had ridden for a half mile, Prophet halted his horse.

"This ain't right," he said. "Duvall didn't come this way. The tracks have thinned, and I don't see any that look like Duvall's."

"Are you sure?" Louisa asked.

"Yeah, I'm sure," Prophet said, offended that she'd doubt him.

He reined Mean around and headed back the way they'd come, Louisa doing likewise.

They'd turned onto the left fork and had ridden about ten minutes when they heard a rifle crack.

Prophet jerked, startled, and halted the lineback dun. "Sounded like it came from over there," he said, nodding to the right of the trail. It was too brushy and hilly for fast riding in that direction, so Prophet gigged the horse into a forward trot, looking for a cross trail. When he found it, he turned onto it and gigged Mean into an immediate gallop, Louisa following suit.

As Prophet rode, he heard three more rifle shots. He prayed that McIlroy had not run into Duvall. The shots were sporadic enough to belong to a hunter, but Prophet didn't think so. A cold prickling at the back of his neck told him that what he'd feared had come to pass.

The lineback ate up the trail, running hard and blowing with determination, its muscles working beneath the saddle. At Prophet's right and a little behind, Louisa spurred the Morgan, crouching forward over the horse's blowing mane, her hat bouncing against her back, her blonde hair blowing straight out behind her.

A ranchstead opened ahead as the rifle cracked again. Someone was standing in the cabin's doorway, extending a rifle. There were two more men in the yard. They were both prone. One appeared dead. The other, Prophet saw as he approached the edge of the yard, was McIlroy.

The deputy lay in a twisted heap, legs curled beneath him, both shoulders and his left leg bloody. He was reaching for his revolver lying several feet away. The man with the rifle stepped out from the cabin. He was a tall, bearded man dressed in black, and he was moving toward the deputy as he cocked the rifle.

"Duvall!" Prophet yelled as he jumped from his horse. As Mean veered to the left, Prophet clawed his revolver from his holster and hit the ground on his belly, extending the gun before him.

As Duvall swung the rifle toward Prophet, the bounty hunter fired. He didn't have time to take careful aim, however, and his slug sailed wide. Shots rang out to Prophet's right. Turning that way, Prophet saw Louisa. She, too, had dismounted, and was firing from one knee.

A tree obscured her view, and her shots missed their mark. Duvall fired one round at Prophet, blowing dirt in Prophet's face, and one round at Louisa. Then he wheeled, bounded up the porch steps, and disappeared inside the cabin.

"Get that son of a bitch!" Zeke shouted, his voice pinched with pain.

Prophet looked at Louisa. "Cover me!" he yelled.

He stood and ran to the cabin, his revolver in his right hand. When he'd bounded onto the porch, he jumped to one side of the door. Sliding a look inside and seeing no one, he ran inside, gun extended, hammer back and ready to fly.

There was a small sitting area before him, a kitchen to the cabin's rear. In the kitchen, an outside door stood wide. Through the door came the sound of hoofbeats as a horse thundered through the brush.

Prophet turned and ran back onto the porch.

"He's got a horse!" he yelled to Louisa. But she must have heard, for she was already atop her Morgan and galloping past the porch, heading east, her expression savagely determined.

Prophet knew it would do no good to caution her to wait for him, so he ran through the dust she'd kicked up toward McIlroy, who lay on his side, staring after Louisa. The deputy bared his teeth in pain.

"How you doin', kid?" Prophet asked, dropping to his knees beside the young lawman.

"I'm all right," McIlroy said. "Get after him!"

Prophet shook his head with frustration, inspecting the wounds in McIlroy's shoulders and thigh. "Can't leave you," he said. "You'll bleed to death."

"No, Lou, you gotta get that son of a bitch!"

Prophet was about to respond when he heard, "I'll tend him."

Turning to his right, he saw a woman walk toward him from the barn, a boy with trembling lips hanging back behind her. The woman was pale and disheveled, about thirty years old. Wide-eyed and ghostly, she moved stiffly toward Prophet.

She was most likely the woman who lived here. And the man lying several yards away, dead, and whom the woman seemed to be trying hard not to look at, was no doubt her husband. Duvall had terrorized and devastated another family.

McIlroy grabbed Prophet's wrist, rasping, "She'll take care of me, Proph. Get after him!"

Prophet glanced at the woman again. He saw that, despite her obvious pain, courage shone in her eyes. He nodded at her and ran over to Mean and Ugly, who milled in the trees and brush beside the cabin. Forking leather, Prophet yelled, *"Go!"*

He and the horse were off at a gallop, Mean's front hooves bolting high as his back legs bent and sprang.

It was a hard ten minutes later when Prophet, cresting a rise, saw Duvall galloping about a half mile ahead, crossing a shallow valley. He was following the pale ribbon of a wagon road looping around to the south, and Louisa was just behind him, the Morgan's head down, planting its hooves like a fine Kentucky racer.

Deciding to cut straight across the loop, Prophet reined Mean off the trail, through some thick brush, into a gully, and up the other side. When they were on the tableland again, Prophet gouged the horse with his spurs. The barrel-chested steed put his head down, digging deep in his heart for speed, as though he sensed the urgency of Prophet's plight.

They were too close to Duvall to let him get away. He'd only kill again.

The horse galloped hard for a mile. Prophet reined him to a halt atop a long ridge spiked with brush and shale. Leaping from the saddle, Prophet quickly snagged his Winchester from the boot and gazed down the bluff, at the road curving below.

Duvall was galloping around a bend, his Appaloosa

slowing with fatigue. He disappeared behind a rock, and when he reappeared, Prophet dropped to a knee, brought his Winchester to his shoulder, and snugged his cheek up against the worn walnut stock.

He lined up the sights slightly ahead of the galloping rider, so the slug would take him through the temple. That's not what happened, though. When Prophet squeezed the trigger, Duvall's horse dropped to its knees. Its ass flew up over its head, and so did Duvall, slightly ahead of the scissoring rear hooves.

Watching Duvall careen head over heels through the air, Prophet grunted, "Damn. Led him too much and didn't account for the crosswind. Poor horse."

He ejected the smoking shell, slid another into the firing chamber, and brought the rifle to bear once again on Duvall, who'd fallen in a heap about ten feet before the horse, which lay twisted and dead on the trail. Duvall was moving, trying to get up. Prophet wanted to drill him, but his chance of hitting him from this distance was slim. Besides, Louisa was now approaching the outlaw, and Prophet didn't want to risk hitting her instead.

Cursing, he ran for Mean and Ugly.

Meanwhile, Louisa reined the Morgan to a halt on the trail, swinging the horse sideways as she reached for her revolver. Before her, Dave Duvall was climbing to a knee. His parson's clothes and hair were dust-coated, and his eyes were bleary.

But he'd managed to draw his revolver, and as he glanced around, blinking and trying to clear his head, he saw Louisa and clicked back the hammer of his Colt.

About twenty yards away from the outlaw, Louisa raised her own gun and fired. The slug tore through Duvall's left forearm, shoving him several steps backward and twisting him around.

Duvall looked at his arm with surprise. "Why, you shot me, you little bitch!"

Louisa slid out of her saddle and walked toward Duvall, extending her pistol in her hand. Her face was a mask barren of all emotion, her jaw set, her eyes cool. Her hat was hanging down her back and her hair was ruffled by the breeze.

"That's right, I shot you," she told the outlaw, who'd swung back around to face her, his gun still in his right hand, its barrel down. Pain shone in his eyes, but there was a grim humor there, as well.

"That's just the first bullet I'm going to drill through your hide," Louisa said.

Duvall gazed at her, curious. "Who are you?"

"Remember Sand Creek, Nebraska, Mr. Duvall?"

Louisa waited to see if the name of her hometown meant anything to him. When no light of recognition shone in his eyes—he'd killed so many people, ruined so many families, after all—she decided to help him.

"There was a family there, in the country along the creek. Happy, God-fearing farmers. My parents, my brother, and my two sisters. Your gang rode in, shot my brother and father, and raped my sisters and mother in the tall grass by the creek."

Louisa was using the cold steel of her anger to remain calm, but her lips trembled slightly as she remembered.

"I was coming back from selling eggs to the neighbors, and I hid in the weeds when I saw the smoke of the fire. I saw it all."

Her voice cracked, and she waited a moment before continuing. "I heard the screams of my mother and my sisters while you and your men . . . while you . . ."

Tears flooded her eyes. Through them, she watched Duvall raise the barrel of his Colt. She ducked as the gun flashed and cracked, the slug zinging past her ear.

Then she fired her own revolver. Duvall stumbled back as though punched, dropping his pistol and clutching his right shoulder with his left hand.

"You *bitch!*"

Louisa took three steps toward him. "It's not nice to call a girl names, Mr. Duvall. I have four bullets left. Where would you like them?"

"You goddamn whore!" Duvall raged. "I chew little sluts like you up for breakfast! I bite your damn toes off!"

"Your dining days are over," Louisa said calmly. "For good."

Duvall's eyes were bright with apprehension. He glanced at his gun on the ground.

"Go for it," Louisa said, reading his mind. "I'll see how big a hole I can blow through your hand."

Duvall lifted his gaze again to hers. The outrage was slowly leaving his eyes, replaced by fear. Unable to believe he'd been bested by a girl, he flushed with bewilderment. Small sighs and grunts of pain escaped his lips.

He stood slouching, knees quivering. Blood oozed through the fingers of the hand cupping his wounded right arm. His hat lay near the horse, and his sweaty hair was peppered with seeds and dust. His black clothes were gray with filth.

As miserable as he appeared, he flashed her a smile, the Handsome Dave grin that dimpled his cheeks and set girls to blushing. "Y-you don't want to kill me now, do you?" he said. "I mean, I got money in those saddlebags, and you and me . . . we could have us a tail-up time in some city."

His eyes gave her a lusty twice-over, and his grin widened as his confidence grew. "Why, sure we could. We could have a grand ole time."

Louisa stared at him dully. Then she clicked back the Colt's hammer and raised it.

"No . . . *wait!*"

Duvall threw up his arms and lowered his head, cowering. Louisa drilled a bullet through his left knee. Duvall screamed as that leg buckled and he fell on his ass, writhing and grabbing the wounded leg, cursing for all he was worth.

"Do you remember them now, Mr. Duvall?" Louisa asked him calmly. "Do you remember the family you murdered?"

He gazed up at her, blinking and swallowing, sweat troughing the dust on his face. He nodded slightly. "I remember."

"I'm the girl you left without a family," she said. "My name is Louisa Bonaventure." She fired the Colt again. It jumped in her hand, drilling a hole through Duvall's right knee.

The outlaw stiffened, throwing his head back, his mouth widening as he screamed.

"No!" he bellowed. "I'm sorry . . . Please! Don't kill me." Sobs racked him as he begged, *"Please, don't kill me!"*

He lay back on the ground, drawing ragged breaths through his mouth.

"Please," he said, sobbing. "I'm a young man. I've made mistakes, like we all have. I beg you, miss. Please, please, please have mercy on me."

"I believe that's what my mother and sisters asked of you, didn't they?"

Duvall lifted his head, his brown eyes glowering up at her, filled with pain and outrage and terror.

Louisa winced angrily as she fired the Colt. Duvall had jerked sideways, however, and the slug sailed wide, plunking into the sod. He looked up at her, a cunning light in his eyes, and lunged toward her. She brought the Colt to bear again, and fired.

The slug took Duvall through his groin, throwing him

back down and evoking a scream so loud that the rest of the world seemed to go silent.

"All right, have it your way," Louisa said tightly, after she'd listened to the man's wails of utter anguish. "I won't kill you, after all."

She'd let him die slow, let him wallow in his pain while he bled to death. Give him time to remember the cries and the anguished faces of those whose lives he'd claimed. Lives like those of her family.

Louisa holstered her revolver and turned toward the Morgan, which had skittered some distance away. She stopped suddenly. Prophet sat his lineback dun behind her, watching her gravely.

They shared a long, meaningful gaze. Then Louisa walked over to her Morgan and mounted up.

She sat staring off pensively, her eyes wide and deep. Then tears filmed them and her shoulders convulsed with a relieved sob.

"It's all over, Louisa," Prophet said.

She nodded. "I'll see you back at the farm," she said. "I'd like to ride alone for a while."

Wiping her cheeks with her gloved hands, she gigged the Morgan into a trot, riding north.

Prophet watched her.

"Help me!" Duvall crouched over his bloody groin, chin lifted toward Prophet, his face streaked with tears. His plea was that of some wounded beast.

"All right," Prophet said quietly. "It's more than you deserve, but here you go."

He drew his Colt and drilled a neat, round hole through the outlaw's forehead. Duvall slammed back against the ground, dead.

Prophet turned his horse around and rode back toward the farm.

EPILOGUE

PROPHET WOKE THE next morning as a pearly dawn glow touched the farmhouse window. He looked around at the dusky sitting room, where he and Louisa had bedded down on the floor. It was only him here now, however. Louisa was gone, her pillow still bearing the imprint of her head.

McIlroy was in one of the two bedrooms, where he'd slept after the woman, Maggie Delaney, had dug the bullets out of his limbs, dressed his wounds, and put him to bed. Mrs. Delaney and her son shared the other bedroom, which she had shared with her husband until Handsome Dave had come calling.

If only Prophet and McIlroy could have gotten to Duvall sooner, Maggie Delaney's husband would be in his bed right now, and not in the grave Prophet had dug in the meadow behind the house.

Prophet tossed his single blanket away and climbed to his feet. Hearing something outside, he moved to the window and looked out.

Louisa was standing in the shadows by the barn. Her black Morgan, an inky shape in the gloomy light, stood with its saddle and bridle on. Louisa appeared to be strapping her rifle boot to the saddle.

What in the hell was she up to now?

Prophet stepped into his jeans and, forgoing his boots and shirt, walked outside, crossing the hard-packed yard in his bare feet, the dirt still cool and damp from the dew.

"Louisa, what are you up to now?"

She turned to him, then turned back to the tie straps on her rifle boot.

"I'm pulling out. I meant to be out of here before you woke." She shrugged her shoulders slightly. "I figured it would be hard, saying good-bye to you, Lou."

Prophet looked at her, frowning. "Where are you heading, Nebraska?"

Shaking her head, Louisa turned to him. "No."

Prophet waited. When she didn't say anything, he said, "Where, then?"

She shrugged again and looked off. "Here and there. Wherever the badmen are."

Prophet's features soured with even more bewilderment.

"I'm gonna try my own hand at bounty hunting, Lou," Louisa said, smiling and gazing into his eyes with resolve. "I'm gonna hunt men like Duvall . . . men who've murdered families like mine. Men who've caused heartache in innocent folks like me and the others Duvall and his gang turned into widows and orphans. I don't know where I'll start yet, but I'll start somewhere."

Prophet shook his head. "Louisa, that's plumb crazy. Bounty huntin' ain't no life for a girl. You go back to Greenburg and settle down with that Nugent kid. He'll set you up with the kind of life you were meant to have."

It was Louisa's turn to shake her head. "No, Lou. I'd like to do that, but I'm not fit to be anyone's wife, not after what I've seen and done. This seems like the only life for me now. Maybe later I'll settle down with a man like Riley, but for now I have to ride the owlhoot trail. Call it a calling, if you like."

Prophet couldn't believe what he was hearing. Before he could espouse more words of objection, Louisa put two fingers on his lips.

"I know it sounds crazy, but what else do I know how to do that might make some change in the world?"

Prophet took her hand in his and held it while he said, "Stay with me, then, if you want to hunt bounties. You'll be safer with me than on the trail alone. You're a girl, for chrissakes—a beautiful girl!"

Again, Louisa shook her head. "I have to ride alone, Lou. I can't be dependent on you or anyone else. Maybe someday I'll feel secure enough to depend on someone, but not yet. If what I've lived through has taught me one thing, it's that."

He was about to speak again, but she stopped him with a kiss, throwing her arms around his neck and mashing her lips to his. It was a long kiss, and she seemed reluctant to break it off. When she finally did, tears filmed her hazel eyes.

"Good-bye, Lou," she said, her voice cracking. She turned abruptly and climbed into the saddle. She looked at him and said, "Maybe we'll run into each other down the trail again, eh?"

Tears rolling down her cheeks, she gigged the Morgan into a trot away from the barn, leaving the yard, heading west.

She called over her shoulder, "Say good-bye to Riley for me, will you?"

"Louisa, goddamn it!" Prophet called after her.

Only her horse's hoofbeats answered, softening with distance.

Frustrated, Prophet rammed the back of his fist into a corral post and stared through the dust she'd kicked up in the yard.

"Fool girl," he called. "You're gonna be the death of me yet!"

He stood there, in his bare feet and sleep-mussed hair, staring west for a long time after she'd disappeared.